THE SPANISH BOY

THE
SPANISH
BOY

C.S. REARDON

Signature
EDITIONS

Cover design by Doowah Design.
Photo of C.S. Reardon by Lance Lee.

This book was printed on Ancient Forest Friendly paper.
Printed and bound in Canada by Hignell Book Printing Inc.

We acknowledge the support of the Canada Council for the Arts and the Manitoba Arts Council for our publishing program.

Library and Archives Canada Cataloguing in Publication

Reardon, C.S., author
        The Spanish boy / C.S. Reardon.

Issued in print and electronic formats.
ISBN 978-1-927426-92-0 (paperback).
--ISBN 978-1-927426-93-7 (epub)

        I. Title.

PS8635.E228S63 2016   C813'.6   C2016-904954-X
                                        C2016-904955-8

Signature Editions
P.O. Box 206, RPO Corydon, Winnipeg, Manitoba, R3M 3S7
www.signature-editions.com

For my parents
Margaret Melley Reardon and Frank Reardon

About suffering they were never wrong,
The Old Masters: how well they understood
Its human position; how it takes place
While someone else is eating or opening a window or just
  walking dully along...

— W.H. Auden
"Musée des Beaux Arts"

2004

1

"A what?"

"I said: 'Grief cannot abide…'"

"I got that part, Lawrie." Mel taps his right ear. What good is a hearing aid if it can't help you hear? "Abide a what, though?"

"Mystery. Cannot abide a mystery."

"I see." Grief cannot abide a mystery.

Just like Lawrie to come up with that, out of the blue. Except it probably wasn't out of the blue. Lawrie would have thought for a while about what to say. He likes things to be considered twice, spoken once. Always has.

Mel lifts the cup from the saucer. Plain white, institutional, the lip too thick, not the kind he prefers to drink from. The pool of milky tea has grown cold. The surface shimmers and separates. He replaces the cup and pushes the saucer away.

Beside him, Lawrie studies his wristwatch.

"Time to skedaddle," he says. "I'll miss the traffic if I leave now."

"Traffic's going the other way this time of day. You know that. Anyway, it's July. Everyone's at the beach."

"Still…"

What is left to be said? One more visit ended for another day.

"Mel. What I meant about grief…"

"I know what you meant, Lawrie. You don't have to go on about it."

"Wasn't sure you'd heard me right."

"I heard you."

They have been friends as long as either of them can remember. They are old men now with no time left to waste on dispute.

Lawrie hadn't said what he did to be unkind. Mel's grief has always been his as well. But today of all days. Her birthday.

They follow their established routine today. In a few minutes, the young woman with the tray will come by. She'll say: "Done here, hon?" Mel will nod his head and she'll carry away the unfinished tea. As a child of the Great Depression he was told never to waste food. That lesson has no place here these days. And, besides, it wasn't a very good cup of tea; left too long to steep, bitter tasting.

"I really should go," Lawrie says and checks his watch one more time. He continues to sit beside his best friend, walking stick propped against the table.

Mel wanted to phone him this morning and say: "To hell with the regular schedule, Lawrie. Don't visit today. Not today. You know." He didn't make that call, though, and when his friend's car pulled up to the front of the building he was relieved to see it.

They do not speak her name. They do not touch one tea cup to another and say: "Here's to our birthday girl. Wherever she is."

But grief. What was it Lawrie said? Grief cannot abide a mystery. Well, yes, the punishing need for Mel, for both of them, to know what happened is still there. That is what has not diminished with age.

He thinks of another July morning. The day the world came to Halifax, bringing change along with it, larger and more dangerous than anything he might have imagined, like a snowball rolling downhill, gathering speed and bulk and heft.

1936

2

For all of his sixteen years, Mel Clarey's life has followed an uncluttered path. By common agreement, this son of respectability and promise is destined for a future meant to hold no surprises, no unexpected turns, his life enlivened only by rich and happy moments.

And so on this Saturday in early July, Mel wakes with the unchallenged expectation that he will not be disappointed. Hadn't he assured his best friend, Lawrie Shine, that besides being born, this will be the most exciting day of their sixteen-year-old lives?

The summer heat is building inside his small upstairs bedroom at the front of the house. He stirs and frees his legs from the tangle of bed covers. A still house, the solitude of the half-waking moment, a contentment that he chooses to hold on to as long as he can. This is the way mornings begin for Mel Clarey. "My sleepy baby," his mother continues to call him.

In the dream he had, he and Lawrie were small tidy boys in short pants, on their way to attend their first day of school. Walking between them, guiding them, is Mel's older sister, Edie. The trees lining the street are canopies of green that obscure the morning light. The unfamiliar houses are dark, their windows curtained. When he tries to tell Edie she's taking them in the wrong direction, she lets go of their hands.

"Wait here," she says and walks away from them.

He calls to her, but she's already a tiny figure in the distance.

The two small boys are alone on the empty street. Lawrie shakes his head, crying. Mel's heart flutters with the urgent panic of the abandoned child.

"Mel," is all Lawrie can manage to say to him.

He might tell Lawrie about the dream later, if he remembers. The comical image of the two of them in short pants and their hair neatly combed will make his friend laugh, although Mel will leave out the bit about Lawrie's tears and his own agitated state.

The sunlight through the window moves across the graceful pattern of his room's wallpaper. Its measured progress calms him. One more inch and it will touch the frame of the door. Eight o'clock. But hadn't he set his alarm clock to wake him long before this?

"*Mel!*" Lawrie's shout comes from outside the Clarey house.

He shifts his gaze from the wall to the empty windowsill. The alarm clock he had placed there last night is gone.

"*Mel!*"

They've anticipated this moment for weeks, the three of them, Mel and Lawrie and Edie. They'd sworn to each other: meet at eight o'clock, on the dot. Not eight-oh-five. Eight. Without fail, they'd all promised.

And now he's late, no time to change from pyjamas into trousers and shirt. Seconds matter. Move this instant, or be reduced to the shame of listening to others tell their own stories about this morning. Never mind an alarm clock. History itself should have shaken him awake.

He's down the hall, feet shoved into the scuffed brown shoes he'd kicked off the night before. One sharp rap of his knuckles lands against his sister's door in his rush to the stairs. He takes the steps two at a time and as he runs past the front closet grabs the first jacket that comes to hand. A tug of the front door, a leap from the porch, and the morning sunlight touches his face. The sky is perfect. The only time of the year it looks exactly this way; diamond hard and so blue, cloudless.

"Jeez, Lawrie. Sorry."

"I yelled. Didn't you hear?"

"Only the first two or three hundred times."

Mel's off down the street, ahead of his friend, tugging the brown tweed jacket over his red pyjamas and his loose teenaged frame. Dressed this way, in night clothes and with the dusty shoes on his sockless feet, Mel might be the one member of the Clarey family who'd skipped the lesson on rules of acceptable outdoor attire. He pushes his wavy brown hair off his face and calls to Lawrie.

"Come on. Hurry."

"Wait up, Mel. Edie. Where's Edie?"

"She'll find us. Come on. We're gonna miss it."

"She said she'd be here. So, where is she?"

"Look, I don't know. You know my sister. We can't wait forever."

"But Mel…"

"You know what she's like. She'll be late for her own funeral."

"Don't say that." Lawrie's brown eyes are the softest feature in his boy's face.

"Oh, come on. You know. A big 'yes' one minute and then a '*What? I said I'd do what?*'" Mel mimics a look of horror. "Everybody knows that."

"Maybe, if you…"

"Wasting time, Lawrie. Come on."

Lawrie doesn't budge, though. His eyes search for some sign that one more body might be stirring inside the Clarey house.

Mel moves away with a clumsy backward step, his body jerking like the limbs of a stringed puppet, just as the Clarey front door swings open.

"I'm here. I'm here."

Edie's fingers fumble with the buttons on the raincoat she's drawn on over her pink nightgown. The rubber boots she wears clomp with every lunged step. Her chestnut hair is wild, tangled.

"The alarm clock, you see, Lawrie? My fault entirely. I wanted to be the first one up. So I took it out of Mel's room last night and I guess…oh never mind that, here we are."

Lawrie's heart, already bursting with the morning's anxiety and anticipation, swells to make room for Edie's smile. And something else. His boyhood worship of the older girl is deepening. Lately his entire body responds in the most surprising ways to the sight and presence of her.

"Come on, you two," Mel calls to them, trembling in his impatience.

People flow along the Halifax street like a spring freshet that's burst its banks, past the comfortable houses painted grey or brown, with the occasional rebellious white. The world, for this morning, has taken leave of its common sense and propriety. Arms and shoulders bump and push. Long legs, short legs, pump with effort; the young, the old, all are gathering pace in the direction of the big park. Mel sees intense faces, gigglers, others open-mouthed and gasping to keep up. Many, like him, have rushed out of their houses wearing whatever it was they'd worn to bed the night before. Pyjamas, nightgowns, a work shirt on top, some manner of bed-clothes covering the lower parts; slippers, shoes and no shoes at all.

This is the oddest collection of humanity Mel has ever seen and none is odder looking to him than his sister and his best friend. For the first time this morning, he laughs out loud from pure exhilaration and at the sight of the mismatched pair.

Mel knows that only Lawrie would have put special thought and care into what to wear for this occasion. He looks at his friend's trousers, so carefully pressed, and the short-sleeved shirt, perfect for the day's approaching heat. On Lawrie's feet are his signature argyle socks and polished brown brogues. And he would have spent a precious minute carving a gully through his thick dark hair, willing it to stay in place with a butter pat-sized spread of the hair cream he saves for special occasions. A knitted V-neck vest is his curt nod to fashion. All this would have taken time.

Lawrie might as well be saying to him: "History may unfold at its own pace, Mel. It will not dictate mine."

Running beside Lawrie is Edie, her hair jumping and bobbing. It is not red, not brown, but the perfect shade of chestnut.

Not curly, but turning just so here and there, the way it should to frame her long Clarey face. No one says Edith Clarey is pretty, not in the way someone means when they call a girl pretty. What everyone does agree on, though, is that with her hair, her wide hazel eyes and easy smile, she is a head turner.

"Just over 800 feet," Lawrie is saying as he draws closer to Mel. His arms pump as he gasps for breath.

"Eight hundred…three feet…eight inches. To be precise." Lawrie's ankles, weak as long as he has walked and an embarrassment to him now as a teenager, wobble and ache.

"Oh, come on, Lawrie." Edie tugs at his shirt sleeve as if doing this will cause him to run faster.

Lawrie grabs at his shirttail that's worked its way loose. His hair, the part long gone, is alive with every one of his uncertain steps. He's smaller, less hale than his Clarey friends. Sixteen last month and Edie, older only by two years, often speaks to him as if he's much younger. The three joke that their families have known each other since the beginning of time.

"Honestly. Lawrence Shine," Edie says.

The air is close, like the first humid moments after a heavy summer rain. Who is here to notice if she releases one or two, certainly not more than three, buttons on the coat? Only her brother and Lawrie. No one else will fix her with her mother's stare, a silent reprimand for a daughter's rebellious gesture. And her mother isn't here to see how everyone else is dressed. So bother the rules. "It's indecent is all," her mother would say.

Well, bother indecency, too. She'll do what she wants and what she wants more than anything at this moment is to feel the air on her trapped throat and chest. The top three buttons of the coat slip easily through their openings.

The long raincoat she'd pulled on sweeps her calves and restricts her running. And there isn't much she can do about her feet. On the way out of the house, she'd shoved them into her rubber rain boots. Her bare toes grate and cramp against their rough lining.

She grabs one of Lawrie's hands. "You're hopeless," she says and tugs at him.

Lawrie's right ankle buckles. He throws out his left hand to break his fall and lands hard on his right knee. The rough dirt surface of the street tears the spotless fabric of his trousers. Edie lurches backward, landing on top of him.

"Oh, Lawrie," Edie says, exasperated, impatient. She scrambles to her feet and bends down, taking his hand in her own to inspect the damage. Her fingertips tap his injured palm, which is already swelling with grit and blood.

In sixteen years, how many times have these two hands twined like this, in play, in help, in happiness?

"Oh, you poor lamb," she says, and this is what Lawrie loves most about Edie Clarey. She says it as though no one is more important to her in the whole world than him. All trace of her annoyance is gone. Only the caring, big-hearted girl remains. While around them figures and footsteps rush by, Edie makes no move to hurry the two of them along.

"I'm okay, don't worry," Lawrie says. "Doesn't hurt at all." His hand does hurt, though, and quite a bit. But part of being sixteen means not saying so.

"Come on, pal." Mel is alongside his friend and grasps one of his arms. Lawrie plants his foot and its wobbly ankle onto the road and pushes himself to standing.

Mel knows all of Lawrie's mooning over his sister is a waste of time. Edie's attention to the injured hand is as close as his friend will ever get to hearing a declaration of love from her. It's a little sad and sorry to Mel that Lawrie, possessed of so much common sense, could exhibit such a lapse.

"Look," Edie says and raises her arm and points. She waves at some men climbing a ladder and scrambling onto a roof. Windows, open in house after house along Inglis Street, are filled with people leaning out, backs arched and looking up, staring into the empty blue sky.

She laughs and hooks her arm through Lawrie's.

"I'd never've noticed them if you hadn't fallen down. What next?"

Lawrie doesn't care about men climbing onto the tops of houses. He wants to remind Edie that he's sixteen. Doesn't she remember the gift she gave him to mark the milestone? Does he have to say it out loud to her that he's almost a man and not to forget that weak ankles are an established feature of the Shine family?

And as though she heard him speak, she throws her arms around his shoulders, holds him tight and steady as she whispers: "This is just so exciting, isn't it, Lawrie? Just so...*damned* exciting."

Her breath tickles his ear. The hushed "*damned*," a word so unfamiliar to their public vocabulary, has the thrill of a forbidden treat. She takes Lawrie's injured hand and brushes it with her lips.

"There now. All better," she says.

And Edie smiles with her implacable self-assurance, her unwavering conviction that she will be forgiven no matter what the transgression. They all treat Edie that way, family or friend. When it comes to Edie Clarey, they can't help themselves.

"Come on, hurry up, or we'll miss it," Mel says. They're approaching the junction where they'll turn right, along with the others still flooding into the streets, and head south towards the big park.

Edie glances over at Lawrie, still doing his best to keep up.

"What else do you know about it, Lawrie?"

His mouth is dry with fatigue and exertion. He inhales some of the damp air and pulls his tongue away from the roof of his mouth.

"Okay. Can carry a crew of about sixty. Depending, I guess, on how many passengers. Of which there's room for up to..." He struggles with his breath. "...Seventy-two."

"And what else?"

"Approximate travel time. Lakehurst, New Jersey to Frankfurt, Germany. Or vice versa. About sixty hours. Depending on winds. Of course."

Edie takes two more strides before planting a heel and spinning to stare at him.

"Get away. Not possible. In the air? *For sixty hours?* Without stopping anywhere?"

"Well, really, Edie," Lawrie says. His throat is clutched by the sight of the pink collar of Edie's nightgown exposed by the loosened raincoat. "They're crossing the Atlantic Ocean. Where could they possibly stop?"

She laughs, not at all embarrassed at having asked such a foolish question.

"Edie, knock it off, will you?" Mel says.

If his sister had taken the time to read more, as much as he and Lawrie had, they'd be in the park by now, not lagging behind the others on the street.

He and Lawrie have anticipated this day since the newspapers began reporting on the floating sensation, the *Hindenburg*. The giant airship, once used to threaten London when the whole world was at war, is now revolutionizing the way people move across the planet. Seventeen trans-Atlantic round trips this year alone.

Mel has pored over newspaper reports about life inside the great ship, not bothering with the other stories that are of little interest to him: that fuss in Spain; the talk of the King and some woman; and the strange German man with the funny moustache and crazy-eyed stare.

"Before we continue, I just want to say…" Lawrie tugs at his woollen vest.

Mel could have told him that the garment would be too warm for this time of year.

"…are you sure we're going the right way?"

"I'm following Mel," Edie says.

"And I'm following everybody else."

Lawrie wrestles the trailing shirttail into his trousers and tugs again at the vest. He looks into the expectant faces of his friends.

"Look. I've been thinking about this. You're captain of a German airship, part of the government's fleet, and we know we can't trust the Germans, right? Can we assume they haven't crossed the entire Atlantic to drop some people off in a New Jersey cow field and then take a few holiday snaps of Point Pleasant Park on their way home? I mean, think about it. This is a…"

"…military plane," Mel says.

"Exactly. So stands to reason, doesn't it, that their interests…"

"…are military."

"And so…"

"They're on a mission."

"Precisely. A mission. And what's the one thing in Halifax that could possibly be of any interest to them? The one thing?" Lawrie waves a bloodied index finger in their faces for emphasis.

"Only one thing?" Mel asks.

"So obvious," Lawrie says. "The dockyards. They want to know what we've got, how many ships, the Navy, how big it is. What work's going on. Think about it."

"We're in the wrong place."

The chance for Mel to be able to say for the rest of his life that he saw the *Hindenburg* fly over Halifax is slipping away. He doesn't want to see the big machine from a distance. He wants to be close enough to feel his hand run along its smooth envelope.

Edie kicks off the airless rain boots and begins to run in her bare feet, the boys a step behind. They head north and east this time, closer to the grey harbour and its docks and ships. Lawrie wills his ankles to find a physical resolve, just this once. They run until they have no more breath and beneath the raincoat, the tweed jacket, the knitted vest, their clothes cling to their bodies like second skins.

And as if conjured by magic and with a great "ahhhhh" from the crowd, the colossus appears above them. The moment that drew all these people out of their homes and into the street has arrived. Dazzle, on this scale, is a once-in-a-lifetime thing.

Among the crowd, the three friends stare transfixed at the sight of the world's most extraordinary machine. They marvel at the pace and shape of change, captured in a single undefined thought: that nothing in their world will ever be the same.

Mel had tried to imagine the resonance of the ship's rotors. He'd thought of the most frightening sound in his limited world, the roar and hiss of the dragon bearing down on St. George. But this monster doesn't roar. It floats, a gigantic lazy football-shaped balloon issuing a steady humming drone. Or perhaps it is the hundred beating hearts of the people around him that he hears, their gasps of breath, in and out.

Here is a world made wild, set in motion by the improbable and, until today, the unthinkable. Edie hears a whirr and a click of spinning cogs, the syncopated notes of a jazz quintet, the scuff of leather-soled evening shoes moving across the ship's dance floor. How many shining points of light in the heavens has Edie already wished on, begging for an adventure such as that?

Lawrie is the first of the three to notice the swastika painted on the *Hindenburg*'s tailfin.

The machine floats a thousand feet above them and yet seems to brush the treetops. It blocks the bright morning sun and envelops the crowd in shadow. Mel stretches out his arm and is sure he can feel his fingers brush the fragile fabric of its skin, feel the shudder as the rotors work and spin. In a schoolboy prank, he touches the glass of the gondola and leaves his smeary handprint for the fussy captain to see and curse all the way home to Germany. The ship flies above them, as close as their imaginations can bring it and as far away as the stars.

Around him, the crowd is hushed at the sight of the spectacle, like the congregation of a church at a particularly reverent moment.

Edie's hand grips her brother's arm. She is somewhere inside the airship, hidden in its rooms, its dining hall, on its dance floor with the grand piano made of aluminum to lighten its load. She is sailing away to another land with people more fascinating than any that surround her here beside the Halifax harbour.

She bends her head, brings her lips close to Lawrie's ear, and whispers: "How's it stay up there like that?"

Her chestnut hair brushes the boy's cheek. He smells her soap, something clean like the fresh cream crowning the milk just after the paper lid is pulled from the top of a new bottle.

"Hy…hydrogen gas. Very dangerous to use, of course, very flammable, but very useful. As you can see."

Edie's eyes haven't left the airship. Her mouth and its line of fine freckles along the upper lip that Lawrie has never been close enough to notice before form a lazy, preoccupied, and soundless "Oh."

His meagre reply has satisfied her, as though all she needs to know about aeronautical engineering and the scientific properties of certain gases is contained in the two-word explanation of "hydrogen gas." Lawrie's limited but confident answer has shut the door to the flow of Edie's practical curiosity.

The *Hindenburg* drifts above them like a passing cloud carried away on the wind, except that this cloud has people in its core. Edie leans into her brother's shoulder.

"I wish I was up there with them, don't you? I wish that so much. To go away, leave here, have a kind of life. How romantic. How exciting."

Mel feels her fingers dig into his arm.

"They might as well be on the moon," she says and her hand drops away.

The immense ship adjusts its course to the east, over the dockyards, over the Navy ships as Lawrie said they would, and moves on to its true path home. The steady drone leaves with it and is replaced by a low murmur of voices, the onlookers finding their tongues and their senses as if waking from a fantastical dream.

Someone nearby lets out a whoop and the spell is broken.

Women pull at their various coverings, suddenly shy at appearing in public in nightdress and robe. Men run fingers over bed-shocked hair and shove shirttails into whatever kind of trousers they happen to be wearing. Children, barefoot, wearing only pyjamas, run round and round the crowd, shouting and laughing. Mothers clutch their children's hands and hurry homeward. A buoyant trail of sons, brothers, husbands pause to light cigarettes and saunter along behind them.

The three friends turn and begin to walk home through the thinning crowd. They glance over their shoulders for a last glimpse of the *Hindenburg*, drifting like a balloon let loose from a backyard birthday party.

Edie bends, close to Mel's ear: "One day I'll fly away with it."

"Oh, don't say crazy things, Edie."

"You watch. One day I won't be here. I'll go away and have big adventures. And that's where I'll be."

"That's crazy talk. How'd you ever get on the *Hindenburg* anyway?" It isn't the possibility of his sister riding on the big ship that makes Mel a little panicky when she says this to him. Rather, it's the notion that his sister will not always be there beside him.

She touches her lips to the side of his face. "Don't worry, though. I'll always come back to you."

"You better," he says.

"But Mel…" She pinches him through his wool jacket. Conspirators, their mother calls her two younger children. "You got to promise. You're never to tell. It'll be our secret. What I said. Now promise me." And she digs her fingers deeper into his side.

I can keep a secret, he'd often said to Edie.

Promise? she'd say.

Promise, he'd reply.

Last year, when they'd pricked their fingers with a sewing needle and mixed the drops of their blood, she'd said: "Now you'll die if you ever, and I mean ever, tell anyone my secrets," and she'd placed a sloppy big-sister kiss just below his left cheekbone as if to seal their pact.

He wants to laugh at her. It's all right to promise. That's just Edie being Edie and saying things that she never really means.

"Okay, okay. I promise."

"No one. It's our secret. Say it, Melville Clarey. It's our secret."

"Okay. Our secret. You're gonna come back, though. Right?"

"I will always come back to you, mister. If it takes forever, I'll always come back to you. That's my sincere, cross-my-heart-hope-to-die, promise." And with a final dig at his ribs she swings out her arms and slings them across the shoulders of her brother and her brother's best friend, a discarded rain boot dangling from each of her hands.

"Okay, boys," she says. Edie has taken to calling Mel and Lawrie "boys," not so much because they are boys, but because it makes them, all of them, sound a little dangerous, like a gangster's moll in the movies she loves so much.

"What now, boys? How do we top that?"

"I have to go home, clean up for shul." Lawrie's examining the palm of his injured hand. "I'll be late as it is."

"You think you might not be the only one a little late to church today?" Edie says.

"You don't understand. I'm probably the only one who's been out looking at it."

Lawrie knows his parents didn't venture outside their house to glance skyward. He left them this morning laid out on their bed, like two murmuring corpses.

The *Hindenburg* might as well be Ottawa's answer to their repeated pleas for compassion for the relatives who didn't leave Germany years ago when they had the opportunity or the money or common sense to do it. "This machine is our future," the grey Ottawa men would write if they bothered to reply to the Shines' letters at all. "Not your rather ordinary Jewish relatives who have no place here in Canada."

The two friends don't discuss this. For Lawrie, to talk about the jeopardy his father's relatives are in makes him feel unsafe in his own quiet city.

"They can get me even here in Halifax," he thought when he saw the swastika on the *Hindenburg*'s tailfin.

"I can't be late today," he says to his friends.

"Well, I'm going to get my hair done. Me and Ma, the two of us." Edie shakes her chestnut head. "Get it tamed. Just for a day anyways. Hey, don't forget it's my birthday. You'll come over for cake, won't you, Lawrie? It isn't a birthday without cake. And bring a bucket of water for all the candles, okay? How'd I get so old, anyways? Eighteen. Jeez. Hey, we should celebrate. We'll go to the pictures tonight. *The Great Ziegfeld.* I'm mad crazy for William Powell."

Edie had heard Jean Arthur say "mad crazy" in a movie the other week. More than anything, Edie told Mel, she wants to be just like Jean Arthur, smart and sassy, but tender of heart, with a little catch in her throat sometimes.

"You know Ma doesn't like us going to the pictures," Mel says. "You know what she thinks they'll do to us."

"You leave her to me. How about you, Lawrie?"

"I'll have to ask and let you know." He plucks at the torn knee of his trousers. "I have to explain this to my mother first."

"And besides," Mel says. "Gus'll be going away soon and we should be spending time with him."

"So?" Edie says. "We'll ask him along. You think just because he's a priest…"

"Not yet, he isn't."

"As good as. Just because he's a priest, you mean he shouldn't be enjoying himself? That *we* shouldn't be enjoying ourselves?"

"It's not that." Mel doesn't know if their older brother approves of the moving pictures. Especially this moving picture. A priest-in-training might be offended by this kind of entertainment. After all, wasn't Ziegfeld in charge of young women, actresses, with bared legs and backless dresses?

Mel nods his head in a way he hopes will make him appear wise. He adds a shrug to be clear that the sight of near-naked female bodies plays no part in what he's about to say.

"You know, Edie, why don't you ask Ma? It'd be a nice way to finish such a grand day."

"That's my boys," Edie says and she pulls them tight to her as she takes one last look over her shoulder.

3

Anyone living along Toronto's Baldwin Street knows what can be found at Goldstein's.

The hardware store lacks a specific kind of nail? Go to Goldstein's. Can't find a bit of blue wool for your sweater? Goldstein's. It's the same for food or clothing, even some kinds of medicine.

And if the front of Goldstein's store is the street's indispensable bazaar, its back room is a marketplace of another kind. Talkers, men obsessed with politics and revolution, gather to exchange ideas while they smoke, drink tea and argue.

They assemble at night after the front door of the store is locked, entering through the alley at the back of the building. There is no need to advertise what goes on inside. Who on this street, urchin or cop, doesn't know about the back room at Goldstein's? But everyone is wary these days, so the men arrive along the clandestine path of the back alley. They come in twos and in threes or, in the case of Micah Gessen, alone.

On a close, humid August evening Micah emerges from one world and enters another when he crosses Baldwin Street; from the silence of his father's tailor shop to the clamour of Goldstein's. He is always one of the last to arrive, a lesson learned early on. If he enters the room too soon he runs a risk of being trapped by a chatty type desperate for neighbourhood gossip and Micah does not trade in gossip. And, besides, there is nothing in his life worth gossiping about.

In more prosperous days the room was used for storage, when people had real money to buy what Mr. Goldstein was selling. These days, empty wooden shelves line the walls and a collection of donated chairs and stools, even wooden crates turned upside down, crowd the floor. This is where the regulars sit: the talkative hotheads, the studious types, the veterans of old conflicts, and the few for whom the confines of the noisy place is the best entertainment they'll find of an evening.

Someone has propped open the door leading to the alley, hoping to coax fresh air into the cluttered room. A single bare light above the door is an irresistible draw for flying nighttime insects. Micah can hear the spit and crackle of their bodies hitting the hot bulb.

He takes a seat on the last available chair, not especially sturdy, but like everything else here, more resilient than it looks.

The talk of the room tonight is about a distinguished visitor coming to their city, a famous author, who will speak about Franco and Spain and the fuss there that only a month ago was confirmed as a civil war.

Micah doesn't recognize the writer's name. How famous could he be? He motions to the man sitting next to him, an ancient asthmatic, whose whistling wheeze is easy to hear even above the noisy chatter of the assembled group.

"This guy," Micah says to him, "what's he famous for?"

"You heard the man say 'writer,' didn't you? So books, I'd say."

"What kind of books?"

The asthmatic studies the cup of hot tea someone has passed to him. "The usual. Life. Death. Purpose. What would you expect? He's French. Pass the sugar, please."

Micah doesn't care about sugar. "Tell me what you know."

The old asthmatic draws in a laboured breath. His tea will be cold before he can make it suitable for drinking. He looks at Micah's face with its fine features and solemn dark-eyed stare. He's not intimidated by one thin youngster whose only weapon is an unfocussed determination to make everyone understand how angry he is. Still, the old man is inclined to move away and find someone else who promises to be better company for the evening.

"Would a little 'please' or 'thank you' hurt?" he says to Micah.

"I just want to know who he is, this guy," Micah says.

"And I'll tell you. First, my sugar. Yes?"

A mother might have taught this boy a few manners. And a mother might have told him to get a haircut. Among the hard types in Goldstein's back room, the boy's black curls are regarded as a bit show-offy. The old man knows that if Micah wants to do the work that must be done, he shouldn't draw attention to himself in this way. Everyone says these things about Chaim Gessen's boy. But he is who he is. Everyone says that, too.

Micah makes an impatient gesture to the person holding the box of sugar. He passes it to the old asthmatic and sees something as unfamiliar to this room as a bulging wallet; the man is smiling. His parted lips reveal an unsteady row of yellowed teeth.

"Thank you," the man says and holds Micah's gaze. The old eyes are watery, as though he's close to crying, but more likely a result of his chronic cough or the smoke-filled air.

"You're welcome," Micah says.

The asthmatic stirs his tea with a spoon being handed around.

"You see? The sky didn't fall down."

He flicks the spoon, careful not to let any drops stain his pants, and holds it out to Micah, indicating with a jerk of his chin that he should pass it on.

"It's my birthday," Micah says. The words are out before he can think about what he's said. The man's smile had jolted him and shaken loose the words before Micah could hold onto what he'd sworn to keep to himself.

"*Mazel-tov.* How old?"

Hadn't he said enough? He won't tell this man one more thing. But the lone admission of the day's significance has made it impossible now for Micah to hold back what he wants only one other person to acknowledge.

"Nineteen."

"Nineteen. Hunh. A good age. So tell me, this is how you celebrate? You come to Goldstein's to sit with this bunch?"

There's no point Micah explaining that he hasn't celebrated any birthday for many years, not in the tailor's home.

"I want to know about this foreigner, this writer."

"What's that?" The asthmatic cups a hand around his ear.

"Please."

"Sure. Then I'm happy to tell you what I know. But first…"

The old man reaches into his jacket pocket and takes out a small package, flat, about two inches by two inches, wrapped in shiny pale green paper. He holds it out to Micah.

"A little something. To mark your special day."

Inside are four small squares of chocolate. In the heat of the back room and inside the man's pocket, the chocolate has softened, leaving smears of brown across the paper.

The old man always carries candy with him. He tells himself the sugar helps with his asthma and chocolate is his favourite medication.

"It's good, always, to have a little with you. For whatever. You never know when you'll meet someone turning nineteen."

Micah is unsure what to do. Eat the chocolate now or later? Is he expected to share it? He breaks off one of the squares, warm and slippery to his touch, and puts it in his mouth. The sudden sweetness on his tongue surprises him. The tips of his index finger and thumb are daubed dark brown. Should he wipe them on the paper or is it acceptable to lick them clean? He rests his smudged fingertip on his lower lip. The old man says nothing, and nothing again, when Micah's tongue flicks and brushes away the chocolate.

"And not all at once. Save some. We need to make things last these days. You'll thank me later."

The boy's mouth works around the dissolving treat.

"Or you can thank me now. You decide."

"Thank you," Micah says. He wants to put the rest of it in his mouth, all three squares at once. He knows he should do as the man advised and leave some for later. And eating all of it now might be considered impolite or greedy. He knows at least that much about manners.

"This writer," Micah says. "What about him?"

The asthmatic blows across the surface of his tea and he sips. He's all business, this boy. It was a good thing to do, though, giving him the chocolate. When he asked this last question, his voice wasn't so harsh, so demanding. A little sugar works wonders.

"Oh, he's a smart one, this Frenchie," he says. "Fellows like him, you'd think they were movie stars, the way they're treated over there. In Europe." The man waves a hand in a direction meant to indicate east and the Atlantic. "This one, the writer, they say he might as well be that Clark Gable fellow, he's so famous there. And they say he looks as good as he talks." He raps his chest with a fist and swallows, struggling to draw in more air. When he was younger, his fighting days had been limited by these weak lungs and on this evening the thick cigarette and pipe smoke is troubling him more than usual.

He takes another sip of the tea. The hot liquid helps with his voice.

"They send these guys out to talk to the rest of us. Spread the word. Get us all worked up. You know. That's why he comes here. Not here to Goldstein's, I mean. Oh no. Although I'm sure he'd find us quite good company."

He struggles for breath and listens for the thin whistling sound that will assure him he has enough air in his lungs to keep speaking.

"He's not coming here, where, I don't have to tell you, we'd certainly make him welcome. No, no. He's at the university. With the other smart ones. And the police. Probably half the audience is police looking for Reds. Like us." He wags a finger, making it clear that he includes himself and Micah in that group. He holds an arm to his face and coughs into his sleeve.

Micah nods at all this, no sign of the pleasure that being called a Red has given him. The chocolate may have softened his voice. His face is as hard as ever.

The old asthmatic isn't the only one in the room who feels a little sorry for the motherless boy with the difficult father. But there's enough sorry to go around these days. What makes this one so special? Still, the asthmatic wonders if putting a hand on Micah's shoulder and mumbling a few kind words might help him. And say what, exactly? That one day Micah will understand that life is a struggle for everyone, not just him. That you make your happiness with what you have and where you are. Don't go looking for it under rocks too heavy to lift by yourself. He says none of that. The boy has been a stranger to life for too long for such thoughts to make any difference now.

Everyone in the back room of Goldstein's knows the story of Micah Gessen. How his family had moved to the tiny flat above the shop on Baldwin Street in 1918. How Chaim's wife, the mother of the infant Micah and pregnant with a second child, died in the influenza epidemic. Soon after, the tailor's parents and a beloved sister were gone. The loss of the people he loved most weighed so heavily on Chaim that nothing, not even the demands of his dark-eyed son, once the cause of so much joy, could lift him above the least of what was needed to get through a day.

Goldstein's is Micah's release from his father's hushed world. Here, amidst the clatter of ideas and voices, is an explanation and remedy for injustice. And here, on the night of his nineteenth birthday, he hears the name of the French writer of important novels about discovering purpose in life and in death through political action. A Parisian intellectual who lived the good life has gone to Spain to fight. His is a world away from Micah's and now he's coming to Toronto to talk.

"I'm interested in this guy. What he has to say, I mean," Micah says to the old asthmatic.

"Then go. Enjoy. Watch who you talk to. That's the only advice I'll give."

Micah nods, as though considering what he's been told. His thoughts are with the package and its three remaining squares of chocolate that he balances in the palm of one hand.

Later, in bed, he'll eat the rest of it with care and savour the taste. When he's swallowed the last sweet morsel he'll run his tongue over the pale green paper to remove the remaining thick smears of the melted treat. As he does that he'll consider where to dispose of the paper so that his father won't find it.

≈

On a warm late September evening, Micah closes the door of the tailor's shop to begin his walk to the university.

He's spent the last month, while waiting for the visit of the French writer, in the library reading his novels about the purposeful life. Micah's plan is to take a place near the front of the lecture hall from where he can observe the writer. What does a writer look like, sound like? When he arrives, the room is full, all the seats occupied. He stands, wedged into the crush of bodies at one side of the room already hazy with smoke and shouted argument.

Not everyone has come to praise the night's guest. Pockets of fascist supporters jostle with defenders of Republican Spain. The air bristles with threats from both sides. This is like nothing Micah has seen or heard in the noisy decorum of Goldstein's with its like-minded quarrels. Something else is happening here. In this atmosphere of barbed insults and muscled rebuttals, he understands that thoughts and actions exist on opposing sides of a ledger marked "good" and "evil."

The air moving through the opened windows and into the room can't ease the smell of bodies and cigarettes or the heat that has built up throughout the day. Micah scans the crowd, remembering the old asthmatic's warning to watch for police.

"Look around," he'd advised. "Shoes tell a story. And see who's been to the barber."

Micah peers over shoulders to search for the shoes that are not cracked and spent like his own, but sturdy, and that glisten with a polish that speaks of practised attention to duty. Under the edges of neat haircuts and inside perfectly still heads, eyes strain from side to side. These are the police, the quiet men, morosely relaxed, smoking as though they have no urgent need to ration their tobacco.

At the front of the hall a door opens. Two men and a woman enter and stop to soak in the raucous salute of applause and catcalling. The famous author is tall and slightly stooped as one would be who spent his days at a writing table, Micah assumes. He wears a well-cut double-breasted dark blue suit with a red scarf tucked into the open neck of a white shirt. He runs a hand over his high forehead and through thinning dark hair, so long it curls over the collar of his shirt. A thumb and index finger pinch the corners of his dark eyes above the bridge of his long narrow nose. It's a face of lines and shadows, framed by a jaw left unshaved that day, a lack of resolve for a tedious chore perhaps or the deliberate effect of someone come to talk of war. The second man, small and tweedy, holds up his arms to signal quiet and begins to speak. The crowd shuffles in its impatience. The old asthmatic had been right. The man's words are as pointless as introducing Clark Gable to the crowd at a movie premiere.

The third figure, the woman, a blonde, is tall like the writer and in her high heels has no trouble matching his height. She settles on a chair at the side of the stage and pulls a shapeless linen coat around her as though she alone is unaffected by the uncomfortable warmth of the room. She folds her arms in front of her and crosses what Micah believes are the most perfectly formed pair of stockinged legs he's ever seen. The audience is subdued at last and not by anything the nervous little man at the lectern is saying. As the woman leans back and shakes her head of loose blonde hair, a soft collective sigh rises from the crowd. If politics can't unite them, the woman will.

The famous French writer surveys the room, stilled in anticipation, hands and voices ready to object or applaud. He speaks in precise, accented English.

"First, I must tell you how very grateful I am so many of you feel a deep caring for Spain's agony. I say *merci* and *gracias*. And welcome. In particular, I say *bienvenido* to the members of your fascist police who also must deeply care about Spain to come here tonight."

Many in the crowd cheer his words and pump the air with closed fists. A fevered few have come to hiss at the Red devil. Left sitting, sullen and uncomfortable, are the quiet men, the observers who will consign their thoughts to their written reports later tonight.

"Communist piece of shit," someone yells. Bodies scuffle as voices, loud and passionate, beat back the lone insult.

The writer's talk is a banquet for the hungry Micah. Seville, Barcelona, Madrid. The names feed his hunger.

In a voice used to creating dramatic emphasis, the writer speaks of massacres and the deaths of innocents. Special praise is reserved for the heroic strangers travelling to Spain to fight the tide of fascism drowning Europe and threatening the world.

"Those of you who want to help," he says, "I beg you, go to Spain."

With that final flourish, the writer and the blonde woman leave the stage. A few strained voices begin to sing the "Internationale." Their efforts are swamped by the competing howls of the fascists and the wave of overheated bodies making their way to the door, desperate to escape the room's suffocating heat and to feel fresh air on their faces.

Micah wants only to be away from the smell and touch of the other bodies. He needs a quiet spot, to breathe in the night air and be alone until he can trust himself to speak without screaming.

Around the side of the building, on a step near the back entrance, he leans against a round stone column. Behind him, a door opens. Light spills across the lawn. He hears voices, a man and a woman speaking French, low with weariness and something else, two people exchanging casual confidences.

The famous man puts a cigarette to his lips as the blonde woman reaches into the pocket of her linen coat. Micah hears the snap of the match igniting and sees its light illuminating their faces. The writer inhales and leans his head back to expel the smoke. The woman slips the fingertips of her hand under the cuff of his jacket sleeve and leaves them there, resting on his wrist.

A hot wave of embarrassment climbs up Micah's neck and face. He has seen people exchange hugs and kisses before, seen handshakes and slaps on backs, arms around shoulders. But he has never witnessed a gesture of such intimacy and, having seen enough, he rises from his place to leave the two of them to their solitary moment.

1937

4

The great eye takes in her every move. She expects to see it blink at any moment. A nagging Cyclops of a thing. Ten minutes to twelve.

Her father had placed the large round clock on the wall several months ago, in September, not long after Edie began working in the office of Clarey Glass and Paint. The clock was Charles's not very subtle reminder to his daughter that employees are expected to arrive at a specific time and, thereafter, observe the accepted hours of a working day.

She'd watched her father prepare to hang it; taking his time folding his jacket, pulling over a chair for more height, hammering the nail into the solid wooden panelling.

"I have a wristwatch right here," she'd said to him and tapped its thin gold bracelet. "That I've been able to read for quite some time, you know."

Charles had ignored her, climbed down from the chair, pushed the plug into the wall socket and stepped back to admire his skill as a handyman.

"I guess there's nothing more to say then, is there?" Edie had said. "Except that great long cord dangling down the wall ruins the look of the place. Makes us look messy, don't you think?"

Charles moved the chair back to its place against the wall. He picked up his jacket and, smiling, left his daughter with her sole companion in the room, the unnerving eye. The timepiece remained there into Edie's first autumn as the new receptionist of

Clarey Glass and Paint, through the winter months, and into the new year.

Now, in late April, it observes her as she arrives every morning and, she's sure, judges her the moment she stands to leave.

Ten minutes to twelve. Ten minutes until the great eye allows her to leave for the dinner break. Ten minutes until she can forget answering the phone, making the tea, the pointless conversations she's obliged to participate in when anyone walks into the office.

All morning, her father has been in town talking the business of the Clarey Glass and Paint Company. In these hard times, when the once bustling building has been transformed into a warren of empty offices, Charles is the entire sales department and because of that, often gone. In his absence that leaves one other person, besides Edie, present and in charge and that person, the bookkeeper Raymond Gillis, is nowhere in sight.

Nine minutes to twelve and still no one to witness a tiny slippage of duty.

Edie Clarey is a young woman of certainties, and she is certain there is nothing that can be accomplished in nine, almost eight minutes now, that can't be done later; answer a phone that rarely rings anymore, fill envelopes with reminders of outstanding bills rather than original invoices, or greet the few customers who visit. All of that can wait.

She leaves her desk to look down the hallway off the reception area. The door to Raymond Gillis's office is open. From where she stands, Edie can see his tidy desk and senses the emptiness of his room.

"I had to go tell them it wasn't time to knock off yet." Raymond's steady tenor ricochets with the clarity of a motivated priest pronouncing from the pulpit. He'd entered the reception area from outside like a spectre, with no warning of approach. Not for the first time, Edie wishes the company bookkeeper was a little more ghostly vapour and a little less flesh and blood.

She's heard Raymond described as "good looking" and he is, in a solid, broad-shouldered way. He has a head of thick brown waves, cut too short on the sides as men do these days to save on trips to the barber. The effect emphasizes the square outline of his sharp-edged face. His blue eyes remind Edie of the sapphire in her mother's wedding ring. His skin, its pinkness depending on mood and situation, is clean-shaven and clear. His looks, along with his steady employment and precisely observed manners, make Raymond a good catch for any woman. Not for Edie Clarey, though. She's in no hurry to set her line to hook the young bookkeeper.

"Who, Raymond? You told who it wasn't time to leave?"

"Our gentlemen in the warehouse. You'd think they didn't have to work for a living." He hesitates and adds in a rush: "M'dear."

Edie hears the flutey tone of hope in his last words. He uses them to lend a depth to his youth and to assure his employer's daughter that when her father is not on the premises, he's more than capable of filling the void.

"Jobs're precious these days, Edith, as we all know. Like gold. And those men have no respect for that if they're just looking for opportunities to slack off."

"What d'you mean?"

"Smoking!" His voice is raised to a pitch guaranteed to register with her as indignation. "I caught them smoking near the warehouse. They know that's forbidden. All that flammable substance in there. Paint, you see. Could go up like that." And he snaps his fingers to emphasize the point.

"Can't be too careful once you know the history of this city and explosions." He tugs at the cuff of his suit sleeve. "My dear." His triumph in the warehouse registers as two scarlet smudges across his pinched Celtic cheekbones.

"They work hard enough, Raymond. They know what they're doing," she says. "My father wouldn't keep them round if they didn't. Not when so many are looking for work. As you say."

"Yes, well." The scarlet smudges spread. "With all respect, I've often thought your father's heart may be a little too tender at times."

"Tender enough to take you in."

The red flush of Raymond's face deepens. Her words, intended to defend her father, have succeeded in wounding the bookkeeper.

"You refer to my situation, Edith."

"I didn't mean..."

"My uncle served many loyal years as the numbers man here at Clarey Glass and Paint. His illness afforded me an opportunity to step into his shoes..."

"I didn't mean to say..."

Raymond takes a step back and places a steadying hand along the frame of the door. "I hope you're not implying that I'm nothing more than a charity case. We both know your father well enough. If he didn't think I could do the job, he wouldn't've hired me."

"My father. As you say. He's very tender of heart."

"Quite so, Edith. Nor does he allow sentiment to get in the way of business. And I believe it was the businessman who made the decision to take me on when my uncle's bad health forced his retirement."

Edie had overheard her father telling her mother that Raymond wasn't to be faulted for the work he did or any lack of attention to detail. But she'd also noted the hesitation in her father's voice. Beyond citing the young man's diligence and intelligence, Charles had nothing more to say about him.

"If you say so, Raymond," Edie says as she glances at the Cyclops eye.

This talk with the bookkeeper has taken five minutes of the precious nine. It's not where he's from, his Cape Breton accent, or how he dresses or cuts his hair. That might bother others. Not Edie Clarey. Something else about him makes her uneasy. For a girl so used to attention, who delights in being at the centre of her family's happiness, she finds his awkward politeness and serious attempts to engage her embarrassing.

"I gotta go." Edie pulls open the desk drawer. She takes out her purse, fusses with it, opens it, jabs at its contents with her fingers, and snaps shut the clasp.

Raymond looks over his shoulder at the clock.

"I haven't heard the noon gun yet."

Edie has come to understand that Raymond is helpless against the temptation to do this sort of thing, monitor aloud the comings and goings of employees. She wonders what kind of glum home with its sombre parents created this sad young man, this self-appointed enforcer of office rules.

When she makes no reply, Raymond signals with a wave of his hand that if she wishes to go, she may.

She pulls her coat and scarf off the wall hook and struggles inside them. When he reaches out a hand and holds up a corner of the coat to guide her arm into the sleeve, she says nothing.

Raymond heaves his sturdy back against the doorframe so that Edie must turn sideways in order to squeeze by him. Her gaze is cast down, her long straight eyelashes outlined against her pale winter skin. As she passes him, so near that the soft wool of her coat brushes against his hand, she is certain he's not breathing.

Edie's mother had taught her children that, above all, they must remember their manners. "A simple 'no thank you' never hurts," she'd instructed her children. The words fight to stay inside Edie when she has to say them to Raymond. As she brushes past she whispers, as much by instinct as discipline: "'Scuse me. Please."

She pushes open the front door as the boom of the noontime cannon echoes from the distant Citadel. He had kept her there until the precise moment.

At the warehouse, Edie unlocks the small side door and steps into the dark interior, quiet in the absence of men. Today is payday and Raymond must have spent part of his morning handing out the envelopes to the workers. She's observed his routine, the way he sets up the small table, arranges the chair, sits and addresses his attention to the job at hand. He points to a spot on the sheet of paper in case a man can't read his own name. Once the signature or mark is produced, he hands over the pay packet with the precision of a priest dispensing the wafer.

There is no camaraderie or banter throughout his performance of duty, no effort to draw the natural friendliness of these men to the surface. And they understand that a smile or a pleasantry makes no difference to the worth of the packet's contents.

"Jokes don't help, but glum don't hurt neither," one of them had once observed to Edie and she'd laughed out loud along with him when he said it.

On Fridays the penny-pinching ways of the warehouse men ease for an hour. With pockets fuller than usual, they head down the street for "a haircut," which is to say, the barbershop with its backyard hut and barrels of bootlegged rum. For a few pennies they can make one afternoon of the working week enjoyable. They leave work a little early and will be a few minutes late coming back. That time, stolen from their long hours during the heat of summer and the cold of winter, is the one act of rebellion by the workers that their employer is happy to overlook. This is Charles Clarey's tip of the hat to their hard lives.

Edie pauses to look around at the sheets of glass cradled in the wooden arms. Since she was a child, she loved to stop here and marvel at the illusion created by the light from the high windows, like stepping inside a prism. Today is different though. Today she can't linger.

Her blue bicycle with its wicker basket leans against the wall where she left it that morning. When her father had presented the machine to her, he'd also handed over a length of thick chain and a lock.

"These are desperate times," he'd said to her. "Anybody will steal anything."

As she fishes in her purse for the key to the lock, she looks at the bicycle. The chain has been moved so that the lock is on the side nearest the wall, as if someone had given it a good hard tug and, unable to force it open, tossed it aside.

Were there scratch marks around the keyhole before today? Perhaps her own clumsiness had caused them, perhaps not.

She inserts the key, twists and tugs, and drops the chain and lock into the wicker basket. Once she's pulled the bicycle through the door, she pushes down hard onto the pedal and moves off to begin the cold ride home.

She doesn't look back so she doesn't see Raymond watching her from inside his office. The young man has yet to find his place in the new city, at the first job of any significance he's ever held. No one had expected much from a miner's son from Glace Bay, but the intelligent boy had listened to his father: "Get your schooling, Raymond," the elder Gillis had said, "so's you don't end up working down below beside them MacGillivray boys. You think they tormented you up here, you've no idea what they get up to underground."

The reliable employee returns to his desk to eat the meal prepared for him by his landlady and wait out the hour until Edie's return.

5

Theresa Monaghan kneels, her face close to the wine-red carpet. The once plush wool has given way to bare patches, exposing some of its rough backing. Friday is her day in the Clarey home for dusting and pushing the carpet sweeper. She stares down the length of the runner and marvels how two decades of shoes and children have worn such a path across it.

If she were the kind of woman given to reflecting on the course of her life, Theresa might recognize something of herself here; beneath the smooth comfort, a tough unyielding weave.

Instead, she wonders how much of this damage has been caused by her own attentions. Has she been too thorough in her cleaning? From now on, she decides, carpet sweeping once every two weeks. That little change in routine might mean getting another year or two out of the carpets before they have to be replaced and cost Mr. Clarey some amount he isn't inclined to spend right now.

Satisfied that she's seen the worst of it, Theresa straightens and steadies herself to stand up. Her right knee complains with the effort. She'll keep her thoughts about the carpets to herself for the time being. Although the Clareys aren't as badly off as many families in this city these days, even as some in their own social circle are, Theresa is sure there is no money for extras like new carpets.

The small brass clock on the fireplace mantle chimes the noon hour. Any minute, she'll hear the noises at the back door,

Mel home from school, Edie from the office. They'll be hungry and want their dinner. And Gus, what can she persuade him to eat today? She pauses at the foot of the stairs and listens for any sound from the sick room. Hearing nothing, she moves on.

The house on the lower end of the peninsula has been her home for almost twenty years. In that time, she has never returned to the north end of the city to search for any trace of the world she knew before 1918. That was the year she'd met Mary and Charles Clarey, a young couple with one toddler and plans for more. They were financially comfortable, with the means to support a live-in housekeeper who could cook and clean and help look after children.

She was the young mother of two daughters, whose husband was away, soldiering in France. In her husband's absence, she and the little girls lived with her mother and sister in a wooden house not far from the water. All of that was before the morning in December, 1917.

A priest, familiar with her story, told the Clareys about the hardship case. She hoped the priest had had the decency to warn the Clarey woman about what to expect when they met.

"Try not to stare," she expected he'd said to Mrs. Clarey.

When she arrived for her interview, she introduced herself with the name she had always been called: Marie, pronounced in the Irish way, *Mar*-ee.

She saw right away the look of shock on Mrs. Clarey's face, even so many months after what had happened. And she noticed Mary Clarey's hand tremble as she poured a cup of tea and knew that whatever range of manners the woman possessed, they had not prepared her for this.

The visitor to the Clarey house picked up the baby, the two-year-old Augustus, and placed him on her knees, where he sat, staring in his serious way at the curious sight before him. It was then left to her, in her most matter-of-fact way, to deal with Mary's unvoiced thoughts. She didn't want any questions lingering because she did not intend to address this matter a second time, not for anyone.

She straightened the little boy's shirt and laid out the details of how her life, set on one straight path, had veered sharply to bring her to this meeting at the Clarey house.

"It was a Friday." Her voice was flat, hurried. She wanted to get this over and done with.

"Wash day in our house. My sister and mother in the kitchen. Heating the water on the wood stove, you see. I'm in the front room with my girls. They're on the floor. Three and one they were, their ages, I mean. We're playing with wooden blocks. I hear shouting outside. From the front of the house you can see straight down to the water, you know, the harbour. I remember saying, 'I can't wait till spring when I can get at these windows. They need a good cleaning.' There's a fire, people running, all wanting to have a good gawk. But it's cold outside and, besides, I can't leave the girls, and so there I am, gawking myself. At the window. Safe, I'm thinking."

Two ships had collided in the harbour. One of them was on fire. It carried wartime munitions and was drifting towards shore, closer and closer to the sightseers wanting a front-row seat to the spectacle. The ones who stayed indoors gaped in amazement through the glass panes of their windows.

"Quite a sight, it was," she said, her pale blue eyes dry and unblinking. She wondered if Mary expected her to cry at some point. "When it come, the blast I mean, the noise, well, my hearing was gone for a good long while after that, you see? And the glass, it come right in on me. I shoulda been blinded, too. 'Stead, it just cut me up. Right here. As you can see. That's what that is." And she fingered the puckered blue-black line on her face as though Mary might be noticing it for the first time.

A large shard of glass had incised the left side of her face, from just below her eye to her jawline, leaving the skin of her cheek hanging like a piece of damp laundry on the clothesline.

"And then I don't remember much of anything. I only know what they told me after."

What they told her was that the vacuum caused by the blast had sucked her out of the shattered window, ripped off her clothes and flung her a hundred yards from the house onto the side of a nearby frozen hill. She lay there, naked, drifting in and out of consciousness. From time to time, she woke to find herself lying on her back, her right leg twisted beneath her. A black rain of fuel oil and ash fell from the sky and coated her skin.

"I was a lucky one. That's what they told me and I guess they'd know." Lucky, because she'd been thrown clear, not buried in the rubble of the house like her children, her mother and her sister. And she hadn't been burned to death as others were when the wooden houses, reduced to splinters, were ignited by stove fires. Oh, yes, lucky because she was found after a few hours and taken to a hospital instead of bleeding to death or dying of exposure on the frozen hillside. In the hospital hallway, overwhelmed with casualties, the laceration on her face was cleaned in a perfunctory way, stitched and bandaged. The oil and ash that fell onto her from the sky served as a kind of tattoo ink in her raw flesh.

"They never found my girls. My sister and mother neither. I looked for them after, the girls at least. I hoped maybe somebody might've found them and took them to one of the orphanages."

She walked through hospital wards and the rooms of the makeshift children's homes, one hand covering her wound so that the sight of it didn't shock the smaller ones. There was little chance of that, though. Traumatized, they lay on their beds like dolls in a store window display. She feared her appearance was so altered by her injuries that she might be unrecognizable, even to her own daughters. Although she never found her girls, she never quite accepted that they had died along with their aunt and grandmother in the house that December morning.

Not long after the Explosion, she received official notice that her husband had died of his wounds following the battle of Passchendaele in Belgium. Her family was gone. Her house was gone and all her possessions with it. Not a photo, not a memento of her life remained. All she was left with to mark her life and time as a mother, sister, daughter and wife was the ragged tattooed line on her face, a thin black ribbon of mourning that she would wear for the rest of her life.

She comforted herself by imagining that her daughters had survived somehow and had been adopted by a loving family. When she was out in public, her eyes sought the familiar faces, hair, eyes, expressions, the telltale physical details of her own or her husband's features.

Mary Clarey listened to all this without question or comment.

"So, that's my story," the young woman from the north end said. "Anything you need to know?"

She watched Mary Clarey's face, fixed as a sculpture throughout the telling, soften.

"Your name, Mar-ee," Mary said. "This is the name you usually go by?"

Marie nodded.

To Mary's ears, the name sounded very much like her own. "You must have a middle name," she said.

"Theresa. My middle name's Theresa."

"Well, then, that's what we'll call you," Mary said, and she smiled, the relief on her face evident. A solution had been reached with no fuss or tears. "Just so there's no misunderstanding, you see."

For this visitor to the Clarey home one name meant as much, or as little, as any other. With everything and everyone gone, what did a name matter?

And so the woman known as *Mar*-ee was no more. She had vanished, along with the rest of her family, and was replaced by someone named Theresa.

Soon after that first meeting, she moved into the house of Mary and Charles Clarey and the baby Augustus, or Gus, as he was known. All talk of the Explosion and Theresa's life in the north end was avoided. No one wanted to remind her of the events of the day, especially Mary, who suffered a lingering guilt, never reconciled, that she hadn't asked Theresa the names of her little girls.

≈

The Clarey house is modern, built for electricity and with a large kitchen, big enough to accommodate the long oak table where the Clareys take their breakfast and the noon meals. Evening meals are eaten in the adjacent dining room with its broad mahogany table and matching chairs and sideboard. Theresa prepares all the food and serves it herself in the evening and on special occasions. That's the way she wants it done. No one questions the process or her intent. To live with the Clarey kitchen is to live by Theresa's rules.

She hears the heavy thud against the outside wall and before she can finish counting to three, the back door opens and a breathless Edie steps into the small mudroom off the kitchen.

"I'm not telling you again to stop banging that machine up against the wall. You know what you're supposed to do with it."

Edie pulls the gloves from her hands, one finger at a time, punctuating each word: "And…what…is…that…exactly?"

"You know quite well."

"Pretend I don't. Surprise me."

"You're to bring it properly into the backyard and put it up against the fence. Leaving it like you do, someone'll trip over it and hurt himself one day. You just watch."

Edie waves her gloves at Theresa before shoving them into her coat pockets. Both Theresa and Mary thought the bicycle, Charles's bribe to his daughter to get her to work at the family business, was a mistake. "It's a useless thing for a girl to have," they'd both argued. "The thing will only make her reckless." Nevertheless, it was the price Edie put on doing what her father wanted her to do: slave away in his office for little more than pocket change. The job was meant to keep his easily distracted daughter busy now that she was finished with school. And by paying her the little he did from his own pocket, he kept the cost of at least one salary off the company books.

Edie had been born a year after Theresa's arrival in the Clarey house. After a difficult birth, Mary was confined to her bed to recover. Theresa took charge of the infant, saying: "You leave this little one to me." And so it was the housekeeper who rose in the dark to comfort the crying baby and rock her back to sleep. She later lifted the tiny girl to smell the sweetest of the summer roses and shushed her when Edie's tongue proved too saucy for polite company. From time to time, Theresa reminded herself: "You're not her mother." And: "You're no one's mother." But the love she felt for Edie frightened her. Wasn't it her history that whoever she loved most, died? She wouldn't let that happen again. She believed that speaking in a certain sharp tone would keep the girl at a distance and so out of harm's way. "You may twist your parents around your finger, little miss," she'd warned Edie. "You'll not do that to me." She did not understand the hopelessness of the thought.

"Take your coat off and sit down. Your brother'll be here in a minute."

"Well, here's the thing, Theresa. Dear one." Edie places a cold hand on each side of the woman's warm face. "I'm here to ask you, in the very politest way I know how, to please make me a sandwich."

"I will not. Sandwiches are no good for you. I've made a fish stew for your dinner."

"But Theresa. I want to eat my lunch in the park today. It's such an…invigorating day. And I can't very well carry a bowl of stew to a park now, can I?"

Edie follows the older woman's gaze to the window. They both eye the steel grey of the late April sky.

Theresa's reputation as a cook has travelled far beyond the Clarey household. Her stews, in particular, turn away from the table those with even the most urgent appetites. Overcooked, oversalted, or no salt at all, a gummy mess of incompatible vegetables, simmered in a sauce so viscous the dish could be cleared with a fork. Her bread has a plaster-like consistency useful for little else than toast or bird feed.

"It's still winter outside."

"I'm meeting Laura Schmidt and we're going to be talking…"

"Yes?"

"We're going to be talking about her sister's wedding and things and that's simply the best place, the most convenient, to meet. That's what we decided."

Theresa looks at the girl she thought she knew so well. Edie was the most open, the liveliest of the three Clarey children, but she'd been keeping things from her these days. She's sure of that. Since Edie began working at her father's business she's changed, even how she dresses. She wears fewer and fewer of the good pieces she owns, hands over what she does wear for washing less often. Plain cotton replaces silk, plain wool takes the place of cashmere, and she wears the same brown shoes that she refuses to have polished. She washes her hair less often too and, Theresa is sure, bathes less frequently. And now she wants to eat outside, in a public place, in a park and in the grey Halifax spring that to everyone else still feels like winter.

"You don't even want to go to Laura Schmidt's sister's wedding."

"Why, that's an outrageous claim. Where did you hear that?"

"From you."

"When?"

"Yesterday."

Edie leans down to bring her face close to the smaller woman. The ragged black scar along Theresa's face has never frightened her. It was always part of Theresa, like the colour of her dark brown hair or the faded blue of her eyes.

"Theresa. Please. Just today." The insolent tone is gone. She might as well have said: "I'm that desperate. I wouldn't ask otherwise. Can't you hear what I'm saying? Listen to me." She places her hands on the older woman's shoulders and offers a conciliatory smile.

"Just this once, Theresa. I promise."

"Yes, but, it's never 'just this once' with you, is it? You wanted the same thing last week. I want to know what's going on."

"Absolutely nothing. Just a bit of fresh air after this awful winter is all. Pretty please, Theresa."

They stay like that, the tall girl bent over, their eyes locked, one not capable of giving up what she wants, the other not capable of denying her. Long ago, Theresa's sister had admonished her for being too lenient with her own daughters. After they were gone, she wished she'd spoiled them more.

She removes Edie's hands and with one long stare meant to salvage some sense of pride, moves to the counter.

"Edith Clarey, you don't consider beyond what's staring you in the face," she says.

Theresa had played her part in making Edie this way. She'd helped shape her and now it was too late to change anything. The girl is who she is and today she will get her way one more time. The surrender, however, would not come without one last jab.

"You, miss, are like a magpie. If it sparkles, if it strikes your fancy, you must have it."

"But Theresa, surely that's only human nature."

The older woman's hands smooth away invisible creases from her clean, freshly ironed cotton apron.

"Don't you 'human nature' me, Edith Clarey. What do you know about human nature at your age? Where'd you learn about that sort of thing? Not from the nuns, I'll bet. No, I didn't think so. You want what you want, you do. And it always has to be your way and today."

"Well, why wouldn't anyone be like that? Want what makes you feel good, I mean? It's only sensible." Only human nature, Edie's tempted to say again, and says nothing. She knows too well how far to push this woman.

Theresa saws two slabs off an unhealthy-looking loaf of bread. From the icebox she retrieves a brick of white cheese and chips at it until she has enough to cover the surface of one of the slices. That done, she jams the other on top and places the resulting mess into a napkin and folds the cloth. She holds it out to Edie, who asks, a smile seeping across her face: "Do you suppose I could have some butter on that, please?"

Theresa holds her gaze. "You're lucky, my girl. You don't know how lucky you are."

Edie takes the folded napkin and purses her lips in an acknowledging kiss.

The moment had passed; not a battle, little more than a tug-of-war between two opposing sides, its outcome determined from the start.

"If you see your brother, tell him his dinner won't wait." Theresa's words are lost in the slam of the mudroom door.

≈

From a distance, Mel sees his sister wheel the bicycle into the street.

He calls out to her and she signals with a wave of her arm that she's heard him, but instead of waiting for him to catch up to her, she pushes down on the pedal and rides away.

Not so long ago she would have stopped when he hailed her and waited to hear his news. That bicycle had changed everything. It was taking her away from him more often, putting a physical distance between the two of them.

"You'll tell her later," Lawrie says as he draws up beside his friend.

"I thought she'd want to know is all."

It isn't every day Mel receives the second highest mark in science. Some scholastic fluke, a sluggard response from the rest of the class, put him right behind his best friend in a test Edie had helped him study for. He'd thought of what she'd do when he told her about their triumph, her squeal and her arms flung around him.

"Damn bicycle."

"Like I said, tell her later, Mel. She'll be just as happy. You'll see."

"Why'd she get the bike and not me, anyways? I'm sixteen. I should have my own bicycle."

"I don't know why, Mel. Because, I guess. Ask your father, not me. One thing you need to understand, though. Boys don't have dominion over girls. Even when bicycles are being handed out."

"I'm not saying that." Whatever it is Lawrie meant by what he said. "She doesn't need a bicycle. Not really. Not the way I do."

Mel readies himself for his friend's defence of his sister. Lawrie refuses to listen to anything about Edie that doesn't reflect his own uncritical assessment of her.

"I'm sure she'd tell you what made her the lucky one if you'd only ask her," Lawrie says. "Have you asked her?"

"Don't have to. She wouldn't hear me even if I did. She's so strange these days. Head in the clouds all the time."

Lawrie's dip of his head, a reluctant nod of agreement, is Mel's one small consolation. They've both felt the shift in Edie's allegiance to them. They hear it in her voice, a change of tone, a way of speaking she hasn't used before. She spends less time asking them about what they're doing and more time peppering them with questions about what they plan to do. When the boys stare at her blank-faced, she says: "With your lives, you dopes. What're you going to do with your lives?"

"Edie," Mel said to her the last time she'd pestered him. "Lawrie and me, we're sixteen years old. What'd you know about anything when you were sixteen?" At least that made her laugh. The bicycle hadn't taken that away from her.

"Come on, Mel. I'm hungry. Ask Theresa if you can eat at my place today. Have some good food for a change. That should cheer you up."

6

He waits for her in the big park, seated on one of the large rocks by the water's edge. He watches for the ships that come and go through the mouth of the harbour and listens for the sound of her approach; the racket made by the basket bouncing against the handlebars of the bicycle as she rides over the uneven dirt path.

Michael Green is the name he uses in Halifax. Micah Gessen has ceased to exist for the time being. A name like Micah might draw attention, so keep it simple, he'd told himself. Michael is commonplace enough, and Green is a name that belongs to nothing and to no one, like Black or White or Brown. With a name so ordinary, a man could disappear.

The trail from Micah Gessen of Baldwin Street, Toronto, to Michael Green of Morris Street in Halifax began the day after he'd heard the French author speak at the university.

The next morning he walked to the office of the Communist Party on Adelaide Street.

"I want to fight," Micah announced. "In Spain."

He was offered the opportunity to paste notices of meetings on walls.

"Paste your own fucking notices," he said.

An older woman, a motherly type who worked in the office and felt sorry for the young man and the way he had been dismissed, took Micah aside. She explained to him that it was the older types they wanted, the men from the relief camps, the protestors who'd already taken the blows from the police batons.

Those men were ready for Spain and the fight and, that day, no degree of good intention could camouflage the obvious, that Micah was too young, too untried. What they didn't want were the underfed hotheads with some kind of personal score to settle.

"They're afraid that you young ones," the woman said to him, "that you're just as likely to turn and run as fight. You don't think so now…"

You don't understand, Micah wanted to yell at her. The years of living with his father had toughened him enough.

Spain belonged to him and he'd get there with or without their help.

He raged about his frustration in Goldstein's back room that night. As the gathering broke up, he stood on the sidewalk outside the store and watched one of the regulars light a hand-rolled cigarette. Micah marvelled that the man he knew as Peter drew in the smoke with the hunger of a starving person discovering a three-course meal rather than someone who had spent the evening inside the congested air of Goldstein's.

Peter crooked a yellowed finger at Micah.

"Come here, boy."

Micah had heard the whispers about Peter, a political refugee, they said, from the Tsar's Russia. One night, as the old asthmatic passed Micah a mug of black tea, he told him why Peter never removed the scarf he wore from around his neck.

"To hide the scars," he wheezed into Micah's ear and offered a knowing dip of his head.

"What kind of scars?"

"You know," the old man said and he drew a finger across his throat. "Now he works in an abattoir in the west end. He carries an ice pick with him, always, inside his jacket. You watch. Ready for trouble, that one. To stop it or to make it." The asthmatic made an impatient gesture. "Pass the sugar," he said. He was done with gossip and wanted to drink his tea in peace.

On the sidewalk, Micah moved closer to Peter, although not so close that he couldn't get a good head start if he had to run. He took in Peter's stained grey jacket. His eyes searched for a telltale lump or sharp point that might reveal the hiding place of the ice pick. Now that they were outside and away from the smoky room, Micah was aware of the smell coming off of Peter; cigarettes and a body gone too long between washings. And something else. It was the smell of the alley behind the Gessens' neighbour, the street's butcher's shop.

"Look. You're wasting your time here." There wasn't much left of Peter's accent. He'd worked hard to blend into the new country.

"You go to some other place. Smaller maybe, like Halifax." His voice was low and gravelly. Perhaps it was the cigarettes. Perhaps it was true what his reliable informant, the old asthmatic, had said to Micah about Peter's throat and the reason for the scarf.

"Find the CP, you know, the Communists, there. In those places, they're more likely to take your kind. Kids. Know-nothings who think they know everything. They'll find you a ship that'll get you somewheres close. England maybe. France if you're lucky. Better eating in France. Trust me. Then you go for a little stroll over the Pyrenees and..." He swept out an arm as if the houses and shops along Baldwin Street were about to be magically transformed. "Spain and the all the trouble you want. You listen to me. That's the best advice you'll get."

Micah decided to take Peter's advice.

≈

The night Micah left Toronto, he waited until his father was sleeping, a difficult enough task since the tailor didn't snore; silent even in sleep.

His father didn't trust banks. Chaim hid his wealth in the basement, underneath the stairs, behind the pile of clothes belonging to his wife, the mother Micah couldn't remember. He decided that he would take only $25 of his father's savings. The tailor could spare that. What did he spend his money on, anyway? But once Micah opened the metal box, he understood the reality of what cash was available on Baldwin Street. He fingered the paper and counted eighteen one-dollar bills. Those he rolled into a handkerchief and placed in the rucksack he'd purchased at Goldstein's. He left the coins. There were some other papers lining the bottom of the box. One of them was his birth certificate. He folded that and put it in the rucksack, too.

He returned the box to its hiding place and crept up the stairs to the door, where he hesitated. Micah had intended to write a note and leave it on the counter for his father to find in the morning. But the effort of trying to reduce his reasons for leaving to one thought, one paragraph, became so overwhelming that in the end, he wrote nothing at all. Let him find out from the group at Goldstein's, if he even talked to them. He tried to imagine his father's reaction when he discovered his son's absence and the missing money. All Micah could summon was a shrugging of the shoulders as Chaim hung the tape measure around his neck. With a drawn-out sigh, the tailor would begin one more day's work. His sense of inevitability about what life had intended for him, to lose everyone who meant anything to him, would then be complete. With that final thought Micah left his father's store and Toronto.

≈

Micah arrived in Halifax the autumn of 1936, looking for work. No one thought that the slender young man had the strength to move and lift and winch. They told him to ask at Clarey Glass and Paint anyway. The old man who owned the place, they said, had a reputation as a soft touch. So that's where Micah turned up, neat and clean, despite the way he'd been travelling, which was hopping freight trains and walking and sleeping rough. He'd taken care to appear as presentable as possible, which wasn't always easy to do these days. He hoped he appeared honest or honest enough looking, something else that it wasn't always easy to be.

The owner of the glass and paint business happened to be in the office that day, listening to his bookkeeper explain that they were a man down in the warehouse. One of the workers had up and left, Raymond told Charles Clarey, without bothering to give notice. He'd taken his last pay packet and not returned. That sort of thing occurred with some frequency. The other workers said he was headed west and they shook their heads as they relayed that news. No one was sure that things were any better for jobs out there. If you believed the newspapers, things were worse.

As Raymond explained all this to Charles, a bored Edie sat nearby, feeding a pencil into the rotary sharpener fixed to her desk. She cranked the arm of the device and listened to the satisfying grind of the wood as it was pared away.

Raymond wanted to show his employer his talent for thrift and planning by making the point that to save a little money they might forget about replacing the departed man.

What he planned to say to Charles was: "We'll drive the men that're left a little harder to make up for the lack of a body. No one's likely to complain." Those were the words he was readying to speak out loud, but never delivered.

Before he could make his point, the boy arrived and interrupted him.

"If you don't mind," Micah said in a clear voice that made everyone turn toward him. "I'm looking for work. Any kind of work."

He'd taken off his flat cap and held it with both hands, leaving it to dangle in front of him.

Charles looked him up and down, taking the measure of him, assessing his appearance.

Edie paused, her hand resting on the handle of the pencil sharpener, and studied the young man with the fine features and the large eyes, so dark they seemed black.

"Name?" Charles asked.

"Michael Green."

Charles prided himself in knowing that part of his success as a businessman was taking advantage of a situation when it was presented to him.

He gestured with the papers he was holding. "Raymond Gillis, meet Michael Green. He'll do to replace that body we need in the warehouse, yes?"

And with a quick shake of Michael's hand to seal the deal and a dip of his chin, Charles left the room, grateful that the distraction had provided him with an excuse to cut off another one of his bookkeeper's attempts to impress him.

The pink stain on Raymond's face burned red. He had wanted to show his boss that despite his youth and inexperience he could do more than add and subtract numbers. He wanted to be sure that Charles understood he was also capable of reasoning and planning. Instead, the intrusion had left him embarrassed. And this boy, standing in front of him, did not appear to be very grateful for his bit of luck and timing.

"Well, I suppose it's done then. We'll need some information from you, for payroll and such. I'm in charge of all that. You'll give the information to Edith here. Edith?"

Edie stared expressionlessly and, so unusual for her, wordlessly, at Raymond.

"We need a staff form completed." He rubbed his thumb and middle finger together, meaning to make a snapping noise. His hands and fingers were moist, too smooth to get the proper grip and make a satisfying popping sound. He turned his useless gesture into a sweep of the air between Edie and the newcomer.

"You'll give Edith the details, Mike."

"Michael."

"As you say. You can write, can you?"

"I can write."

"Well, then…"

"All right, Raymond," Edie said.

Michael looked at her for the first time. He had some appreciation for insolence in the face of authority.

"Well, then." Raymond straightened, pumped his heels twice and went off to his own office.

Michael resisted laughing at this unusual bit of luck in a city he'd known less than forty-eight hours. He'd landed a job when everyone warned him that there were no jobs to be found.

Edie cleared a space on her desk and pushed the form, along with the freshly sharpened pencil, toward him. Without asking and without hesitation, Michael pulled a chair away from the wall and placed it so that he faced her. He picked up the pencil and began to write. There was no pause as there was sometimes when someone who couldn't read or write well, or at all, was confronted with this task. Edie had learned how to ask in those cases if she might help and wrote down their name and address for them. Some, she came to understand, found this too shaming and she never hesitated to tell them it was fine if they preferred to take the form home with them and return it to her the next day. This boy didn't hesitate. He even held the pencil as though it was no stranger to his hand.

As he wrote, she read the upside-down words. Michael Green. Morris Street.

"I don't know the number of the house," he said. "I just moved in this morning. I can let you know tomorrow."

Edie heard none of the roughness of language, saw no ingratiating smile for the boss's daughter, that she was so used to these days. His words were simple, direct, educated even. Someone from away. She was meeting more and more strangers these days, although none quite like this one.

"That'll be fine," she said and added, hoping she didn't sound too rough, "Don't forget."

Micah nodded, put the chair back against the wall and looked at her.

"You need something else?" she asked.

"When do I start?"

"Oh, well, tomorrow, I guess. Tomorrow morning."

He continued to stare, no smile, such a serious face, one not used to laughter. Not ungrateful for what had happened to him here, just all business.

"Time?"

"Eight. Be here at eight." She thought her voice too loud, as though she was giving orders or trying to teach a disobedient child the right way to do things. "And don't be late," she added.

The words sounded rude, not like her at all. "You'll ask for Joe Dan. Mr. MacLean to you. He's in charge. He likes everyone to be punctual. He's very particular about that, so more like quarter of eight, I'd say. To get on his good side."

"That won't be a problem for me. I'll be here early enough," Micah said.

"And don't you forget to tell me about the street number."

Micah nodded and put the cap on his head. He left without a "thank you" or a "goodbye."

She had noticed that his jacket was worn in places and probably not warm enough for Halifax's raw weather. And there were no mittens or gloves either, not even a scarf.

≈

As he waits for Edie to arrive in the park, Micah eats the stew that the landlady of his boarding house prepared for him. Everyone eats stew these days. It's a real Depression meal bolstered by endless loaves of cheap bread. Today's offering is made up of vegetables and beans. Fridays mean no meat, someone had told him. When he asked why that was, he received a one-word explanation: "Catholics."

The lunch bucket with the stew is on the ground beside his feet. He forces himself to eat less and less these days, never finishing what he's been given. Some days, he eats nothing at all at midday. He wants to get used to the feel of hunger, its pains and, above all, its purpose. In the same way, he does without anything that could protect his hands and neck from the cold. He needs to harden himself to these discomforts, although he's finding the sharp pangs of hunger difficult to ignore. And Micah hates the cold. As a boy he huddled close to the small stove in his father's tailor shop during winter months, leaving his spot only for school or chores or to sit at the table to share a silent meal. Keep the body relaxed and don't tense up, someone had told him at a recent meeting. But his body is rigid and a fine trembling runs through his chest and down his legs and arms.

To the other warehouse workers this new boy, not given to talk, but not unfriendly either, is something of a mystery, and Micah's looks have only deepened their interest in him. His surname, Green, is ordinary enough and he is dark in the way some Celts are dark. He's thin in the way everyone is thin these days from never having enough to eat. This might exempt him from the warehouse gossip, but it doesn't. The dark hair, someone remarked, there's too much of it and don't they think it has a strange curl to it? The lips are a little too full and too red for these lean times. His eyes, though, have them truly puzzled. Dark hair and blue eyes, green eyes, hazel eyes, brown eyes. They've seen all the combinations for people with ordinary names like Green. This boy's eyes are different; so dark that they could only be described as black.

And there's something strange about him that is not like the other foreigners they'd known. There had been a Ukrainian once and after him, a Finn, both from out west and biding their time, waiting for ships to take them to Stalin's Russia where, relatives assured them, there was plenty of work. Those men had been big with broad shoulders and muscled arms, miners and farm boys who lifted the heaviest loads without complaint. And they shared something else: they were uncomfortable standing about when it came time to take the morning and afternoon tea breaks.

Someone else recalls a Greek man and a Lebanese, both dark-eyed like this boy, but shorter and sturdier than the slender fellow from Toronto. And those ones had loved the tea breaks, if not the tea, and loved to talk. So in those ways they are not at all like Michael Green. The new boy keeps to himself and, although not unfriendly, he takes his dinner breaks alone and never accompanies them on their weekly excursions to the barber's bootleg hut. He prefers the solitary chores to the ones that require teams and he isn't awkward with paper and pencil, often volunteering to fill in the forms to keep track of inventory: paint cans in, paint cans out, panes of glass, rolls of wallpaper.

Micah is aware that he is the subject of some curiosity among the men. What they or anyone else thinks of him is their bother and none of his.

The warehouse men are satisfied to harvest sparse clues about him, at their leisure, and not rush to any hasty conclusion since no one among them wants to be seen to pry. And the subject of this Michael Green helps fill the time. He keeps their minds away from their hard lives, whether it is the sick baby or the worried wife or the longing for those left behind in Cape Breton or some other place.

So there is a tender pinch of disappointment for them the day Ralphie Campbell announces to the warehouse that the key to the riddle of Michael Green lies in the little book he carries with him, tucked inside his jacket pocket.

The book, Ralphie informs them, is Spanish. "Not Spanish, as you'd say. Not exactly. More like, *about* the Spanish language."

"He's Spanish then, you're saying, Ralphie."

"Of course it don't mean that. Not necessarily." These men are so keen to twist anything he says. But it was done. From that day on, Micah Gessen or Michael Green, was known to all in the warehouse as "the Spanish Boy."

≈

When he goes to the office to give Edie a copy of a notice of delivery, he never pauses at the door the way most of the others do before entering. He makes no attempt to ingratiate himself. He strides in, right up to her desk, and hands her whatever it is he's carrying from the warehouse. His hat remains on his head when he stands in front of her, the only woman on the premises, and the boss's daughter to boot. There is no smile or scraping of the foot. This isn't rudeness. It is the unhesitating expression of someone daring her to attempt a reprimand for his disrespect. He only lingers in the office when Raymond is nearby.

The bookkeeper dislikes Micah calling him Raymond rather than Mr. Gillis. He took his complaint about Micah's attitude to

Mr. Clarey who, he thought, for such a no-nonsense businessman, could be worrisomely lax about certain aspects of discipline. Charles told Raymond that he had no intention of firing or talking to anyone for the act of referring to another employee by his first name.

The bookkeeper, knowing he owes his job to the good graces of this man, didn't press the matter. He had weathered similar slights as a child when his fevered studying put him ahead of what his teachers knew. They, in turn, ignored the precocious boy and took some small delight in the playground bullying of him by the MacGillivray twins, Peter and Paul, waiting longer than necessary to intervene in the one-sided punch-ups between Raymond and his tormentors. So many years on, he felt the same sting of dismissal as he stood before Charles.

The seed of his antipathy for Micah was planted, took root and grew within him, a little more each day.

≈

The sharp sound of the tinny bell startles Micah.

"How about that?" Edie arrives, hatless and chestnut hair loose, one leg stretched out to scrape along the ground as she slides to a stop.

She flicks the lever of the round bell attached to her handlebar and the thin sound rings out again.

"Like it? Got it yesterday. My brother, Mel, he put it on for me. I love it." And she makes a show of ringing the bell one more time.

"How much did that cost?"

Edie has never quite found the thing that makes him laugh or smile. And something else. Who is this young man who doesn't encourage her own happiness?

"Ten cents. At Summers' Hardware. That's not much. Is it?"

"Do you know what ten cents means to some people? Do you?" The physical discomfort of the cold and his hunger feeds his anger at the girl and her new toy.

"Ten cents is enough money to buy a piece of meat to feed a family," he says. That might be an exaggeration, but what does this girl know about the cost of anything? "A piece of clothing to keep someone warm, or just to have something to cover their nakedness."

Edie blushes. She always blushes when he uses words like "nakedness" or refers to parts of the body other than useful remarks about the most obvious appendages. One day he shocked her into speechlessness when he told her he admired her breasts. For days after that, whenever she passed a mirror she glanced at their curve in the reflection.

"Well, I thought I might save a life. Let people know if they're in my way, or..."

Micah has turned away from her and stares at the far side of the harbour. The other workers call this kind of weather a dirty day. In the seven months he's lived in Halifax he's seen a lot of dirty days. The list of what Micah misses about Toronto is a short one. At the top, he'd put "sun."

She lowers the bicycle to the ground and sits beside him.

"I have a sandwich. Would you like some?"

"I've eaten enough." He taps the tin lunch pail with the side of his foot.

Never a thank you, she notices. Will she ever get used to that? Other days, she's listened to Micah talk about what he believes in and why. She heard the word "communist" for the first time from him and about him and regarded it all as harmless talk that could not touch her or her family. As much as he had explained to her, she was left with practical questions she was afraid how to ask. Does he not say "thank you" because he's a communist? Would it be all right if she continues to do so? She might do it anyway as a kind of perverse rebellion.

"I can't say it's a very good sandwich. Just some cheese. Theresa isn't much of a cook. Which isn't such a bad thing, is it? Means we all eat less, my family, which means she buys less food which means someone else can buy it."

"Edith." Like Raymond, he never calls her Edie, as her family and friends do. "The very fact you have a maid…"

"She's not a maid. I've told you. Not really a maid. She's been with us forever. More part of the family."

"A member of the family who's paid? That unconscionable."

"Uncon…is it?"

"Lacking scruples. Unethical. Ruthless, even."

"Okay, okay. It's just that you don't understand. We love Theresa. We really do. She's one of us. We're crazy about her. And, besides, if she was very unhappy, she'd've left us by now. Wouldn't she?"

"Did it ever occur to you she has nowhere else to go?"

Edie has never told Michael about Theresa's life. He doesn't know about the Explosion that took everything from her and how kind her mother and father were never to mention that trauma or the disfiguring scar that made it impossible for Theresa to get another husband, never mind a job outside the Clarey house. Michael might be right that Theresa has nowhere else to go, but why would she want to leave? Everyone loves everyone else in the Clarey house. Nothing is more simple or straightforward to her. She wonders again what kind of home this boy comes from that he doesn't understand that. He never speaks about a mother or father and refuses to say if he has brothers or sisters. He is unhappy in that way people are when they insist they're perfectly okay and say nothing more. "Happy" is not the word that comes to mind when she thinks of Michael, although Edie knows he's clear about many things she's not clear about. He has rules and beliefs and that must count for something, not unlike her family's Catholicism, although Catholics, she's decided after spending time with him, have heartier appetites and dress better than communists.

She breaks off bits of the bread and tosses them to the scavenging ducks. Everyone and everything is looking for scraps these days.

"The fighting's getting worse in the north," Michael says.

Edie knows better than to ask him to go over one more time who is fighting whom and for what. He's told her that he goes to the library whenever he has the time. He devours the dispatches from Spain, printed in the local papers, and he listens to the radio reports whenever he can convince his landlady and other boarders to turn away from the trivial entertainment shows they love.

"If I don't get there soon, it'll all be over."

She nibbles on the cheese from the sandwich and watches the ducks nudge the lumps of bread she's thrown to them. Even the ducks are suspicious of Theresa's baking.

"Any word on that?"

"Just a matter of waiting for the visa. And a ticket and a boat."

"If you'd let me go with you…"

"Well, you can't. I've told you why. You've no passport. No money. No visa. And what would you do once you got to Spain? You can't fight. I mean, how would you even get on the boat?"

"I'd stow away."

He tosses his head back and what sounds like a chuckle and then an outright laugh bursts from him. She's said words at last that amuse him, although she wishes it hadn't been at her expense.

"We'll take my bicycle," she says. "Take turns riding it or ride it together."

"What? And ring the goddamn bell the whole way?" Michael shakes his head. "You're ridiculous." His black eyes shine at her, bright and hard, like pieces of glass trapped by the sun. "Completely absurd," he adds.

If Edie possessed the capacity to hate, she would have hated him at that moment. There are lots of things she could do once she gets to Spain. Not everyone has to shoot a gun.

"And besides, our dear government has passed a law. They've made it illegal for any Canadian citizen to fight in a foreign war. Even if that war means overthrowing fascism. Who's the fascist now?"

"If you'll just risk it…"

"Stop it, Edith. That's an end to it." Michael bends and picks up the tin container and the remains of the stew. "I'm getting back to work. You remember what work is, don't you? That place your father owns, where he makes money so you can have a maid."

"She's not a maid. We love Theresa."

He's gone before she's finished the thought. She tosses the uneaten sandwich onto the ground, for the indifferent ducks to do with as they wish, and picks up her bicycle. She'll take another route back to the office so that the two of them don't arrive from the same direction or together. That possibility doesn't bother Edie, since she's spent most of her adolescence being dutifully disrespectful to her parents. What she does know is that the two of them being seen together bothers Michael in a way she'll never understand.

7

From the window of his second-floor office, Charles Clarey's eyes sweep the late-afternoon harbour. He seeks any hopeful sign that shipping traffic has increased since the last time he looked, which happened to be this morning. There is no such evidence of that now and he knows there will not be for many days to come. Ottawa has pumped some money into the Navy, keeping the port buzzing. Government contracts and a few construction projects have added breath to his own business for the time being. The best hope for a boon to salvage the city's wretched economy lies with all that fuss in Europe. A little war might help, he thinks. A small one, not lasting too long, no real dying or killing involved, of course, just a punch in the arm to boost the economy.

He'd spent the morning up the hill in town, visiting the businesses that Clarey Glass and Paint has supplied for as long as some of them have had their doors open. Nothing came of his efforts. Little ever does these days. Only a friendly chat, a gentle commiseration and a cup of tea. How many cups of tea did he down this morning? More than he thought healthy.

Charles is the third generation of Clareys to run this business and they all had their stories of hard times. All Charles wants is to keep afloat long enough, through the choppy water, until the storm has passed and calm is restored. He knows his reputation is a good one as honest, straightforward and smart in the ways of business, a good man to deal with.

Among Charles's generation there had been occasional attempts to identify or create a kind of family motto. "Sacrifice," "family," "king" were all mooted for inclusion without consensus ever being reached. The efforts fell between those Clareys who believed that mottos, as a rule, elevate a family's social status and those Clareys who thought it wasn't possible to improve on the words spoken by the founder of the business, Charles's grandfather, the Irish immigrant Leo. Leo was known as a man with an eye for spotting an opportunity. During one particularly unsettled time in the city's day-to-day business life he was seen smiling and when asked why, said: "Because there's money in confusion."

The old man had hammered his personal ethos into all the Clareys: be faithful to family and church; be dutiful to family and community; be generous to all. So if a motto has to be written, Charles believes it must be some distillation of Leo's ethos. "Family, faith, duty" is the one he silently carries within him. But mottos do not print money. There is no possibility of prosperity coming soon short of an upheaval like war and, following his grandfather's observation, the potential for lucrative confusion.

Charles wanders into the reception area to see if his daughter can provide a diversion for him. Placing the young and inexperienced girl in this job carried its own risks. Her skills are only impressive in her lack of them and her tendency to become distracted is recognized by most as an aberrant charm rather than an education gap that needs closing. In spoiling his only daughter, he has ensured that the necklace of responsibility will never weigh down her long pretty neck. He is aware that Edie is a girl endowed with good manners, endless enthusiasms, and who lacks any pressing curiosity beyond the information that serves to answer her most urgent query: "I want this. How can I have it?"

Charles and his wife had seen to it that none of their three children, in particular their only daughter, ever struggled with unhappiness or want. This approach to childrearing informed the entire family's attitude to Edie. In the pursuit of the Clarey standards—family, faith, duty—Edie was allowed to observe them all and yet be burdened by none.

By having her work in the office, Charles hopes that at least some of his own discipline might tame her. Edie is wild, although not in the way that's meant when people speak of "wild" females. She had gotten away with too much when she was younger. We should have been harder on her, Charles tells himself, the way we were with her older brother. But there was too much delight to be had in watching her play, never sitting still, never quiet. She is so unlike all the Clareys in that way and for that reason, they all want to be a bit more like their Edie. By letting her remain untamed, they allow themselves to share a sense of her wildness without having to face the consequences of being wild themselves. Charles scoffs when he hears Edie referred to as "a daddy's girl," although it is true. He only has to feel his heart tighten in his chest when he looks at her to know that.

"Penny for those thoughts," Charles says. "What's got you so absorbed out there, my girl?"

She hunches her shoulders and stretches her back, stiff from sitting in the wooden chair and from the boredom of the place.

"Have you got something for me to do, Pa? There's nothing for me to do here except this filing and that won't take any time at all." She pats a thin collection of paper on her desk.

"If it won't take any time, then why don't you do it?"

"Well, then there absolutely wouldn't be a single thing for me to do. This way, there's at least something I know I have to do before I leave. It gives me a purpose."

"Is that so? And in the meantime, you stare out the window."

"Waiting for the ships to come or go. I like to watch them."

"You'll have a wait. Fewer and fewer of them these days." He puts his hands in his pants pockets and bounces on the balls of his feet. "Your great-great-grandfather was about your age when he sailed into this harbour."

Charles loves telling the family story about the teenaged Leo, sailing alone from Ireland, no friend or family with him during the terrifying crossing. He draws out the details of Leo's first sighting from the ship's deck of this rough and dirty outpost of Britain's colonial system. And with each telling, he delights in watching the expression on the faces of his children, not unlike the look caused by the throb of pain from a persistent tooth ache.

"Yes, yes." Edie claps her hands together. "We know that one."

Edie adores him, all his children do, in spite of his tendency to repeat the same stories. He wonders, though, does it ever occur to his daughter that he has many other things to talk about? All she has to do is ask. But she never does, so she never hears him talk about what occupies most of his days: the business, that mess in Europe and his older son's wordless, worrisome unhappiness.

His daughter has the best of the Clarey looks—the hair, the height, the wide hazel eyes. There's no mistaking that. The rest she inherited from the Sullivans, her mother's family—the good skin and the straight nose.

"I came to tell you…" Charles pauses because he has nothing to tell his daughter, but now that he's standing in front of her, he's compelled to say something.

"I came to tell you…that it's all right if you want to leave a little early today."

Edie reaches for the desk drawer handle to retrieve her purse.

"Not yet. And don't pout. 'A little early' I said, since it's a quieter day than usual. And not until you've finished that filing. Is that clear?" This is as stern as Charles ever manages to be with her.

Edie nods and purses her lips in what she hopes is an extravagant display of obedience.

"I want you to…go talk to your brother, Gus. He's been so low since he's been home from school. Cheer him up. It's not good for anyone to see him like this."

"When can I go?"

"As soon as the filing's done. How long will that take you?"

Edie trills the edges of the thin collection of paper with her thumb, looks at her father and tilts her head as if to say that an entire day could hardly hold enough time for the chore.

Charles removes his hands from his pockets and adjusts his glasses, although from where to where is undetectable.

"As long as you do it. First thing tomorrow morning, latest."

Charles Clarey had not become a success in business without first learning to be flexible.

8

One. Two. Three. As many times as Gus Clarey counts the bills, the number and amount does not grow. The three dollars and some coins he scraped out of his pockets lies on the bed beside him. How to transform the amount, make it swell, like a financial loaves-and-fishes story?

He's still weak and wants nothing more than to lay his head and body back onto the pillow.

"Take it slow," he'd been advised by the doctor. "Pneumonia takes it out of you. It was a near run thing with you and we must respect that."

But Gus was insistent. He'd marked this day on his calendar. One month since he'd arrived home. Today he would dress in something other than pyjamas. He told himself he'd walk around, test his legs and arms for strength and resist all commands to return to bed.

"Augustus." Theresa is at his bedroom door, a dusting cloth in her right hand. In her left arm she balances a folded bundle of two shirts, some socks and underwear, freshly cleaned and ironed.

"I don't really care if you say you're feeling better. It's too soon. You'd do well to listen to me."

"I'm fine, Theresa. Better than anyone knows. Let me do this one thing for myself. Please."

"You'll wear yourself out and end up right back in bed. No matter what I tell you to do, I suppose. And what are you doing there anyway? Counting your fortune?"

A little joke had grown up between them since Gus announced his intention to leave Halifax for the seminary in Antigonish. No family fortune for me, he'd told Theresa. Just the simple life of a parish priest tending his flock. Another kind of fortune, he assured her, awaited him. And Theresa, who had not believed in any God since the moment she awoke naked, bloodied and childless on a frozen field in the city's north end, nodded and patted the arm of the tall young man. She didn't want to tell him what she had discovered that day in December 1917. That faith can collapse in the face of catastrophe as easily as it can be lost while someone is sleeping. Some are born with it, some are born to it.

"Yes, my fortune," Gus laughs. He doesn't move from where he sits on the side of the bed.

"And you intend to do what exactly with it?"

He smiles at Theresa, not one of those broad toothy Clarey grins, but a tense lipless expression. "Hop a ship to Borneo?"

"Not a train to Antigonish?"

She puts the clothes onto the seat of the armchair and brushes back the thatch of brown hair that has fallen across the young man's forehead.

"You've no temperature today. I still wouldn't go far if I was you. So Borneo's out of the question. A few more days before you start wondering when to go back, I'd say."

Gus had arrived in Halifax a month ago, in a private ambulance Charles had hired. The principal of the seminary had informed Charles by telegram that his oldest child was ill with pneumonia and that home might be the best place for him until he could heal and come back "when his strength has returned to him."

"Yes, possibly a few more days. That should do it."

"And some more beef broth. I'll fix a new batch for you to drink. That seems to be helping."

"That'd be lovely. I'm sure it's helped me." Theresa's broth is well-known as a fatty concoction studded with suspicious lumps.

She smiles with pleasure at his words, deaf to the delicate lie, and leaves the bedroom to continue her dusting and tidying.

From downstairs he hears the sound of a door slamming. Probably Mel home from school and looking for something to eat in the kitchen. Unlike the rest of them, Mel seems to have been born missing a sense of taste. This is the only way anyone can explain his willingness to clean a plate of Theresa's cooking.

It isn't his brother who has come home, though. He recognizes the rhythm of the footsteps, the long-legged lope, two stairs at a time.

"No running," he hears Theresa say as Edie skips past her down the hall.

She arrives breathless and drops onto the bed beside her brother, planting a kiss on his warm cheek. The cold air clings to the coat she hadn't bothered to take off when she entered the house.

"How's gloomy Gus today?"

"You're sitting on my fortune."

"What?" With a squeak she stands and stares at the paper and coins.

"What're you doing with that? Priests don't need money. Office workers need money."

He puts his hand over the paper and coin before she can reach for it.

"I'm not a priest yet and what do you know about what priests might need money for anyway?"

Edie laughs and unbuttons her coat. "Oh, you'd be surprised what I know. You're feeling better then. First day out of bed. On the mend, as Pa will undoubtedly say." She picks up the clothes from the armchair, tosses them onto the bed beside her brother, and falls down on the soft springy seat.

"What are you doing home so early?"

"Time off for good behaviour. Pa took pity on me. There's nothing to do there."

"I'm guessing it wasn't pity he took on you. You have him wrapped around your little finger. Always have. What Edie wants…"

"Oh, that's just mean, Augustus. Say, I'm a working girl. A working girl who doesn't get paid, I might add, except for a little pocket change."

"And a nice new bike."

"That was a gift."

"More like a bribe."

"Jealous, jealous. Isn't that one of those sins? Never you mind. I live in fear that bike will be stolen one of these days. Why, I'm sure someone tried to pick the lock this very morning. You watch, it's going to be stolen and then what'll I have to show for all my hard work?"

Edie holds up a hand, index finger and thumb touching to form a circle that she presses to an eye. She closes the other and stares at her brother like that, his face framed in her fingers. Here is Gus, the one who loves to laugh and is a great tease, who is the source of many of Edie's happiest childhood memories. The dependable older brother, the dispenser of sage advice, so reliable and trustworthy and, as a typical Clarey, duty bound.

Edie did her best to entertain him as he recovered. She read to him, at first from some of the books he'd brought with him from the seminary. Little books, thin books, with tiny print that made her eyes hurt from squinting, books with words she didn't know and couldn't pronounce.

"Am I supposed to know what these words mean?" she'd asked him. "Because I don't. Even when they're mixed up with words I do know, I still don't get what it's about."

She settles back into the armchair, her eye continuing to observe him through the cupped hand.

Where had he gone, the brother she knew so well? Not just to the seminary in Antigonish. Edie misses the brother who laughs and tugs at her hair and jabs her ribs to hear her squeal. He hasn't grown up at that school for priests, she thinks. He's grown older and sadder. All he seems to be these days is sad. The one who could out-talk and out-argue anyone once keeps to himself these days.

"Would you ever steal anything?" Edie says.

"What? Steal? I suppose as a rule, no. If I had to…"

"Had to?" Her hand drops from her face. "*Had to?*"

"I mean if I was starving. If circumstances were such that it was the only way I, or my sister, I hasten to add, could survive. If it was a matter of life or death, feeding my family, when there was no other way, then it might be acceptable. At least, understandable. Only as a last resort, of course."

"And what if you believe that someone just doesn't deserve to own something? That it's not rightly theirs because they have so much already and someone else might have hardly anything at all."

"Is that really a good enough reason, Edie?"

"And if you believed, oh, I don't know, property is…well, if you really believed that owning something is *like* stealing."

"Stealing from whom? What's going on here?" Gus had never heard his sister discuss any subject more complicated than the price of dresses at Mills Brothers.

"Well, if, say, you believe that it's stealing for someone else who doesn't have…whatever it is you have."

"Edie, who've you been talking to?"

"No one." She waves her hands and the serious look on her face dissolves into a smile. There again is the Edie they all know, bright as a star, sparkling like a rare jewel.

"Are you planning on stealing something of mine, sis?"

"The only thing you have worth stealing is that belt of yours."

Gus touches the leather of the Clarey family heirloom cinched around his waist, the belt made by Leo, their great-grandfather, who'd worn it for all of his adult life and passed it down to his son and that Clarey to Charles. Charles had declared it no longer fit to be seen as part of respectable business attire and put it away in its wooden box, where it remained, coiled like a sleeping snake. Years of regular polishing with oils had kept it supple and free of cracks. When Gus prepared to leave for Antigonish, he'd asked to take it with him. Edie, never having understood the notion of rights of inheritance and used to getting whatever she wanted, knew only that an object of great beauty and utility had slipped from her grasp.

"Perhaps someday you can have it," Gus tells her. "Someday if I'm told I can't take anything with me after ordination. Maybe that day. And if Mel doesn't mind."

"Oh, Mel won't mind. I just know he won't. He's not the sentimental type. Not like me." And with that she tosses Gus a complicitous smile. He acknowledges it with his own grin and all at once feels better than he has for weeks.

From downstairs, they hear the kitchen door open and slam shut and the voices of Mel and Lawrie.

"The two musketeers home from their wars," Gus says. "Friends for life, those two." At least he can take comfort from that.

9

Three long tables crowd one wall of the room in the basement of the parish church. On top of one is a neat hand-lettered sign reading Ladies. To its left, the table with its sign, Men; to the right, Children. Late this afternoon, as Mary Clarey and two other volunteers were about to close up, a bundle of used clothing was delivered. She shooed the others away, told them to go home, and assured them that she didn't mind looking after the additional chore. She prefers having the place to herself, and she likes the calm that comes from the precise rhythms of sorting and folding.

On the table marked Ladies, someone had placed a small cache of handkerchiefs, new and with small purple violets embroidered into one of the corners. Mary's thumb strays over the tidy thread of cotton flowers. Edie would love them and, for a moment, she considers taking them home. But no, they weren't put here for her to choose and she's done enough to spoil her daughter. Someone else will see the pieces of linen and will fall in love with them or find them useful.

There are never enough of the items they really need, warm coats and boots for winter, dresses of any shape or style. Women, Mary's discovered, don't like parting with their wardrobes. This reluctance to sacrifice is one of the troubling curiosities she'd discussed with her husband.

"You'd think women, mothers, should understand better than anyone," she'd said to him.

Charles had looked at her and worried again that his pretty, fragile wife was affected too much by this church work she was doing. She volunteered there because that's what the Clareys and Mary's family, the Sullivans, did. Their grandparents and great-grandparents had arrived in Halifax all those years ago with nothing and someone had been there to help them. You do what's right for others. It's that simple to Mary.

Charles had patted her hand and placed a dry kiss on her forehead. "You fuss too much, my dear. Remember, you're good enough as you are."

She wants to believe her husband's words, that she is good enough. She steps back to take one long last look at the tables. There is nothing more she can do here. Still, she hesitates. Mary had come to the church today to sort and fold, but something else holds her there. Too many times she has put off what needs doing and it cannot wait one more sleepless night.

She pulls on her coat and turns the light switch to off. With her fingers gliding along the smooth wall of the familiar darkened hallway, the reluctant penitent finds her way upstairs.

≈

Father O'Neill's white head is bent in silent contemplation. Mary watches him and wonders how long he'll be locked in that state. The priest isn't praying. He's nodded off, sitting there, and if it wasn't for the enormous bulk of his belly propping him up, he might have toppled over long before she arrived.

The subject of the corpulent priest was another one she'd raised with her husband last Sunday, after mass. "How is it this one is so fat when so many others haven't flesh on their bones to keep them warm?" she'd asked Charles.

"You're unusually critical of that one, aren't you," Charles had replied. "Are you thinking for Lent it might do him some good to take on Theresa as his housekeeper? Perhaps forty days and forty nights of Theresa's food might diminish him. And humble him. Hmmm? Is that what's on your mind, Mary?"

She studies the priest, fascinated by the roll of solid flesh that bulges over his collar and keeps his heavy head balanced, preventing it from dropping to his chest. He's a mean old thing and lazy, too, she suspects, concerned with his own comfort more than those who need the comforting. She longs to tell him that his very presence mocks this place.

A soft snore and a faint whistling leak from the old priest's mouth and nose and fill the still air of the church. She wishes again that Father Comeau hadn't been called away. The young Acadian was such a sensitive man. He started the used-clothing drive and organized the once-a-week soup kitchen before he was moved to tend a bigger parish in Montreal.

In his stead, the parish received Father O'Neill, a journeyman confessor content to count off the days until his retirement by observing the most obvious duties and little more. His sermons bore Mary. And he's an impatient man, as likely to snap at someone's question as answer it. She doesn't like him. This is one of the unresolved sins that haunts her visits to the confessional. How is she expected to confess to her priest that she harbours unpleasant thoughts about that same priest? And now she must prod this sleeping bear, beg a favour, and hope he doesn't growl at her.

Mary, it has long been observed among her circle, is the delicate Sullivan blossom planted among the tough Clarey weeds. But this flower has not survived as long as she has in that pasture without being pollinated by some of their strong will.

She kicks the end of the pew.

A harsh snort rises from the priest and she hears the soft whistling sound again. The man will sleep through the Second Coming. Mary walks to the nearby tray of votive candles, grasps it with both hands and shakes. The collision of metal and glass echoes off the stone walls of the church.

"What are you doing there?" Two large hands run over the bloodhound face. "Oh, it's you."

"It was crooked. I straightened it."

The priest moves his head from side to side, stretching out the stiffness in his neck. "Well, you've interrupted my prayers, you and your straightening. I hope you're happy now."

Not so much happy as very satisfied. "I'm so sorry, Father." Another lie to add to her list. She steps towards the pew on careful tiptoe, hoping he will interpret this as an offering of humility.

"You should be sorry. I'm a busy man these days."

"Of course you are. We all know that, Father." There it is again, a little lie, the prideful pretense of pretending to be something she isn't. Well no, not so much a lie, she tells herself. More like a harmless hypocrisy. Even though Mary is not a brave person, her visceral dislike of this man fills her with something that resembles courage.

"Since you're here now, Father, I wonder if you'd hear me out. I have a small favour to ask. Only a very small thing, you know, but so important to me."

The watery eyes, as leaden-coloured as the ocean on an overcast day, assess her. She knows that to him she is only Mary Clarey, the small and fragile-looking woman, wife of the affable businessman and those three great galumphing children. He'll take in and judge her neatly combed light brown hair, waved with such care by a professional hand even during these hard times. He'll notice her pretty china-blue eyes and, on her head, the navy beret with the single colourful feather.

"Only a minute of your time, Father."

"Only a minute." He sighs with the weariness of someone who cannot understand why he alone has been given so many burdens. "It's what they all say. What is it then?"

Mary is little more than a type of woman to him, the sort he's dealt with for decades; the volunteer types, certain that their unremarkable sacrifices have earned them the right to tell him how to do his job.

"I'd like you to hear my confession."

The loud cough of his laugh sounds like a shotgun in the empty place. "I do confessions on Wednesday and Saturday evenings. This being a Friday, you've the unique distinction of being both too late *and* too early."

"This won't take long…"

He closes his eyes and raises a great meaty paw, as though about to swear a sacred oath. Isn't this what they all say, and after that, doesn't he find himself pulled into something that takes all day?

"Rules are rules, Mrs. Clarey," he says. "We'd have no order at all in this world if we didn't have rules. You need to consider that for a minute."

Humbling herself in front of this man makes Mary weary. Weary from the strain of being polite in the face of his rude dismissal of her and from the days and nights of worrying about an ailing child and what Gus's illness had driven her to do.

"Father, please. It's an urgent matter. I wouldn't bother you otherwise." She pauses, wanting to be sure that the church is empty of any sound before she says what she knows she must. Mary was not born a cunning person, but her years beside her husband, the resourceful businessman, have taught her some useful lessons.

"Father, I've come to you seeking forgiveness."

The priest's hooded eyes widen and fix her as though she has only at that instant come into focus. What did he hear in her voice that makes him sit up and shake off the interrupted nap clouding his watermelon head? It isn't simply Mary's urgent request that impresses itself on his lazy mind because during his priesthood, he'd had the good sense to ignore countless similar pleadings. No, it isn't that. In this woman's voice, soft as a whisper, he hears the sound of someone needing him, and only him, to free her of a great guilty burden.

Mary's words, "seeking forgiveness," have ignited the wick of the priest's somnolent spirit. With the ingrained reflex of a boxer responding to the bell, he grasps the back of the pew in front of him and shifts his great bulk to upright. Wordless, filled with purpose, he strides towards the back corner of the church and the curtained wooden boxes.

≈

Inside the confines of the confessional, Mary kneels and makes the sign of the Cross.

"Bless me, Father, for I have sinned..."

The rattan screen separating her from Father O'Neill is the only reminder of her notional anonymity.

"...my last confession was one week ago."

Over her words comes a low rumbling sound. A thunderstorm. So unusual in these parts and at this time of year.

Through the screen, in the dark of the adjoining cabinet, the shadowy hands of Father O'Neill rest on the hillock of his noisy stomach. Friday is the day his housekeeper, Mrs. Zinck, prepares her finnan haddie with its cream, onions, potatoes and the delicious salt of the smoked haddock.

The widow Zinck is often found in the basement of the church, keeping Mary company as she sorts and folds. As well as being renowned in the parish for the miracles she works in the kitchen, Mrs. Zinck is cherished as a dispenser of holy gossip. She spares no detail about the dining habits of her priests, and her Friday finnan haddie, she once confided to Mary, is a special favourite of Father O'Neill.

"Tell me what's troubling you now, Mary." The priest's burnished baritone fills the wooden space.

"I've..." Mary draws in a deep breath. "My son, Augustus, my oldest. You know he's studying for the priesthood, Father."

"It's common knowledge. What else?"

"He's been very sick. Very sick. We thought..." Her voice drops.

The shadowy form of the priest leans close to the screen to catch her words. She wants to ask him if he has observed that the truly guilty speak like this, with their voices low and hard to make out. Is it that we can't bear the thought of God hearing us, she wants to say? There is one other, more practical, reason. Hushed voices don't breech the fabric of the confessional's curtain to entertain any curious ear waiting in line for their turn.

"But you prayed, didn't you, Mary? We all prayed for your boy and now he's better, I hear. Your own husband told me that. You won't lose him after all."

She hears again the rumble of the priest's impatient appetite. Mrs. Zinck had entertained Mary about Father O'Neill's love of her fish stew and her fresh baked bread. She warms the loaf, she told Mary, before she places it on the dinner table and watches the butter slide from the priest's knife onto the white flesh of the bread. Only then does he tear apart the slice and dip it into the hot yellowed cream. So partial is Father O'Neill to this Friday dish that he often requests they start the evening meal a little earlier than usual.

"You're right, Father. I did pray for Gus," Mary says. "Many people prayed and I am so grateful for that. What it is, you see…I need to tell you what I prayed for."

"Go on." His impatient tone presses her to pick up her pace.

Her hands fumble with her purse. Where is that handkerchief? She could stand up right now, claim a sudden illness, flee the confessional and the church without ever telling the priest what she'd implored him to hear. At home she could go about her business with no one the wiser about her shameful escape. But Mary is a dutiful daughter of the Church and will do what her conscience demands.

"I asked God to spare Gus…"

"Well, of course you did, we all did that."

"I asked God to spare Gus…and take someone else in his place."

A startled shuffle of robe and body fills the hushed cabinet.

"You're saying have someone else die rather than your son? Is that it?"

Mary dabs at her overflowing eyes and presses the handkerchief to her face. The priest is right, of course, but if someone must die, why must it be her own child? Who, she had asked herself, could take his place? In her mind, she held an incomplete vision: someone very old, prepared to leave this life at last, or another, perhaps no longer able to endure the suffering of a terrible illness. Whatever the circumstances, she reasoned, wouldn't it be a kindness to release any one of those terminal cases from their earthly obligations?

"You need to understand, Father…you can't know how desperate I was. A mother's desperation."

"And what is it you want me to do about that right now?"

He is leaning so close that his ear is brushing the screen, straining for her faint words.

She must get this over and done with, say the words aloud that will convince him, convince herself, that she understands what she did was misguided or worse.

"I was w-wrong to ask for that," Mary says. "I-I need forgiveness for what I did." Did he hear the slight stumble when she spoke? Had she given away, with her words, her own lack of sincerity?

She hears no sound from the other side of the screen. Is there one more thing she needs to say to hurry this process along?

"What I asked God to do for me, Father," Mary says, her voice clear now, striking the mark she is aiming for, "I want to take it all back."

Father O'Neill had assured his faithful reporter, Mrs. Zinck, that his years as a priest have granted him authority on certain matters. And as such, it is his duty to set a parishioner straight on subjects near to his heart. On this day Mary has touched on one of them: what one may or may not ask of God.

"Let me see now if I understand this." Father O'Neill's voice is steady with confidence. "You want to take back a bargain you made with God himself and return it like a dress that doesn't fit to the department store? Am I understanding you, Mrs. Clarey?"

"Father, please. I only wanted my son to live." Mary's voice wobbles with each word.

"And you were willing to let someone else die in order for that to happen. You do acknowledge that, don't you?"

"Father…"

There is a dry rustle of his clothes as he sits up. No need to lean in to her now.

"We don't bargain with God, Mary. Ever." The baritone voice is strong and unhesitating. A shame to waste such a moment on an empty church.

"And tell me, Mary. Did you happen to include yourself in that list of people God could do without? Did you? Were you willing to make your own sacrifice? Because I haven't heard you say that."

"I was wrong to bargain. I've said that." Her soft hiccupping sobs prevent any further defence.

Some Catholics are too Catholic for their own good. Mary had heard Mrs. Zinck quote Father O'Neill on that very subject.

The priest straightens himself, moves his head to hear the satisfying click in his stiff neck, and clears his throat: "As penance, you'll say an extra round of the rosary every day. Two. Two extra rounds of the rosary every day. For a week. Two weeks. And I want you here, kneeling in this church, as you do it. And make sure I see you."

"Yes, Father."

The familiar voice of surrender; the adult who kneels to confess and leaves as the child.

"Am I forgiven now for what I did, Father?"

"That remains to be seen, doesn't it? I'm not the one to tell you that, Mary. It's in your heart, isn't it? What you've done and what you need to do."

Mary is sure his voice has softened. Perhaps there is some good there after all, and even this man can feel remorse for the harsh tone he first took with her.

"Now let me hear you say a good Act of Contrition."

"Oh, my God, I am heartily sorry for having offended Thee…"

Another low roll of thunder covers Mary's words as her final "Amen" fades into the gloom around her.

The priest pronounces a rushed benediction and, that completed, brushes back the curtain to ready his exit.

"Hurry, hurry," she wants to say to him.

"If it's comforting you're wanting, Mary, I'll leave you with this. I've had people tell me some pretty rough things in the course of what I do. As for you, well, I have to say what you've done ranks pretty low on the scale of despicable acts."

Mary presses her handkerchief to her mouth.

"Not like some others in this parish I could mention. And not like those ones…like that Mussolini fella who must be a Catholic given his name and where he lives. Imagine what's on his mind when he's in the confessional. Give me five minutes alone with him, I tell you. I'll sort him out. Stop all this foolishness that's going on over there. No. You're no Mussolini, Mary."

And with that, Father O'Neill heaves himself to standing. The sound of his hard-soled shoes on the floor echoes off the stone walls. As he opens the door to the sacristy, he's sure he can already smell the aroma of Mrs. Zinck's bread warming in the oven.

Outside the confessional, Mary is relieved to see that she is alone, no other person to witness her shame. In the empty place, she kneels and begins to recite the first prayers of her penance.

10

Fish soup is the usual Friday evening meal in the Connelly boarding house on Morris Street, an act of deference to the Catholic majority around the table, as well as the house's owners. Micah watches as Lydia places a bowl of boiled potatoes beside the tureen. If the soup alone is not sufficient for the boarders, they can fill themselves up with potatoes and bread. In the Connelly house, there is no shortage of potatoes and bread.

Lydia's arm brushes Micah's shoulder as she withdraws her hands. He dips his head and hopes that no one else at the table noticed the moment of familiarity.

"Serve yourselfs," she says and moves towards the adjoining kitchen, where, along with her mother, she'll eat her own meal, close enough to hear the state of conversation or complaint.

"Thanks, as always, Lydia dear," one of the men calls after her.

She smiles and walks on. Of the ten men seated there, eight pairs of eyes follow Lydia out of the dining room. She takes care with her looks, her fashionable clothes and short bobbed hair, a shade of blonde that has some professional help. And, in her figure, these lonely men see a plumpness made that way for touching and holding.

One of the boarders makes a soft grunting noise, followed by a few sniggers and a lone rebuke from the young man seated at the head of the table: "That'll be enough of that," Raymond Gillis says.

Micah's gaze is fixed on the empty bowl in front of him. He had eaten only half of his lunchtime stew and his hunger pains are now sharp and insistent. He's come to anticipate the Friday evening fish. The Connelly women are decent cooks who take care to provide quality as well as quantity to their boarders. For that reason alone, Micah's happy to have found this place.

He'd been pointed in the direction of the boarding house soon after he arrived in Halifax several months ago.

"Not the best, you know, but clean," he'd been told. "The Connelly women run a tight ship and the rent won't kill you neither."

He went right away to the house on Morris Street and knocked on the solid oak door of the large white Victorian. An older woman answered. Tight brown curls gripped her head, framing a face that had faded over the years from pretty to what one of her boarders described as "not unpleasant."

"I understand you've a bed no one's using right now."

"I've just the thing," she said to Micah and invited him into the foyer with its high ceiling and imposing staircase. The walls might have shimmered once with the shiny newness of the expensive floral wallpaper. Age ensured that any pattern and any suggestion of quality had diminished. The wide planks of the grained floors sighed under their footsteps.

The widowed Mrs. Connelly (her boarders could not agree on her first name) owns the boarding house. Along with her daughter, Lydia, she keeps it clean, cooks the meals, and makes sure that only respectable types are accepted to live under their roof. Tenants are told to pay their rent in full and on time and observe the basic rules of cleanliness. And they must be sufficiently schooled in manners to cause no trouble for their hosts or anyone else. Drink of any kind is not tolerated. The Connellys want everyone to know that, above all, they are women with standards.

Beyond these prejudices, the mother and daughter do not judge their clients.

On that day Micah first arrived, Mrs. Connelly had led him to the kitchen where she opened a door and stepped aside.

He peered into a tiny windowless room. The narrowest of cots, suitable for one slender body, was the sole piece of furniture. Above the cot, a short plank of wood was affixed to the wall with rough metal brackets. Anything that didn't fit under the cot could be stored there. A bare light bulb dangled from the low ceiling.

"How much?"

"Two dollars. Payable every Friday. First week in advance. No exceptions. You get your meals for that and all. Laundry's extra. Single rooms're usually more'n that, but seeing as…" and she waved her hand in the direction of the cramped space.

From boyhood, Micah had heard the haggling that went on between vendor and customer in the shops of Toronto's Baldwin Street. And he'd heard similar pleas the short time he'd been in Halifax, everyone trying to outdo another with sadder and sadder stories justifying the need to save a penny. He would not be one of those.

"Would it be convenient if I moved in right away?"

"There's a dollar charge for a front-door key," Mrs. Connelly said. "You lose it, there's not another. Your money back neither. You miss a meal, no discount. No visitors, except in the parlour. No drinking. And no talking back. All that understood?"

"Understood."

"Well, go get your things and you can move in."

"It's all here." Micah adjusted the rucksack from Goldstein's that hung from his shoulder.

"It's settled then," Mrs. Connelly said. "Cup of tea to seal the deal, dear?"

"Yes, okay," Micah said. "Thank you."

"I'll put the kettle on. You can leave your money on the kitchen table."

After Micah had settled in, he learned of his room's history. Its original purpose was as a storage closet. When the house was being readied for boarders, the resourceful Mrs. Connelly, keen to squeeze a dollar from any available corner, emptied it and declared it fit for habitation. The last occupant of the space had woken one January morning to find his blanket coated in a stiff covering of frost. He had asked Mrs. Connelly for a reduction in rent. She'd offered him another blanket.

"You should be paying me to sleep in there," he'd shouted at her and left without paying what he owed for the week. She had felt just bad enough not to run after him. The room had remained vacant until the day Micah knocked on the Connellys' door.

The terrible cold during the winter months was a hardship for him. On the worst nights he took his blankets and thin pillow and slept on the kitchen floor in front of the stove, still warm from the evening meal's preparation. He lay curled there, like a family dog seeking his creature comfort. It was Mrs. Connelly's habit to rise early to stoke the stove's fire for the morning tea and bread. Her step on the stairs was his signal to gather his things and return to the room. He didn't want her thinking he wasn't tough enough to endure whatever conditions the tiny chamber of winter horrors forced on him.

Despite all this, Micah is content with his situation, where, for the most part, he's left alone. It will do until the day when he lies on another bed in another cramped berth on his way across the Atlantic.

≈

The Friday evening meal of fish soup and potatoes makes slow progress around the table.

As the resident of the Connellys' largest single room, for which he pays top price of $3.50 a week, Raymond Gillis believes this accords him the table's seat of responsibility. He takes his time spooning the steaming fish soup into his bowl, spearing the potatoes for his plate before passing the dishes on to the other boarders. In the small spare cottage of his Glace Bay boyhood, Raymond and his mother waited for their food until his father had finished eating his meal. Only when he'd risen from the table and nodded his assent did the son and wife help themselves. This was the way it was done.

Around the Connelly table, once the bowls are filled, plates heaped with potatoes and bread, one more torment remains for the hungry men. They wait as Raymond clasps his hands and lowers his head. This is the signal for everyone, if Catholic, to begin the recitation of the Grace prayer and if not Catholic, to sit in quiet contemplation of something else, even if it is what a pain in the arse Raymond Gillis is for making them endure this routine every bloody evening.

"Bless us, O Lord, and these Thy gifts…"

Some at the table mutter along with him, others fidget.

Lydia leans against the frame of the kitchen doorway, arms folded, head tilted rather than bowed. Micah stares at her, allowing the smallest twitch of his mouth to let her know that they both have the measure of Raymond Gillis. Lydia knows she has judged the black-eyed boy well. This is someone she can trust to keep her secrets.

"…forever and ever. Amen." With a deep sigh of satisfaction, Raymond picks up his spoon, nods his assent at the others, and dips his spoon into the soup.

≈

"Honestly, Edith, do you have to do that sort of thing at the dinner table?"

Edie glances at her mother and falls back against her chair. "Later, mister," she murmurs to her younger brother.

Mel struggles to put back the tangled shirttail that Edie has pulled loose. The fact that he has grown up and out in the past year and is now taller and heavier than his sister hasn't halted the habit of her assaults on his teenaged dignity. Anyone but Edie, he tells himself, anyone but Edie and, boy, they'd be in trouble. He glances at his mother and smiles, lifts his hands as if to say "what can a boy do?"

Mary understands. Mel is the sweetest-natured of her children, loving and trusting; a sensitive boy who has never given her a moment of worry.

There is little that cheers Mary more than the presence of her children. With Gus joining them at the table for the first time since his pneumonia brought him home, and after the easing of her guilt at the confessional that afternoon, she might describe herself this evening as being in a state close to happiness. Her oldest boy is still pale and his deep cough continues to trouble her, but to have him here fills her with relief.

There had been other children than the three gathered at the table, the mourned ones that didn't live longer than a few months inside of her. She never stopped blaming herself for their loss. She was sure that what happened to them was caused by some fault of her own, some internal flaw that she was responsible for. Priests counselled her to accept the miscarriages and to find her comfort in God's plan. She sought release from pain in daily prayer.

Gus's illness had driven her to the desperate pleas as well as a personal penance: she had refused food for most of the day and insisted that she deal with the most incorrigible of the indigent cases at the church. She had hoped that doing this would build a protective wall between her sick child and a hungry fate.

And tonight for Mary, at this table, is the proof of an understanding God: Augustus, moving steadily along the path to restored health. Her sacrifices had been worthwhile. The threat of losing her oldest child has passed.

"Edie says someone tried to steal her bike today," Gus says.

"Gus," Edie's fork clatters against her plate.

"Oh, sorry. Was that a secret?"

"Be careful with that fork, my girl. You'll crack the plate," Mary says. "I never liked that bicycle."

"It's good exercise for her." Charles holds the platter Theresa, standing beside him, has given him and levers a fillet of some white fish onto his plate. What is it? Taste, if it holds such a thing, might give him the answer. He passes the dish to his younger son and eyes a bowl of boiled white potatoes and a lifeless vegetable that might be carrots.

"What's this about stealing, Edie?"

"Oh, nothing. I happened to mention it to a certain trusted older brother. I guess he must've skipped class the day they taught secrets of the confessional. What I said was, looks as though someone fiddled with the lock."

"In the warehouse?"

"Well, yes, where else, Pa? In the warehouse."

"Don't take that tone with me, my girl. Put it in one of the empty offices from now on."

"I can't do that." The platter of fish reaches Edie, who removes one small piece and passes it to her mother. "I won't do that. What would I be telling the men? That I don't trust them, that's what."

"Well, someone…"

"Well, nothing, Pa. I won't do that. They'll be thinking I'm a snot…"

"Edith."

"…a snot. And I'm not."

"Not a snot?" Mel sniggers into his hand.

"A snot, she's not." Gus leans back his head and laughs.

"You two," Edie says.

"Stop it." Charles brings his hand down on the table.

"Oh, come on, Edie." Gus's voice rasps from the effort of laughing.

"You're no fun anymore," says Mel.

"All of you, stop it. Edith, you know if this one goes missing there won't be another. If you're so attached to this bike, you'll watch out for it."

"Well, what if someone has a greater need for it than me?"

"If you feel that way, I can certainly ask around. I'm sure I'll have a taker for it in no time." Charles winks at his younger son.

"I appreciate your thoughts and your suggestion, Pa. I'll keep it in the warehouse just the same, thank you."

"Can we forget about that contraption now and eat?" Mary had argued against Charles offering her daughter a bribe to work at the business and was most unhappy about that particular bribe. She worries about the appropriateness of females riding bicycles. Never mind the physical harm it could cause her, it's the look of it and what people might say. Edie's reputation for extravagant behaviour is no family secret. What Mary never says out loud is that she fears the bicycle gives her daughter too much independence. She is a headstrong girl who has never been reined in. Mary blames herself for that, too.

Charles joins his hands and bows his head, the signal that all talk must stop.

"Bless us, oh Lord, and these Thy gifts which we are about to receive from Thy bounty…"

He nods at Augustus. It's the turn of the one so long absent from the table to finish the prayer.

"…through Christ our Lord…"

"Amen," comes the chorus, followed by a flutter of hands making the sign of the Cross. No one hurries to eat except Mel, whose failure to develop any distinction between good food and Theresa's food is well known in this family and makes every meal for him something between a duty and a pleasure.

In the doorway, Theresa folds her arms and turns back into the kitchen where her own plate of food awaits her.

11

The two teenaged boys meet in the dim evening light on the stone path running alongside the Clarey home, evening meals eaten, schoolwork finished.

"You paid what for that?" Lawrie asks.

"A nickel." Mel rolls the small white tube between his index finger and thumb, careful not to dislodge any more of the fine dry tobacco threads. He hears the faint crackling sound of the aged weed under his fingers. "Ricky Gilchrist was selling them out back of school today. Don't worry. I've spent money on more foolish things."

"Oh? Like what?"

"Don't be a pill, Lawrie."

"Look, the money's yours, okay? Not mine. But a fool and his money. You know what they say. Purchase in haste, repent in…"

"In what?"

"Well, something that sounds like that."

Lawrie pulls his collar up around his neck. Because the sky stays lighter for much longer at the end of the day now, he'd convinced himself that the evenings must be warmer, too.

"I do see this, however, as a significant step in your personal development."

"How so?" Mel hasn't taken his eyes off the cigarette.

"Your attempt to be unconventional. So unlike a Clarey. I think it suits you."

At sixteen, almost seventeen, Mel's conviction that he needs to fashion an older style, more in keeping with his looming adulthood, had driven him to hand over the nickel to his classmate for the cigarette.

"It's not a sin, you know, Lawrie. I won't have to spill about this one in the confessional."

"How about the sin of disobedience to your parents?"

"Not this one. Not technically. They've never actually told me *not* to smoke."

"Look, it's really not your Catholic hairsplitting that concerns me. I'm worried you-know-who will walk out here any moment…"

Mel slips a hand into his jacket pocket and takes out three wooden matches. "I'm betting on her not counting these every night before she leaves the kitchen."

"So, come on then, light up. Let's see how this works."

Mel rests the cigarette on his bottom lip. The thin paper absorbs what little moisture is there. If he removes it, one of them, paper or lip will not survive intact. And the cigarette has an odd taste, not pleasant at all. He's reminded of one of Theresa's burnt supper offerings.

"Maybe if Ricky'd given you some tips to go with that nickel…"

"Okay, okay."

Mel strikes the red bulb of a match against the wall and touches its flame to the cigarette.

"Now, Mel. I can only go by what I've seen in movies, but I think you're actually supposed to draw on it. You know. Just putting a match to it won't quite…"

"I got it," Mel says. The words, issued from his fused lips, are a mumble. The thin trail of rising smoke causes his eyes to water. His tongue curls away from the acrid taste in his mouth.

"Maybe there's a less dangerous way of cultivating a world-weary image," Lawrie says. "One that doesn't involve holding an open flame to your face."

Mel mumbles something.

"What? You're busting?"

Mel's trying to laugh, but he can't open his mouth. He's reminded of the moment when he first touched his tongue to an icy metal pole. He tugs at the cigarette to get it away from his mouth, get the smoke out of his nose, his eyes. The fine skin of his bottom lip tears and stings as the paper comes away with it.

"Not 'I'm busting.' I said, 'it's disgusting.' Tastes like…"

"…like you put a burning weed inside your mouth?"

"I suppose."

"Well, I think you're an awfully brave man, Melville Clarey. Most people I know don't have an ounce of such courage. Attempting a feat like this in broad daylight…"

"It's as good as dark."

"…with his parents mere feet away. That's real nerve."

Mel drops the lighted cigarette on the ground and crushes the burning tip with his shoe.

"And you know, Sherlock, it's bad form leaving the evidence where you-know-who can find it."

"I'll say it belongs to you. Poor Lawrie. Taken leave of his senses."

"Good try. Who'll believe that?"

Mel picks up the crushed tube and puts it in his pocket.

"I guess I'll have to find some other way to age."

"Try hair tonic. Very few fatalities. Can we go inside now? April in Halifax. Not exactly standing-around-outside weather."

The two walk to the back door of the Clarey house and into the small mudroom.

"When's your dad going to break down and get a radio, Lawrie?"

"No time soon," Lawrie says. "Jack Shine isn't one to have his pocket picked for something you'll soon be tossing out with your trash, he says."

"Not a great track record that way?"

"I think he's still pretty sore about misjudging the electric razor."

In the kitchen, Theresa is finishing the tidying up. If there is a cleaner kitchen in Halifax, no one can say where it is.

"Lovely evening, Mrs. Monaghan."

Theresa, head down, arm working to remove a stain only she sees, isn't concerned about how the Shine boy addresses her.

"I better not be smelling what I think I'm smelling."

"Wood smoke, Mrs. Monaghan. April, and people've still got their fireplaces going. Imagine."

Mel wants to laugh, but his injured lip hurts when he moves it.

≈

Charles's habit is to close out the evening reading his newspaper in the front room. With a cup of tea beside him, he listens to the symphony of groans and gurgles from his stomach as his eyes scan the front page. Spain takes the boldest headline: a town called Guernica is in ruins. German and Italian planes flew over the city and dropped bombs on the civilian population. Hundreds, maybe thousands, are dead. No one is certain of the exact number.

"Holy hell," Charles mutters. Aeroplanes used for that sort of thing. What new ways to kill people will someone dream up next?

He remembers the German airship, the *Hindenburg*, flying over Halifax last year. Now that the big machine is making regular trans-Atlantic runs, what can stop a war in Europe from coming all the way to Halifax? What if someone armed it with bombs? Twenty years ago, the Germans tried to do that over London. Those clowns, Hitler and Mussolini, are just crazy enough. Charles missed out serving in the last war because of his poor eyesight. He'd accepted a metal helmet with the letters FW, Fire Warden, stencilled on it, ready to deal with any war-related emergency. For four years he carried the helmet with him wherever he went, proof to anyone who glared at him that a Clarey man was not one to shirk his wartime duty.

Preparations for the new king's coronation are underway, he reads. And one of the little princesses, Elizabeth, is very excited and looking forward to the ceremony. Pope Pius XI has a painful, swollen leg. A fifteen-year-old girl in Utah gave birth to twins. What the hell is that doing on a newspaper's front page? Or the story about a young movie actress who committed suicide in a New York City hotel room? Stories meant only for the inside pages. What else? Ireland has a new constitution, and in a small box at the bottom of the page, he reads that Dizzy Dean is promising to win twenty-five games for the Cardinals this season. At last, a story worth reporting.

An editorial runs the full length of the left side of the front page, no doubt stoking the city's fires of discontent in order to sell more papers. What are they pushing today? "The Essence of Democracy" reads the headline. Charles skims the paragraphs. They shout about "great accumulation of wealth in the hands of a few people." Jesus, that's rich. Who's got the great wealth? Give it to me, he wants to say to them. I'll see that it's distributed properly.

A gravelly cough from nearby interrupts his reading.

"Can I get you more tea, Pa?" Gus asks.

"I'm fine. Tea is the only really good thing that comes out of Theresa's kitchen. I don't want to spoil myself."

Gus smiles. "Her food allows us to appreciate so many other things."

His son has become so holier-than-thou since he's been at the seminary. The boy is smarter than some of the things he says these days. Maybe it's just a phase, trying things on for how they sound.

"How are you feeling, Gus? Take a seat. You on the mend?" Charles moves his feet from the footstool and Gus sits, perched on its edge as though he's eager to be away at the first opportunity. His hands, joined as if in prayer, are wedged between his knees, his shoulders hunched.

"Gus."

"Pa?"

"I asked you how you're feeling."

"Well, Pa…"

"You're feeling well?"

"No, it's not that I'm feeling well. I was just thinking out loud, saying 'well,' not that I'm actually well, if you see what I mean."

"I see." Charles doesn't, though. "If not actually well, then, how would you describe your health?"

"Not bad, is what I'd say, I guess."

"Fever?"

"No fever."

"Bit of a cough, still."

"As you can hear." Gus gives a small reflexive bark to emphasize his point.

"Strong enough?"

"Like a kitten, really."

"I see." Charles doesn't see that either. "Got a letter from your principal the other day. I didn't want to bother you about it while you're still in bed."

Gus looks at his father and his shoulders straighten.

"What'd he say?"

"Usual stuff you'd expect. Wanted to know how you're coming along. Wanted to know when they might expect you back. That's not exactly how he phrased it. He wanted to know *if* you're coming back."

Charles has been in business long enough to be able to read a customer.

"Is there something you'd like to tell me, Gus?"

The son runs a hand through his brown hair. After weeks of no visits to the barber, it touches his collar; long enough to tuck behind his ears or obscure his expression when it falls onto his face. He has always been so fastidious about his appearance that this change, not quite slovenly, more unkempt, is one more worrisome sign that not all is right with him. Gus was an obedient boy and even as a child, thoughtful and attentive. Teachers loved the young student and priests were never happier than when the conscientious boy served beside them at mass. He looked out for his younger brother and sister, warned Edie when her parents were losing patience with her. Family, faith, duty. Gus embodies Charles Clarey's personal motto. He is such a dutiful son, so much a Clarey in that way, Charles tells himself. So, what is troubling this least troublesome of his children?

"Pa, you know illness can be hard on a person. Lower your defences and all and sometimes not allow you to think straight. About the right thing to do, I mean."

"A little confused?"

"I guess you'd call it that."

Gus stops, as though that one observation is the sum of all he has to say. His hands go back between his knees and his shoulders hunch again. The father and son sit, each waiting for the other to speak first.

"Done." Mel lopes into the room, Lawrie close behind him.

"Evening, Mr. Clarey."

"Lawrie."

"Homework's done, Pa. For both of us. So. Time for the radio. Yes?"

"Mel, this isn't such a…"

"No," Gus says. "Really. Let them listen to the radio. It's their reward, after all. We'll talk later, Pa. It's not all that important. We've got lots of time. Only me fretting." And he rises, leaving his father with the newspaper and the two friends crouched in front of the radio, watching the glow from the tubes light up the dial.

"Boys, don't dig your shoes into the carpet. Get something to sit on. Otherwise, Theresa'll have a fit. What's that I'm smelling?"

"Wood smoke," the two answer in unison.

"Your father's right," Theresa says, patting Gus's arm as they pass in the doorway. "I'm going to have some big fit unless you do as he says and give that carpet a break."

Mel and Lawrie pull over a bench. They sit so close to the radio that their ears almost touch the front of the machine.

If Charles had not been left so preoccupied with what was bothering his oldest child, he might have smiled when he looked at the faces of the teenaged boys. They are such a mismatched pair, always have been, in looks and in interests. The younger son is almost the same height as his older brother now. Charles had bought Mel his first razor last year and the two had spent an enjoyable morning in the bathroom discovering and re-discovering, on his son's fuzzed face, the art of shaving. It was a touching rite of passage that he had looked forward to and took great pleasure from.

"Mind if I join?" Theresa says, although there is no real point in asking. The room is as much hers as anyone else's. She sits on the sofa, turns on the table lamp next to her and draws her knitting out of a faded brocade bag. When Gus arrived home so sick, she'd gone to the yarn store to buy wool for a patterned vest. "You know how cold it gets in Antigonish," she told anyone who asked, even though she'd never once in all her life ventured off the Halifax peninsula. The colours she'd chosen, a vivid green, yellow, reds and blues made up an unholy garment. This, however, was her gamble. If God, or whoever it is other people believe control these things, is courageous enough to let Gus wear the sweater then he must also have the courage to let the boy live.

≈

At the top of the stairs, Gus pauses to catch his breath. The yellow light from the door of his parents' bedroom cuts a triangle into the wine-red carpet. His mother is seated on the frilled bench in front of her vanity, head bowed. For as long as Gus can remember, she spends a little time there most nights tending her fingernails with the tortoiseshell-handled instruments that lie on the tray on top of the small oval table—the tiny scissors, the metal file, the two chamois brushes used to finish and buff. Her hands, Mary says, are her best feature. The nails are left unvarnished. She believes their simple symmetrical beauty, with their delicate white half-moons, are more eye-catching than any colour she might cover them with. She regrets that none of her children, in particular her daughter, can exhibit such hands as an inheritance. They all have the Clarey hands, too large, too long-fingered, suitable for piano playing if necessary, never as objects of admiration as are her own.

Gus leaves his mother to her moment of solitude and contentment and continues down the hallway. He can hear the murmur of radio voices from downstairs and his brother's and Lawrie's accompanying laughter. The door to his sister's room is almost closed. A sliver of light lets him know that it's all right to give a faint knock and push it open a few inches.

"Edie?"

She looks up from her bed, her long frame stretched out, shoeless, sockless in the chill of the house.

"God sakes, Edie, aren't your feet cold?"

She looks down the length of her body and wiggles her toes. "I'm toughening them up."

"Whatever for?"

"We all need to be tougher these days."

She's propped up against the many down pillows that cover her bed, still wearing the brown dress with the white collar and cuffs that she wore to work. Her chestnut hair, allowed to have its own way after a day of controlled brushing, fans out from her head like rivulets of water running away from its source. The book she's holding rests against her ribs.

"What've you got there?"

She tilts the book so that he can read the title on its spine and laughs as her brother's eyebrows rise.

"Edie, I figured you more for Groucho than Karl. Don't let Pa catch you with that. What're you doing with it anyways? Not your kind of book, is it?" He has no idea what his sister's kind of book might be.

"Well, someone in this family has to be on top of things to understand what's going on in this world."

"And you think we don't understand? But Karl Marx? I'm amazed you even found a copy in this city."

"It belongs to a friend. He loaned it to me."

"Okay." Gus sits down on the only chair in the room, the narrow gold-painted excuse for seating in front of Edie's vanity.

"And what have you learned from Mr. Marx?"

"Lots."

"Like?"

"Well," Edie swings her legs over the side of her bed and faces her brother. "Like I said…lots of things."

"Name one."

She looks down at the book, her right index finger sunk into its pages to mark her place.

"Well, for instance. Mr. Marx doesn't see the need to put pictures in his books. There aren't any pictures. Not one. Can you believe it?" she says and laughs again.

Gus joins her and soon a cough, rumbling up from his chest, leaves him red-faced and breathless.

"Gus?" Their mother's voice, tight with concern, carries down the hall.

He breathes in, waiting until he can speak without causing another coughing spell.

"Don't worry, Ma. I'm okay." There is no reply. She's already gone back to her nails, back to the soothing clip, file, polish.

"Who gave you the book?" he asks.

"Doesn't matter. Someone just as concerned as I am about the way things're going, you know. Too few people having all the money."

Gus wants very much to mock her again. That Edie, raised in comfort, always so concerned with how she looks and what she's wearing, is now expressing a conscience, is as funny as it is charming. In her sweet way, she is embracing ideology with as much enthusiasm as she hugs her brothers and family. She loves too much and too easily. Now she's asking him to believe that her boundless enthusiasm for loving things includes ideas as well as people. Edie's time in school ignited no academic fires, even with the soft curriculum of the convent school. The nuns praised her athletic ability, her talent for raising spirits and amusing others — they didn't know what the drama club would do for a star after Edie graduated, they told her parents — but not much else.

"I know what everyone thinks about me. There's more here, you know," and she taps her forehead. "More than the likes of you ever give me credit for."

"And clearly someone else thinks so, too."

"That I have substance."

Oh, you have substance, Edie, he wants to say. Look in your closet. There's a ton of substance in there. We made you like this. It's our fault that you have no ambition beyond what you find within the confines of this easy Clarey life. We've missed something about you, though. What we call high spirits is really some kind of fire that burns inside. We shake our heads over the things you do, the things you say. Our parents despair about the state of your manners and behaviour. Now, something or someone is stoking that fire. And what a shame it is for us not to be part of it.

"So, tell me, sister, what'll you do with all this learning?"

"I'll make a difference. Make people's lives better. Don't look at me like that."

"Like what? It's just that this is all so sudden."

"You've been away, you know. A lot happens to people when you're not looking."

"Keep your voice down. We don't want Ma worrying we've got a Red living under the roof. How'd she ever explain that to the neighbours? Are you a Red, by the way?"

"You can make fun of me all you want, Augustus Leo Clarey. My life is changing. All our lives are changing. I can feel it. Something will come of this. You watch."

She shivers in the cold on her bed of eiderdown and fresh linen. For Gus, life without the buoyant presence of his sister is not worth living. His sister is no Red. This will pass, in the way that all of Edie's enthusiasms do. Whether she sets her wheels on the Clarey track or not is up to her. Here's one thing we never understood about you, he wants to say to Edie. Your imagination makes you too big for this house.

"When are you going back to Antigonish?" she asks him.

"I'm not sure."

"When you're feeling better?"

"I'll let you get back to your reading." As he stands, the narrow gold-painted chair creaks under the shift of his weight. "This is an old thing," he says and pats the chair. He might be referring to how he feels about himself.

"Well, I hope you never get better. Not if it means you going away again."

You are so lovely, he wants to tell her. He watches the arch seriousness of her face fade. No matter what she chooses to do, what will always remain is Edie, the loving sister.

"Good night, sis," he says and leans down to kiss the top of her head.

"Will I have to call you Father Gus when we're very old? Will my children have to call you Father Gus?"

"Call me what you want. When we're old it won't matter. I'll let you get back to your reading, Mrs. Lenin. Don't start any revolutions while I'm asleep, okay? Wait till I wake up. I want to be there to see it."

"Har har. Night night, Gussie."

And with that, he leaves her and closes the door to her bedroom. Down the hall, he can see his mother, head bent, arm pumping, buffing each nail until it glows.

≈

What little Micah has learned about Lydia, the younger of his two landladies, has come from her in terse points of detail. There are no late night strolls down memory's smooth path for this woman. "What was, was," she'd said to him not long after they became acquainted. "I've no interest in plowing that particular field again."

She married as a young woman and had no children. When her husband died of cancer she moved in with her mother to help run the boarding house. She wanted nothing more of marriage.

"I'm not against the institution itself, you see," she told Micah. "It's that I loved him a little too much. He spoiled me for anyone else that way. I do miss his touch something terrible, though. That's easier to replace than himself."

Those who have heard Lydia's thoughts on the matter think this a shame because she is an ideal catch for someone. She's still young enough and pleasing to look at and sensible, not given to unsettling mood swings. A few men have courted her in a determined way, yet she refuses the most tempting bait, preferring her own arrangements.

She does not take her lovers from the boarders in her own home. She doesn't want her mother's business acquiring a certain reputation. The single exception to this rule is the dark-haired boy with the black eyes living in the cramped space off the kitchen, the one who says his name is Michael Green. In the way he keeps to himself, Lydia recognizes her own way of doing things. There isn't much risk of this Michael, or whoever he is, talking about what they do together.

"Doesn't your mother ever want to know where you've gone?" Micah wanted to know.

"She's ears like rocks these days so she sleeps right through. Never stirs until five when that alarm clock in her head goes off. Couple of times she found me sneaking back into the room. I give her the usual. Bathroom. Checking to see if the dough's rising. She's a dear and I love her, I do. Really. And I thank God she's clueless."

When she'd asked Micah his age, he'd said right away: "Almost twenty." She told him she has never had a lover so young. "I don't like to take advantage that way, you see," she said.

Two bodies don't fit easily onto Micah's narrow cot, so the kitchen is where they transact their business, stretched out in front of the warm stove. And a business is very much as it seems to both of them. Goods offered, goods accepted, concluded in a satisfactory way, neither feeling cheated. At its conclusion, there is no lingering.

This night, though, he startles Lydia by catching hold of her wrist as she straightens her nightgown and prepares to leave.

"There's no time to do it again," she says. "And, besides, this floor's killing my back."

"I know. Just stay for a few more minutes. Please?"

Lydia has a soft spot for men who say "please" and "thank you." Her late husband had such good manners. She likes this boy for that and for the way he doesn't try to impress her as so many others tried to do. And one thing more: he possesses a softness that she recognizes in herself, a tender wound caused by loss or longing.

"Just lie here," he says. "That's all I want. Only a few minutes. Nothing else. Please."

Lydia lies back down, their two heads balanced for space on the hard square of unyielding pillow.

Micah slips his hand under the sleeve of Lydia's flannel nightgown and finds her wrist. His fingers rest there, a band of warmth across her smooth skin where he feels the slow steady beat of her pulse.

12

"You're no use to me."

"I'm not sure I've even heard of it. How can I be expected to know every street and corner of an entire city?"

There is no breeze coming off the harbour today and for the minutes they sit in the park they can believe that the warmth from the day's sun means they've felt the last of winter.

Micah's lunch pail is on the ground beside him, untouched. Nerves have taken away any appetite. The moment he's anticipated since he left Toronto months ago is so close. Today, Edie's presence, radiating her characteristic good will, rattles him. He wants her gone except that he needs her, she can be helpful to him.

Go to the yellow house on McCully Street, he'd been told. The yellow house close to Robie Street. The one with the dark green door and the blinds pulled down all the way. That house.

"Good to know," Micah said to the man who issued the instruction. "Where's McCully Street?"

"You want to get to Spain so bad," the man said, "you figure it out."

Micah understood. If the yellow house on McCully Street eluded him, he wasn't going to find his way to Spain. There is no boat ticket for the unresourceful.

"Edith, you need to find out for me how I get to this McCully Street."

He is accustomed to seeing her face wide-eyed and smiling, not set the way it is, mouth pulled down, her gaze focussed not on him but on some distant point. Has he misjudged her all this time? Did he mistake her girlish enthusiasm for a lack of will?

"Why should I do that?" she says. "Ask one of your warehouse friends."

Micah is not used to such resistance from her. He needs her to do this one thing for him. He won't beg her. As difficult as it is for him to wheedle or cajole, he must find a tone that will bring her back to him.

"You know they're not from here most of them." He drops his voice as though he must take care not to be overheard, even though the surrounding crowd consists of a dozen hungry ducks. "You know that, Edith. And besides, I don't want those men gossiping about what's my business, not theirs."

She's slow to answer him.

"What's in this house, anyways?"

"My boat ticket and visa."

Edie tears at the thick slab of bread and tosses the pieces on the ground.

"Who are they? The people in this house."

"The ones who arrange these things. Look, if you don't know how to do this…"

"No." Edie almost shouts the word. The ducks give a startled squawk and scatter. "I'll do it. I mean I can do it. There's a map in the office. A map of the city. I'll find it and write out directions for you."

"That's my girl," he says and smiles at her. She isn't his girl, but he finds a strange delight in watching her face light up when he says it. Girls like Edith Clarey were not part of his life growing up in Toronto. There were only the ones like him, children of parents who struggled to make a living, and find a reason to feel at home in their new country.

Schoolgirls, the ones who possessed a little spirit, had teased Micah for his dark curls and for the state of his clothes. Shouldn't the tailor's son be dressed better than the rest of them, they said? Not with patches at knees and elbows like their own. He wanted to ask his father then how it was possible that young girls controlled young boys in this way and yet grew up to be little more than slaves.

His father had not prepared him to understand that what a person wants and what a person feels, though often contradictory, can co-exist inside one heart. How was the motherless boy to know that he didn't have to choose between the excitement in his chest, like the beating wings of a small bird, and the recoil of embarrassment at their attentions? So, Micah ignored the girls because he was shy in the way all young boys are shy of young girls. And he ignored them because that's what he sensed his father would tell him to do — keep to yourself — if his father had been the kind of man to dispense advice.

In time, the girls turned to someone else and the absence of their voices and smiles had the sting of a betrayal for him.

Beyond the Connellys' kitchen floor, Micah is no better educated in the ways of men and women than he had been as the schoolboy surrounded by tiny temptresses. There was no future for him with a girl like Edie. He told himself that it was only her persistence that kept her close by him.

"Can I come with you?" she said.

"Can you…?"

"To the house, I mean. Just to the house. To get the ticket and visa."

"No." He's done with compromise. By asking her for directions, he's offering her a chance to show the extent of her loyalty. Micah wants his next answer to sound as rough and confident as he means it to be. He wants her to feel not slighted, but hurt. If she won't do this one small thing for him, he won't waste any more effort to persuade or convince. He'll break away from her in the same way he's doing without food or comfort. And if she asks why, he'll tell her: "Because it's good for you." This is his father's legacy to him. He conjures the sound of Chaim's voice: "You see? By doing without, you became stronger. And now look at you. On your way to Spain."

"I'll be quiet. I promise. I won't embarrass you."

"I said no." He doesn't know who or what is inside this house. There is the danger that police agents are at the meetings he attends and know all about his quest. They'll arrest him and anyone else with him.

"Embarrassment has nothing to do with it," he says, although to have come this far and be stopped on a street called McCully is more than he could bear. No, she certainly can't come with him.

"You need to understand how dangerous all of this is. Good people risking their lives every day for a cause. You've got no idea."

Micah's rough talk finds its target. Edie's hazel eyes scan the surface of the water.

"Fine," she says. "I'll find you the street. Come by the office before you leave the warehouse today. I'll have directions for you."

She drops the rest of her sandwich on the ground and shakes out the napkin.

He knows there is something he might say to her, some small consoling phrase that could ease her unhappiness. But Micah has no idea what those words are. Since the first time they met he treated her one way, the only way he knew, and was confused because he also wished he had the understanding and words to say something else. In that way, he is not so different from others when it comes to Edie. Even Micah can't deny wanting to please her and see her smile.

Edie presses her foot against the pedal of her bicycle and rides away. Since they had been spending these lunch times together, this is the first time she has left before him.

≈

Edie is as good as her word. She has written out the directions to McCully Street in her neat convent-trained hand. And she's drawn a map of straight lines for streets, circles for notable landmarks and arrows for added assurance. She hands it to him, unsmiling. Micah feels a quick stab of what might have been regret for his rough words to her earlier in the day until he reminds himself he's doing a necessary thing for Edie. He's making her understand what real disappointment is like and that, to Micah, is useful if you want to get along in the world.

≈

It's dark by the time Micah approaches the door of the yellow house on McCully Street. An icy spring wind tugs at his cap. He stumbles along the pitted sidewalks with only the faint lights from windows to guide him. All the houses along the street struggle to show their level of respectability in these hard times. Most are in need of some maintenance, a coat of fresh paint, a repair to a sagging front step. When better days return to Halifax, they will resume their status as honest shelters to the hard-working. There's no mistaking the yellow house; the colourful anomaly along the street of grey and brown. Like all the others, it is a two-storey clapboard structure; on the ground floor a front door and a single window to one side. Above, two windows under a peaked roof. A brick chimney stack hugs the wall.

Pieces of paper, a sock sodden in the melting snow, are matted in the narrow patch of grass along the short path in front of the yellow house. The weak light from inside shows the neat repair of a jagged tear in the roll-down blind of the main-floor window. The gleam of a small rectangular piece of metal attached to the dark green door draws Micah's attention. In the nighttime gloom he can just make out the letters etched there: M. & J. Hibbert. He knocks as he was instructed to do. One rap, pause, then two short taps. Who will answer? They might be carrying a gun. He hadn't thought of that. And he hadn't been given a password. Maybe they'll be expecting one. Will they slam the door in his face when he doesn't know how to respond? This might be another test.

A man stops and waits for his dog to finish sniffing at something. Micah hadn't checked to see if he was followed as he walked here. He can't remember if they'd told him to do that. The dog moves closer, in search of the next distraction, nose close to the ground as though he's picked up a suspicious scent.

Micah knocks again at the dark green door, his shaking hand making the last two raps of the signal sound like three.

The dog drops to its haunches, barely ten feet from him. It's a fair-coloured mongrel with a pointed nose and ears that half flop over. Micah doesn't trust animals and has no idea why anyone would want to keep one in a house. If that dog barks, you run, he tells himself.

The door to the yellow house opens. An older woman smiles at him.

"You must be Micah." She speaks quickly, quietly. "You look just like your picture." She puts a hand on his arm and draws him inside the house.

She closes the door part way, leaving just enough room to stand and look outside.

"Lovely evening, Jackie," she calls out.

"Fer Eskimos," Michael hears the dog's owner say.

"No truer words, dear," the woman says. "And Dot's better?"

There's no sound from the man on the sidewalk. He's giving his answer with a shake of his head.

The woman sighs and expels a heartfelt: "Ahhhh. Maybe when it warms up. She'll feel stronger then. The sun always does us good, doesn't it?"

"Hardly remember what it's like," the man called Jackie says.

"As soon as my visitor's gone, I'll bring Dot some soup."

They bid each other good night. She closes the door and turns to study Micah for several seconds. Her eyes are dark and unblinking, made to look larger than they are by the thick lenses of her round wire-rimmed glasses.

"You need to take off your hat," she says at last. Her soft voice has taken on a no-nonsense urgency.

"My hat?" He's come all this way, to the brink of his ambition, to be told to attend to his hat?

"It's very rude to leave it on when you've entered a stranger's house," she says. "Do I have to tell you young people everything? Does no one teach ordinary manners anymore?"

Wordlessly, and without turning her head to look at him, she makes an impatient gesture with her hand. He pulls the cap off his head and follows her.

In the kitchen, she motions for him to take a chair across from her at the worn wooden table. The room is small and warm. The heat from the kitchen stove keeps hot the pot of soup destined for Jackie's wife, although there is no sign of water being readied for a pot of tea, the accepted gesture of welcome. The walls are white, the wooden counters are scrubbed clean and lined with the objects of a tidy and ordinary life. Tidy and ordinary are the same words he would use to describe the woman.

Whatever her age, and she must be ancient, it is unfathomable to Micah. At least seventy. Her grey hair is pulled back from her round face and collected in a neat knot at the back of her head. Soft sloping shoulders frame a thick body. A man's brown cardigan, too big, sleeves folded over at the wrists, covers a faded blue cotton dress. There's a spot at the right elbow that's been darned. Her hands rest on the table, one folded over the other, the joints knobbed with arthritis. The thin gold band on the finger of her left hand was placed there in younger days. It will not come off now unless it is cut away.

Since they took their seats at the table, the woman has not moved her gaze from his face. She taps the envelope under her hands.

"Well. Micah," she says.

"I'm Michael here."

"Your paperwork says Micah, so Micah you are to me."

He thinks of the piece of metal attached to the dark green door. M. & J. Hibbert. Is she the M or the J?

"And what do I call you?"

"You don't call me anything, dear. We won't be talking long enough for that."

"If someone asks…"

"No one will ask. And we won't be seeing each other again, so there's no need for you to know my name. You give me the money. I give you the goods. This is our one-night stand, you might say, dear." Her face alters slightly. She's enjoying herself.

From the inside pocket of his jacket Micah takes out the money he'd put aside from his pay packet, week after long week. He slides the thin bundle across the table to the woman. She picks it up with her left hand, licks the thumb of her right and begins counting the bills with her stiff fingers. Only when she's finished does she hand the brown envelope to him.

"A passport in the name of Micah Gessen," she says. "With the proper visa. The birth certificate you gave us. And there's the ticket. You sail from Halifax to New York and then you board another ship for France. There's no direct ships to Spain these days. And if anyone asks, you're on your way to Paris for the exhibition."

"What's that?"

"A big international fair. Doesn't matter. If they want to know, tell them you're an artist. Going to see the paintings there."

"What if they want some kind of proof? What if they tell me to draw something? I'm no artist."

She shrugs. "Tell them you're a sculptor. It doesn't matter. Tell them it's modern art you do. No one knows what that is, what it looks like. And no one's likely to ask you to do such a thing anyways. They don't care. Chances are, they know exactly where you're going and for what. Just as long as you're on a boat that's headed away. That's all that matters to them."

"So what do I do when I get to France?"

"You dock at Le Havre. Now listen to me. You're on your own from there. You'll find the name of a Paris contact in that envelope. If you've got the money, get on a train and head south for the border."

"And if I don't have the money?"

"Walk."

"There's no other way?"

"You can run for all I care, dear. Hitch a ride. Whatever conveyance gets you there. You won't be alone for long. You're sure to meet others on the ship or in Paris. Once you get to the Spanish border, you find the people who take you across the mountains. I hope you've a pair of sturdy shoes. You wouldn't believe what I've seen some people go to war in."

"And after that?"

She shrugs again as if to say, could it be more self-evident? "You find the war. Or it finds you. As I understand it, that won't take long. Especially in the north these days." She shifts her eyeglasses. If she meant to or not, the gesture emphasizes the point she's just made.

Throughout all of this, the woman's voice never varies in tone. She's friendly enough, but the moment he walks out that door she'll forget everything about him; his name, his address, where he's going. This forgetting is part of her business, what she's trained herself to do. Unless it's him she doesn't like. Taking off the hat without being told might have made a difference, might have made her warm to him. Or maybe she's one of those who don't like Jews. As long as he has been on this quest, from the streets of Toronto to this table in the run-down house on McCully Street, he's rubbed up against them, the ones wary of his motive and intent for reasons as old as history and as recent as that day's indignity.

But no, he's sure it has nothing to do with who he is. For her, and the others, it's who he might be. They watch for spies, for anyone who can do them harm. Trust no one. He understands this because he shares that suspicion of people. And what does it matter to him what this woman thinks? After he leaves this house all of that will cease to matter because what he's wanted for so long is about to happen. Micah Gessen, the tailor's son from Baldwin Street, is going to war.

He holds up the envelope.

"When do I leave?"

"Tomorrow night. The information's all there, inside. Just read it. You're travelling alone?"

"Alone."

"It's best. You've said goodbye to the ones you care for? Left instructions what to do if you don't come back?"

"There's no one."

She looks at him and shakes her head.

"There's always someone, dear," she says.

They sit, staring at each other, Micah hoping for some final flourish, an acknowledgement of the sacrifice he's making, a word of farewell or encouragement. Instead, she leans back in her chair and looks at him, as though taking him in for the first time.

"I have to say, dear, we don't get many of you coming through Halifax. Most go through Montreal. The ones that end up here were usually held back for some reason or other. Too young. Too old. Not strong enough. Filled with good intentions and nothing else. Who knows? Maybe they're right about you. Holding you back, I mean. I guess I'll never know, will I? A body's a body, I say. And if you're willing to risk it, then…" The rounded shoulders move up and down one more time, dislodging a sigh from her.

"I'll be going then," he says.

"It's best not to linger. And I've a sick neighbour's needing her soup."

Micah holds up the envelope. He'll give her one last chance to praise him. "Thank you for this. It means so much to me that I'll be able to fight for the cause. Fight fascism."

Her mouth may have twitched, not quite a smile.

"Yes, dear." She stands up from the table and walks to the front door, this revolutionary hidden among the respectable residents of McCully Street.

Micah steps outside and turns for a last goodbye, but the door to the yellow house is already closed.

≈

Before Raymond hears the front door open or close, he hears the key in the lock. He lies on his bed and listens. Whoever is at the door takes care to make as little noise as possible.

No matter who is entering the house, they all start out that way. If they've been out drinking he hears the stumble on the first step of the stairs. If the first step and the second are finessed, the loose board of the third is the giveaway. The drinkers always try to step over that one, but risk getting stuck, one leg stretched too far, not enough balance or leverage to hoist them over the gap. No sober person attempts that. If there are no footsteps at all on the stairs after the closing of the front door, he knows it's Michael Green heading for his cubbyhole off the kitchen.

He's always apart, that one, apart from everything. It only makes sense to Raymond that someone who talks as little as Michael Green is hiding things. Why else doesn't he join in? He reads books, so he must be smart enough. Maybe too smart for his own good. He watches with those black eyes. And that mouth, pulled up at one corner as though he knows something the others don't.

And he's brazen, this Green character; his silence mocks as though daring Raymond to wonder about him. While the other boarders sit in the comfort of the parlour smoking and chatting, listening to the radio, he leaves the house or goes to his closet of a room to read, or when that space is too cold, sits alone at the kitchen table. No temptation for companionship or friendly diversion ever leads him to seek the company of the other men.

The boarders have given up trying to draw him into their own chatter. Raymond takes a rare delight in prodding him with questions he knows the boy won't answer.

"Cat got your tongue?" he'll say because he knows from the look on Micah's face that the attention irritates him.

In the quiet of the late nighttime house, the sharp click of the key engaging the front door lock carries up the stairs and into Raymond's room. There is no stumble on the bottom stair this time, no grunt of effort to get over the noisemaker of a step. Only silence. Michael Green must have taken off his boots and walked shoeless down the hall to the kitchen.

Another resident of the house is also waiting for the sound of that door closing. There they are, the footsteps from the third floor where only Mrs. Connelly and her daughter sleep. She moves along the hall, past Raymond's door. Her hand reaches for the banister and her feet clad in the dark red slippers, take one step and then another. She doesn't care who hears the groan of the faulty third board on her way to the kitchen.

One night Raymond crouched at the stop of the stairs and listened. As much as they tried not to make the noises, he heard them. What has that despicable boy done to that respectable woman to make her act like this? Disgust fills him until he thinks he might scream.

13

Edie turns the key in the small lock, opens it one more time and rearranges the chain looped through the bicycle's wheels. She's wasting time until Micah's work brings him to the front of the warehouse, close to where she's standing. He's counting flats of paint cans and recording the number on a sheet of paper that lies on the table next to her. It wouldn't do for her to simply march in and demand to talk to one of the crew. She has no authority to do that unless the situation is an emergency and if it isn't, whatever she has to tell one of the workers must wait until the tea break.

"Morning, Edith." Joe Dan MacLean's voice cuts through the bustle and noise of the warehouse. "Anything I can do to help?"

"No." The word comes out with more force than she intends. She wishes she hadn't said it quite that way to Joe Dan, such a nice man, with the smooth manner and voice of someone of natural authority. His offer has nothing to do with deference to his boss's daughter and everything to do with the nature of an instinctively polite person.

"Thank you," she adds, too late to hide her rudeness. She sees over his shoulder that Micah has finished his counting and is walking to where she stands with Joe Dan.

"If that lock is being a bother, leave it. I'll keep a lookout for yer machine," Joe Dan says.

"It's fine. Don't worry. It's just being a little…"

"…individual?"

"…individual this morning, yes, thanks. Don't worry, Mr. MacLean. Really. Almost there."

Micah is drawing closer. Joe Dan stands his ground, determined to be useful and if not useful, then at least friendly.

"We all have days like that."

"Thank you for your offer, Mr. MacLean. Really. It's not necessary."

She might as well have put her hands on the older man's shoulders and pushed him away.

He flicks an index finger against the brim of his cap and without another word, moves off. Micah reaches the small table beside Edith, picks up the clipboard with the tally of merchandise and runs down the column of numbers with the pencil.

"There was no call to be so rude to Joe Dan, you know. He was offering to help. No one else thought to do that."

Including you, she wants to say to him.

"Aren't girls like you supposed to have better manners?"

Edie dips her head away from him so that he can't see her face. This is not what she had planned. She had meant to ask, in a nonchalant way, if the map she'd drawn had been useful to him. Instead, she wants to cry. She tugs again at the chain.

"I only wanted to know…" She doesn't trust her voice to finish the sentence.

The pencil stops and he looks at her at last. "Wanted to know what?"

"The map, if it helped. Did you find…"

"Shut up. Keep your voice down."

"…what you needed?"

"Your map was useful, as things turned out."

"You could thank me, you know. Speaking of manners. A simple thank you is called for, I think."

"If it's so important to you…thanks."

They remain like that, Edie toying with the lock and chain, Micah continuing to scan the column of numbers. At any minute,

Joe Dan might interrupt them, tell Micah to get back to work and stop wasting Edie's time.

"You got what you went for?" she says.

"I did."

"I see." She could end the conversation there and never ask how much time she has left to be with him. She takes a breath, hoping to settle her voice.

"So, when do you leave?"

He's not inclined to tell anyone the details of his departure, especially Edie, but there's nothing she can do about him leaving now. Of all the things he thinks of her, he knows she's trustworthy. She can keep secrets as well as he does.

"Tonight."

"When?" she says.

"Keep your voice down. You can't come with me."

"I could…"

"No. You couldn't. I've told you. I'm going alone. You're a foolish daydreamer. No idea what you'd be getting into."

"And you do, I suppose. You don't know any better than me."

Micah's hand trembles as it moves along the page of numbers and columns.

"Lookit. You've made me forget what I'm doing."

"So what?" Edie says. His sudden confusion has restored the old Edie, the girl so confident of her powers to persuade. "What's your worry? Put down any number you want. If you get it wrong, there's nothing they can do to you tomorrow, is there? You won't be here."

Micah doesn't enjoy being bested by her. She watches him as his hand seeks a place to stop and record.

"All right," she says. "You go. But let me give you something to take with you."

"What've you got that I'd want? You whine you never have money. Other than that, what else helps me?"

"This." Edie slaps the seat of the bicycle.

Micah opens his mouth wide and starts to laugh. Ride a bicycle to a war? She is ridiculous. As ridiculous as she ever was.

"You'll take it then?"

Well, why not? He has to get from Le Havre to Spain somehow.

"You're serious? You'll give me your bicycle?"

Edie gives a sharp nod of her head. "Yes," she says. "You can't let anyone see you take it, though. They might think you're stealing it. I'll have to bring it to you. At the boat, I mean. Tonight."

He might have kissed her then if they hadn't been standing where they were. Instead, he tells her where to be and when to meet him.

"And you don't tell anyone. Anyone. You understand? No brother. No maid. No one."

Edie places a finger to her lips and nods. At last, there is her smile.

"Now, go. I've got work to do."

She runs all the way to the office. Sometimes things have a funny way of working out. Sometimes when you're not expecting it to happen, opportunity walks right up to you and shakes your hand.

If she'd been more attentive to her father's stories of their ancestor, Leo Clarey, she might have recognized the echo of the old man's observation about finding opportunity in confusion.

Edie never listens closely enough to anyone, though. What she sees is her own cleverness bringing her the one thing she wants most.

14

Raymond crouches at the top of the stairs and watches the front door of Mrs. Connelly's boarding house.

The door is where he'll see the one calling himself Michael Green and who evades any questions about where he goes most nights, come in or go out of the house.

Raymond will discover whatever sinful or illegal thing Michael Green is up to and once he has, he won't hesitate to involve the police. The hard times have created a criminal class that treats the city and everyone in it as though they're owed something. It's a reasonable guess that Michael is part of that bunch, perhaps preying on women as they walk alone to their homes. Or he's a thief, robbing people for what little money there is to be had in anyone's pockets. He might be spending time in the illegal drinking holes or leading some kind of double life. Any decent society would side with Raymond and judge Michael Green, and whatever he's doing, as unacceptable.

He stares into the dim light of the front hall and beyond the glassed front door of the house. From above, he hears the strain of feet on aging floorboards as Mrs. Connelly and Lydia prepare for bed and from below, the careful tread of steps down the hallway from the kitchen. Michael Green, his small rucksack slung over one shoulder, unlocks the front door, places his key to the Connelly house on the telephone table, steps outside and closes the door behind him. The only sound is the faint click of the lock engaging.

Raymond moves down the stairs, stepping over the noisemaker of the third board up. He peers through the glassed door and watches the boy disappear into the night.

≈

Edie turns off the lamp on her bedside table. She sees no light from her parents' bedroom or from Theresa's or Mel's rooms. Only Gus's light continues to burns.

Her plan is to wait until she's sure Gus is in bed. She'll sit for the minutes her brother will take to fall asleep. Only then will she begin a soundless trail along the hall and down the stairs to the door and outside.

She forces her feet to stay steady and unmoving as her fingers fidget with the handle of the cloth bag holding what little she'll bring with her. She took her time considering its contents. What does a girl pack to go to a war? Her breaths are shallow and sharp. Her heart beats a quick rhythm as though she's run up and down the stairs several times. A drink of water would be useful to ease the dryness in her mouth, but she can't risk stepping into the hall and being seen by someone who will ask her where she's going dressed as she is.

Has she done the right thing, not leaving a note behind? If she tells them where she's going, her father will have her found by the time she gets off the ship and sent home. She doesn't doubt that Charles, with his political contacts, can do that. Better to leave them guessing about her until she reaches Spain. You can't find anyone in the middle of a war, she reasons. She wants to leave a word or two for Mel to tell him not to worry and that she loves him most of all and that she meant what she said to him that day the *Hindenburg* floated above them; she will always come back to him. If she leaves some words for Mel, then why not Gus, and what about Theresa, and if she leaves a note for Theresa, how will her parents feel, being left out? No, it's best to say nothing to anyone.

Edie runs the palms of her hands along the fine wool of her best coat. When it was time to choose a coat to wear she didn't hesitate to take her favourite, the navy blue. She loves the way the tucked waist shows off her figure and its warmth will make it ideal for where she's going.

A noise from Gus's room. She lifts her head, alert to his footsteps as he walks to the bathroom. A door closing. From the hallway, she listens to the sounds of her brother running the water in the sink, brushing his teeth.

Inside Gus's bedroom, draped over the arm of his chair, are his clothes and on top of them is the family treasure, Leo Clarey's smooth brown leather belt. With a few quick strides she's in his room. This belt will be her sign to them. Gus will know she took it and that she'll return it. That will be his clue that she'll be back and that they shouldn't worry.

Down the stairs, through the kitchen and out the back door, stuffing the cloth bag into the bicycle's wicker basket. She wheels her bicycle along the walk and onto the street. One last look up and down. She is alone. No one to wave to, no one to wave back at her. This is how the future begins. A note left behind could be such a simple thing. "Don't worry. I'll be back one day." What else does she need to say? That she loves them all? That's silly, they know that. They'll just have to understand. When she comes back one day, they'll look at her, stare in amazement, wonder at all she's done and the adventures she's had. No more little girl from the south end. Her life begins tonight and, grinning with the excitement of it all, Edie tightens the smooth brown belt around her waist and balances on the bicycle seat.

≈

At the window of his narrow upstairs front bedroom, Mel jiggles his flashlight. It flickers and the beam steadies. He moves the switch on and off until he's sure it won't falter. He waits for Lawrie, whose bedroom is across the street from his own, and his signal. Every night the boys blink messages to each other. With all the teenaged agitation of a new thrill, they begged for flashlights for birthdays and taught themselves the Morse system of dots and dashes. Neither falls into bed without knowing the other's final thought of the day. These conversations never last long. They need to conserve the life of the expensive batteries.

As Mel kneels and waits in his darkened room for Lawrie's light, he sees a movement in the street.

It's Edie, the bicycle balanced against her hip. She's fixing something around her waist. A belt. He watches as his sister pauses and looks behind her, in front of her, and places her foot on the pedal and pushes down. She wobbles for an instant as the bicycle moves off, so unlike her usual confident ride. She steadies herself and moves along the street and disappears from sight. Where is she going at this time of night? That bicycle has been taking her away from him more and more often. Now where is she off to? He wants to open the window and call to her, but that will only wake everyone and they'll want to know who he's yelling at and why. Doing that will only cause trouble for her. He'll ask Edie tomorrow where she's been and tell her she better be careful riding around alone this time of night. Their parents let her get away with too much. A brother has to look after his sister. He'll talk to her tomorrow. For tonight, as he has always promised, he'll keep her secret.

A blink of light from Lawrie's window draws his attention back to what he's doing there. His thumb moves the switch on his flashlight.

≈

The harbour water is inky black, so unlike the expanse of blue and grey Edie sees from her office window during the day. Ripples from the movement of the tide lap against the hull of the ship. With its peeling paint and rusted hull the ship hardly seems seaworthy. She's seen many vessels come and go, all more impressive, more imposing and certainly more seaworthy than this floating wreck.

The bicycle rests against her right hip. She grips a handlebar and fingers the cloth bag she'll carry with her to Spain tonight. There is no movement along the railings of the ship. The crew is likely inside, out of the cold air, until the last minute before casting off.

Edie thinks again of the note she should have left for her family. Her mother frets over the smallest thing. Look at the noise she'd made about Gus's cold. And what about Mel? How will he remember her? She won't be back for years possibly. Only last summer she and Mel and Lawrie came to the harbour, close to this very spot. They'd gaped and laughed and ahh'ed at the sight of the enormous balloon, the *Hindenburg*. One day I'll ride in it, she'd said to her brother. Maybe when she returns. Whenever that is.

"I wasn't sure you'd show up."

Micah's voice cuts through the hollow slapping noise of the water and through the hum of the ship's engines. He looks as he always appears to her, like a cat on the hunt, tense, in control and ready to spring. Tonight, the dark eyes have a particular intensity and, although he would never admit it, inside he must have the same crazy buzz of anticipation that she feels.

"Well, here I am. Ready." Edie pats the bicycle and pulls the bag from the basket and threads her free arm through its handles.

He stands close to her, the bicycle between them. "You've done well," he says.

Edie's smile slides into her wide loose grin. All discipline dissolves with the sound of his praise. Her shoulders relax and a knee buckles leaving her slouching and eye-to-eye with Micah. The bicycle slips away from her and he holds it, one hand on each of the handlebars.

"You know, I've never even been on one of these things. Never ridden one."

"Oh, there's nothing to it. It's like…"

"…riding a bicycle," he says and the two of them laugh. For the first time since they have known each other, they share a moment that is offhand, instinctive, no art on her part intended to charm or on his to rebuff. The two of them, in that spontaneous moment, had found each other at last and all because of Edie's bicycle. A brilliant idea, she thinks, just the thing. He won't deny her now.

"I suppose I should thank you," he says.

"Well, of course you should thank me. And don't worry. I'll teach you how to ride it."

He looks at her, eyes alert with surprise.

"What? Here? Right now, you mean?"

"Well, if there's time. It makes more sense, though, once we get to where we're going. When there's more time…"

"You're not coming with me. I told you that." He backs away one step, wary of what's coming next.

"Well, you can't take my bicycle, you know, and leave me here. That's not fair at all."

"I made it clear this morning. You're not coming with me. And you were clear you understood. You offered me this bicycle. Didn't you? You remember saying that? Yes or no? You remember saying that?"

Edie nods, her eyes locked on a spot near her feet. She puts her hand on the bicycle's leather seat and draws it to her.

Micah feels the tug of her hand on the bicycle. So like her to do this when something makes her unhappy. Take back what she's already given.

"You don't like it when you don't get your way, do you?"

She doesn't answer. Her eyes are fixed downwards.

"You're a spoiled girl who only cares about what she wants." He had allowed himself to become sentimental about Edie, to feel pleasure in her presence. She had made him weak.

"I know." Edie's voice is little more than a whisper. "I know you think I'm like that. It doesn't mean I can't…"

He pushes the bicycle at her, rough enough that she flinches when it hits her.

"Keep it," he says. "I'm not going to fight you over this thing."

Micah shifts the weight of his rucksack and turns away.

"No," Edie says. "Wait. Here. Take it. I'll tell them it was stolen." She's crying now. Her most precious possession and she's willing to give it to him, even after he's dismissed her. This is hardly credible to her, that she'll have to stay, miss the great adventure and miss being with him.

There is no hesitation in his step as he walks towards the ship.

"Wait a minute. Here. I said it's yours. I don't care."

Edie has been so adept all of her life at seeing, in any situation, a glimmer of light to be exploited for her own happiness. There is no light in the expression on Micah's face. She sees him now as he is, obdurate and unyielding. An unfamiliar feeling stirs inside of her. This is what it feels like to lose.

He takes the bicycle from her, without remark or expression. He picks it up and balances it awkwardly against his shoulder. With unsteady steps, Micah weaves his way up the narrow gangway until he steps onto the ship and disappears from sight.

≈

"S-T-A-N-K-O I-S S-T-I-N-K-O" Mel spells out to Lawrie. Mr. Stanko's science class is a particular burden to him.

"M-E L-I-K-E S-C-I-E-N-C-E," Lawrie answers back.

"M-E L-I-K-E J-A-N-E-T M-O-R-R-I-S-O-N."

The beam of Mel's light wavers. They sign off and, content with their night's wit, put away their flashlights.

Mel tugs at his blankets to bring them up to his chin. He's outgrowing his childhood bed. His little room at the front of the house, always the first place to feel the effects of the variable weather, is colder than the other bedrooms. He listens to the house. Next door to him, he hears the click of Gus's light switch and his brother settling under the covers, and silence. Mel listens, straining for some sound within or without that will let him know that his sister is home. Wherever she was going must be important if she didn't tell him about it. He remembers what she said to him that morning of the *Hindenburg*. I'll be going away, she'd said. I'll come back, but only if you keep my secret about where I've gone. Only if he does that, will she come back.

They have always been so good at keeping each other's secrets, although anything he told her always paled in comparison to what she wanted concealed. One day the two of them pricked their thumbs with one of Theresa's sewing needles and touched them together, the two dabs of blood joining them forever in their pact.

"Now we'll both die," Edie had said to him, "if we tell anyone our secrets."

From the end of the hallway, Mel hears the soft grunt of his father's snore.

Where was Edie going? She'll tell him tomorrow. Wherever she's gone, she means it to be a secret for now. When he sees her, first thing, he'll tell her that he kept this one too.

He struggles as long as he can to stay awake, waiting for the sound of her bicycle rattling up the walk and hitting the side of the house. He waits for the sound of the door opening and the familiar tread of her step on the stairs. Nothing brings sleep faster than trying to stay awake.

≈

Edie stands on the cold empty pier waiting for Micah to emerge and wave to her, signalling for her to come aboard. He *will* do that. He *will* change his mind. She is as certain of that as she's ever been about anything. He will do that for her. They understand each other. Micah is somewhere on that ship, forming the words he wants to say to her, that he was wrong when he turned his back on her. For as long as it takes, she will stand here. Edie pulls the belt tight around her waist, listens to the empty slap of the water against the ship's hull and waits for him to appear because she knows that will happen. She will not be denied.

"This is the night my life begins," she says aloud.

15

"*The Prince and the Pauper?*"

"Erroll Flynn."

"I suppose. If it keeps the boys occupied." Charles digs into his pocket and draws out his money clip. He hands two one-dollar bills to Gus. "I don't know about this, though. How it looks."

"Pa. They need a distraction. This won't hurt them. It may even take their minds off things for a while."

"People will…"

"Talk. I know. Let them. They're going to say whatever they want, whether I take the boys to the pictures or not. The ones who figure Edie ran away, that's what they're like. The truth of it is, no one knows where she is. We're not putting up party lights, after all."

"I suppose." Charles runs a hand across his forehead and over his wavy brown hair. He does this compulsively now, as though trying to soothe himself with a parent's comforting gesture. In the two weeks since his daughter's disappearance, his hair has turned grey at the temples.

"You and the boys go, then. I'll stay with your mother. Did she get out of bed at all today?"

Gus shakes his head. He smoothes the bills with his fingers. This is more money than he needs to get himself, his brother, and Lawrie into the theatre. Half that amount is plenty. Edie's disappearance opened up something in Charles, as if gestures of generosity might help bring her back.

His mother had gone to bed and stayed there, silent and unresponsive. She's in shock, the doctor told them. Try to keep things as normal as possible, he said; sit with her, read to her and try to get her to eat something or at least get fluids into her. If she doesn't come out of this soon, they'll need to talk about the hospital.

Gus did what he thought was useful or what his mother might want. Father O'Neill was called in for bedside prayers. The old priest had insisted, in his lugubrious way, that a sturdy chair be brought into the room for him to sit on.

"The knees, you know," he said. Once he was seated, Gus and Theresa exchanged looks over the bowed white head. They understood each other. The old priest was simply too fat for a kneeling position. Gravity would take him to the floor, but no force other than divine could restore him to upright.

While Gus intoned the prayers along with Father O'Neill, Theresa went to the kitchen to make the tea and slice the cake the priest would be expecting at the end of his visit. She wanted no part of the bedside show. More than anyone else in the house, she understood that Mary was in a place beyond the reach of prayers.

"If only she'd cry," Gus whispered to Theresa one day. She understood that, too.

Theresa assumed the role of nurse, leaving Mary's room only to perform her other household duties. She washed Mary, brushed her hair, changed her nightdress, held her head as the glass of milk or water or broth was tilted to her lips and encouraged her to drink, or at least sip, from it.

Gus knew that not much of anything would make a difference to his mother except the return of her daughter. Normal, the doctor had said. How do you keep things normal when a thing like this happens? Wasn't crying the normal thing to do, given the circumstances? Gus had cried, although not out of grief. He wasn't sure that someone disappearing was cause yet for grief. He had cried out of fear and frustration. There was nothing normal about any of this.

"Take the car, will you?" Charles says to Gus.

"I'd prefer the walk. And it's better for them. They're not getting much exercise these days."

"Take the car."

"Really…"

"Chances are you'll run into someone who'll say something. I don't want Mel being upset."

"Fair enough."

Gus understands what his father means. He's heard it all himself. The well-intentioned condolences, so awkward because no one is sure if they're even necessary, are bad enough. So are the bland assurances of hope, even optimism, that Edie will appear on their doorstep one day, out of the blue, with a rational explanation of where she's been and why. And he endures the ones who speak to him of theories. Maybe she was kidnapped, like the Lindbergh baby. Has the family considered that? Have they received a ransom note? They want to know if it's true what they'd heard: that a ladder was found under Edie's window. Is that so? Was she seeing a young man? Maybe they eloped. Have they seen any suspicious characters walking past the house?

Others venture that a temporary madness had taken hold of his sister as had happened to someone else they knew. Or she'd hit her head and lost her memory, wandered off and will recover from it any day and find her way home, like a straying cat. And there are the ones who stop him to ask, in their indifferent way: "What do you think happened to her, Gus?", as though he enjoys nothing more these days than killing time on a street corner and having a friendly chinwag about every gruesome scenario that has gone through his own mind. Yes, he understands what his father is getting at. He'll drive Mel and Lawrie to the theatre in the car rather than walk there.

Gus finds the boys on the front porch. The weather is warm for this early in spring and they've exchanged their coats and scarves for sweaters. Lawrie had searched his bedroom for a stack of baseball cards, the neglected relics of younger days. They pore over every one, heads close, and speak in low stunted phrases, so different from their usual voluble selves. Mel has become withdrawn since Edie's disappearance, talking little to anyone except Lawrie and spending hours of the day by himself. Gus had thought that if anyone could draw Mel out of his shell it would be Lawrie, but as he watches them he's not sure that even his brother's oldest friend has the power to do that.

He sees his brother and his neighbour for who they are now, teenagers about to shed their boyhoods. In the months he'd spent at the seminary, Gus had missed a crucial turning point in the physical lives of the two of them. Mel seems to grow taller every day. His shoulders are more suited in size to a man than a boy. And Lawrie, at last, is reaching a height to match his age, although with his slender build, he's still small-looking beside his friend. They had been boys right up until all this happened with Edie. In the last two weeks, they have changed, but too fast, like flowers forced to bloom before their season.

Mel and Lawrie are older now than Gus had ever imagined them being. But hadn't everyone aged in the last weeks?

"Come on, you two. Let's go."

≈

Charles had noted to Gus that in the days following Edie's disappearance there had been a small but noticeable spike in sales of paint. And it wasn't the warmer weather that encouraged people to take walks that carried them past their quiet house. The Clareys had discovered that grief is an irresistible magnet for anyone not doing the grieving.

"There's simply no accounting for how people react to a thing like this," he'd said and put his arm around his son's shoulder, hugging him close.

"And I'm not sure what we'd've done without you here, Gus. The pneumonia was a gift we didn't see at the time, sending you home. You've been a pillar of strength for your mother. For all of us. One more shock like this will finish her, I'm sure. She's that fragile."

And so Gus let it go, what he had wanted to tell his father, one of the last nights Edie had spent amongst them. He understands that it is his duty to return to Antigonish and the seminary, although not before his mother's health is restored.

Everything about life in the Clarey house had been routine and ordered for so long. Overnight, their world had become an unpredictable place.

There was all the public fuss. "Daughter of Prominent Halifax Businessman Missing," the front page headline read and below that in smaller type, "Foul Play Not Yet Suspected." Later, the headlines took a dramatic turn. Lurid, Charles called them. "WHERE IS EDITH CLAREY? Halifax Family Suffers Agonies. Reward Offered For Clues." Not even that attempt to shake loose an answer jarred the mystery of Edie's disappearance.

The police paid regular visits to the Clarey house. Reporters knocked on the door and when no one answered, they sat on the front porch and waited for someone to go in or out.

"Want some advice?" one of the cops said to the family. "Somebody better get out there and talk to them reporters, else you'll never be rid of 'em. They're worse'n a summer rash when they're onto a story like this one."

So Gus had opened the door and handed over a photograph of his sister, taken at the time of her high school graduation. Her hair was combed, her white blouse pressed and tidy. She appeared to be a serious individual, a capable girl. Only those who knew Edie well recognized the familiar expression, the one she had just before she burst out laughing. That was the picture Gus gave the reporters, not a family photo where Edie was being Edie, acting up in a way that anyone who wasn't there when the photo was taken or who didn't know her could possibly be expected to understand.

The reporters asked some questions and Gus gave them considered answers. They scribbled in their notebooks and went away, the only evidence that they'd been there a scattering of cigarette butts under the rhododendron bush beside the front steps. Gus was sure he had projected strength and control when he spoke to the men of the press and was annoyed to read later that their reports described his voice as "rough with emotion" when he knew it was the lasting effects of the pneumonia that made him sound the way he did.

A few days after Edie disappeared, two police detectives came to the door and introduced themselves to Gus.

"Wentzell," the older one said, tapping his chest with a finger. "This here's Collins," and he hitched his head so that there would be no mistake whom he was referring to, although there were only the two of them at the door. "We're here about the missing girl."

Gus told them what he knew, including the detail of the missing belt. They gave him a long stare. Some clothes were gone from Edie's room and they made note of that. Why she would have taken a man's belt, though, and such an old one at that, was beyond their reasoning. And Gus telling them about the significance of it and this ancestor, Leo Clarey, who was long dead, made no sense to them either.

"Well, she was very fond of it, you see," Gus said. "A little jealous that she didn't have it for herself." The detectives continued to stare at him. They waited for his further explanation of why they should absorb this point.

"You had to know her," Gus said. "When she wanted something, well, that was it. She had to have it. I'm so certain that if she decided to leave, she'd've taken it with her. She had a plan, I think, is what I'm trying to say."

The younger detective, the one introduced as Collins, licked the tip of his pencil and wrote the word "belt" on a page of his notebook. When he noticed Gus paying particular attention, he put a circle around the word and smiled as if to reassure the Clarey son that he had grasped the significance of what he'd just been told.

And Gus told them about the missing bicycle, too, how much it meant to Edie and how she said someone had tried to steal it not too long ago. Perhaps someone wanted it badly enough to do her harm. He watched Collins make another hesitant note and circle that one as well. The detectives asked a few questions about the bike. In talking things over later, both agreed Edie had probably used it as her getaway vehicle.

As the veteran detective, Wentzell, went over his notes, he told Collins he'd heard people talking about that one, the son who had come home unannounced from his school which happened to be the seminary in Antigonish.

"They *say* it was pneumonia." Wentzell tapped the side of his head with an index finger and winked at his partner.

The detectives didn't pay any attention to Joe Dan MacLean either when he told them that the same day Edie went missing, one of their warehouse workers, a Michael Green, never showed up. He said he'd seen the two of them having a tense conversation only the day before and he wished he'd said something then and maybe all this wouldn't have happened. The detectives nodded and left, wondering why such a sensible-seeming man like Joe Dan MacLean thought they needed to know that. What did a girl like Edith Clarey have to do with a working scruff, and wasn't the young man's sort coming and going all the time, anyway? That bit of information was never recorded for anyone to read or ponder.

There were no other leads after that. No one said they'd seen Edie after she'd gone to her room that night. At least, the Clareys who were talking told the police they hadn't seen her. Mary was incapable of speech. Mel, who was ignored by the police as too young to know or understand anything, had descended into what Gus thought of as a kind of catatonic state. The youngest Clarey whispered monosyllabic responses to the few questions put to him. Whenever their sister's name was mentioned, Mel turned away.

The Clarey house without Edie, even when filled with people, seemed empty.

≈

Gus leads the way to three seats on the aisle of the theatre. He wants to be able to move out quickly if a situation arises, if one of them has to leave or finds the movie upsetting for some reason. You never can tell these days what crazy thing might happen or what anyone might do or say to them.

The lights inside the theatre dim and the screen flickers with the image of the newsreel; the coronation of the new English king and the happy faces of the royal family, the little princesses, the solemn functionaries and the crowds laughing, singing, cheering. That sort of occasion suits Edie. She'd love to be there, shouting, her laugh cutting through the noise, waving small Union Jacks and her enthusiasm for the spectacle energizing everyone around her. Gus's eyes scan the crowd. He sees no familiar face. If she's not there, where has she gone?

The announcer's voice rises and moves on to the next story. This one had happened only a few days after Edie had gone missing. In their dazed state, the family had gathered around the radio to listen to the unbelievable news. The great airship, the *Hindenburg*, had exploded into flames over a field in New Jersey.

"Oh, the humanity," the reporter had shouted into his microphone.

Only last summer the mighty machine had flown over their city. The streets had hummed with the excitement of people rushing to see the flying miracle. Gus remembers Edie and Mel, words tumbling and tripping, as they described the morning. Edie was consumed by the romance of the voyage, the notion that one day she might be able to rise and float above the familiar and the mundane. As she recounted the moment to him, her eyes held wonder and longing for a moment so close and yet beyond her grasp.

In the theatre, Gus watches the death of the same machine; the sudden explosion, the brilliant light of the flames, objects falling, not pieces of the ship, but bodies, human beings so desperate to escape the fire that they threw themselves off the burning structure and waited as death came to them swiftly, brutally, from their impact with the ground.

The ship's burning membrane dissolves like crystals in water. Gus imagines himself standing, with his sister, high up above the ground. The intense heat from the fire burns their skin as they clutch hands and lean out from their perch, arms spread wide as they fall together from the great height. He hears her final scream over the rush of noise in his own head and he's sure at that moment that his sister is gone, never to come back. But what had happened to her, really? Would they ever know? If they were ever going to be a family again, they must know.

Beside him, the boys' faces are fixed on the images of the flames and the disintegrating ship. His brother's face is as it has been for the last two weeks, expressionless, numb with not knowing. Mel's arm reaches up towards the screen as though he's trying to touch it. Gus braces himself, ready to grab hold of his brother and run, but Mel draws his hand back and it drops into his lap. Whatever he had seen there is gone, locked inside him forever.

Beside Mel, Lawrie's mouth is slack, lips parted. Had all of them seen and felt the same presence, sought Edie's face in those black and white images as they remembered her fevered long-ago wish to fly away? Had they shared the same sickening sensation of her loss?

The newsreel ends and the movie begins. Gus had tried to contemplate life without his sister and what it would be like for them if she never came back, if they never knew what had happened to her. In the darkened theatre, he understands what the rest of their days will be like. We'll scan the faces of any crowd we see, he thinks, useless, straining and hoping, condemned to hope.

One life, the easy unvaried path of the Clarey way, has approached an unanticipated bend; another path, unseen and uncharted, has begun.

The three faces are lit by the flickering images before them. They watch the fantasy world unfold on the screen, as remote to them as the real world they are now entering.

1946

16

Mel could have chosen another room to sleep in. Gus's room, or what had been his brother's room, is not being used. There's more space there and a bigger bed, one more suited to his size; a bed for a grown man, not like this one with his head at the limit of one end and his feet outdistancing the other.

But this is the room Mel had longed to return to, the narrow space at the front of the house. This is where he is most comfortable, with the only bed he'd known until he left for England as a teenaged soldier off to fight a war. For almost six years he'd dreamed of coming back to this place with its walls covered in the rhythmic design of climbing vines. When he has trouble falling asleep he counts, over and over again, the number of patterned repeats running from baseboard to ceiling.

Other than his bed, the only furniture in the room is the chest of drawers that holds his new civilian shirts, socks, underwear. On top of that sits the framed photograph he looks at first thing every morning and last thing every night to remind himself that, although he resides in the place of his childhood, he lives an adult's life. From his bed, he can see the image of the beautiful, dark-haired woman holding her baby. His wife, his daughter. What are they doing right now, at this very moment? Is she thinking of him? What does she tell the baby about the father she's never met?

Mel wants his daughter to understand this place and who his people are, the ones she'll know as father and grandparents. He'll begin by showing her this room, explaining to her that he slept here as a baby and as a boy and a teenager, burrowed under blankets in the cold winter months, lulled by the spring wind moving through the trees outside the window, and where he absorbed the still hot air of summer nights. The two of them, father and daughter, will look through the window and he'll describe the boyhood friends signalling to each other with their flashlights. He'll tell his daughter all of that and more, one day soon.

In the years away, he's grown up and out, the width of his shoulders almost matching the width of the mattress. His first night home he'd sighed as he lay on the bed, imagining himself Gulliver in the land of the Lilliputians. Mel never doubted that he would reclaim this room on his return to the Clarey house. The place calms him, reassures him that the continuity he longs for is almost within his grasp.

He is awakened this morning, as he is most mornings, by the movement of his father down the stairs and into the kitchen, where Theresa has brewed Charles's tea and readied his breakfast. Their low morning voices drift up to Mel; their talk of the weather, what kind of day it might be and if it's fair enough to risk walking to the office or is it more prudent to drive the car. Any other subject of discussion depends on what they've read in the newspaper or heard on the radio. They're all relieved that there is no more talk of war.

Charles's established routine is to be at his desk at Clarey Glass and Paint by eight o'clock. Mel joined the family firm on his return from overseas, but his father never presses him to keep the same morning hours.

"After six years in the army," he'd said to his son, "you deserve a bit of a lie-in."

It's not just consideration for his youngest child and what Mel had been through that made Charles say that. He enjoys his solitary morning time as he walks or drives to the office. This is when he thinks about the issues that need his attention.

Mel and his father are similar in that way, in their need to be alone. Maybe all the Clareys are like that, his older brother

Gus more than any of them. Even Mary has something of that in her, always wandering off by herself into another room. The exception, of course, had been Edie, who was truly happy only when surrounded by others and the noisier the better for her.

Mel's bed, for all of its narrowness and age, is soft and warm, a luxury he still hasn't got used to since his return. He stays there until the last minute, until he hears the sound of his father leaving the house. That's the signal for him to throw back the covers and step into the chill of the spring morning.

≈

Once the front door closes behind Charles, Theresa waits for the next cue that her morning is unfolding as it has for the last several months. She listens for the creak of Mel's footsteps overhead as he moves down the hall to the bathroom. Only then does she pour the last of the tea into her cup and fill the kettle with water to brew a fresh pot.

She slices the loaf of white bread and sets aside the end piece. In all the years she's tended the Clarey house, she's never served anyone the heel. That, she reserves for herself, and not because she prefers it to any other part. Theresa does not allow waste in her kitchen. That slice will not be wasted here and not by her.

She no longer bakes her own bread. There was no resistance from her when Charles suggested that in order to ease her work load they get their bread from an outside source. What she serves these days is delivered three times a week. She sniffs each loaf as it arrives, suspicious of its quality. Its lack of weight worries her, not at all like the hefty concoctions she produced for so many years. She was only a little disappointed that the Clareys took to this new, less substantial, loaf with a surprising lack of hesitation or complaint.

Theresa's life has been defined by its routines. It was routine, after all, that caused her to be in the front room of her house tending her two daughters on the morning of the Explosion. And routine had kept her sister and mother in the kitchen that day, heating water for the weekly clothes washing. Next year will mark the thirtieth anniversary of the day that transformed the city and the life of Theresa Monaghan.

Several months ago, Charles had handed her the latest promotional wall calendar for Clarey Glass and Paint.

"Here it is. 1946," he'd said to her. "Did you ever imagine the two of us would live so long?"

As she does with every calendar, Theresa took a pencil and marked a faint 'x' in the corner of one day, December 6th. She needs no other reminder of its significance. The mark is her silent pledge to her daughters that they are not forgotten. This gesture is as close to a place of remembrance as they will ever have. In the time since that day, she has absorbed the sharp insistent pain of her grief until it has become part of her. What remains, what will never ease, is the simple longing for their physical presence.

Theresa created one routine as her life with the Clareys began so many years ago and one more after Edie was gone. When the war came, everything changed again. Mel, along with Lawrie, boarded a troop ship and sailed for England in the late fall of 1939. Gus stood on the Halifax pier and waved them off. The older Clarey boy had been among the first to stand in line at the Armoury to sign up. He'd spent his years in uniform as a chaplain on army bases across the country, as embarrassed as he was anxious, about never seeing the war first-hand. The colony of Newfoundland was as close to the action as he ever got.

In the boys' wartime absence, the three adults settled into a daily childless pattern. Charles took his morning tea and toast and left for the office. Only then did Theresa eat her own breakfast and decide what needed doing in the house that day. At ten o'clock she carried a cup of tea upstairs to Mary and helped her begin her day. That done, the two women went about whatever it was that kept them occupied. Twice a day, at the sound of the mail being pushed through the slot and dropping onto the carpeted floor, Theresa searched for the only letter anyone wanted to see, an envelope addressed with Mel's looping boyish handwriting.

The appearance of a letter from Mel was cause for excitement. His messages were shared with the Shines as were Lawrie's with the Clareys. Over the years, the letters arrived from England and Italy and in the final months of war, Holland. Theresa, not Mary, walked the envelope across the street to their neighbours and reported back on any news from the Shine's house.

An unexpected knock at the front door set her heart pounding, caused her breathing to be smothered by dread. Day after day, year after year, she contemplated the moment she would take possession of the telegram with news that Mel was missing or killed in action. She'd heard the stories from neighbours. Everyone knew someone who had received such news and everyone knew that as bad they imagined the moment would be, it was always so much worse.

Mary left the house less and less often and only for the most essential reasons. Her volunteer church work stopped after her daughter's disappearance. She returned to the church only on Sundays or holy days to attend mass, accompanied by Theresa and Charles. Anything more than that, anything requiring her to stand among a group of people or talk with them for any length of time, was avoided. She never again stepped inside the confessional box and she made no particular remark the day Father O'Neill was found collapsed in the sacristy, dead of an apparent heart attack.

At last, after so many years of waiting and anxiety and anticipation, there was the welcome upheaval to the household of Mel's return, and Theresa struggled to find the necessary rhythm of yet one more new routine. She had to remind herself that her days were no longer torn by panic or hope. The Clarey boys had survived and one of them was living in this house again. Only Edie had not yet come home.

She listens to the sound of Mel's footsteps as he leaves the bathroom and moves down the hall. As happens every morning, there is a pause in this journey, outside his sister's room. When he returned from overseas, they encouraged him to take Gus's room as more suitable for a grown man. Never once did anyone suggest that he might want to adapt Edie's for his own use.

Every two weeks Theresa dusts and sweeps the floor of that room. She makes sure that it is neat and tidy, ready for the day the girl comes back to claim it. She changes the linens on the bed once a month so that when Edie falls asleep that first night home she will do so between fresh sheets. And Theresa ensures that the frail gold-painted chair is drawn back from the vanity and set at a welcoming angle, just so, as though the piece itself awaits the arrival of the long-lost girl.

≈

Mel pushes open the door to Edie's room, taking in every detail of it; the wallpaper with its cheerful pattern of violets, the bed with its soft white covering and the many pillows Edie insisted she must have in order to get a good night's sleep. The vanity and its knickknacks are arranged in a haphazard fashion to the casual observer. He knows this is the way Edie wanted them to be. He waits to feel the echo of her presence. They all do.

Each morning he looks for any clue, any whisper of intuition that might tell him what happened to his sister. Seeing and hearing nothing, he retreats, pulling the door shut until he hears its soft click.

There had been no discussion on his return of next steps. He'd accepted Charles's announcement of his position at Clarey Glass and Paint without question. His feet, he told himself, were where they should be after such a long time away, back on the worn Clarey path.

≈

Mel has two civilian suits, one grey, the other a dark blue pin-stripe. Today, he will wear the grey. He bought them soon after he'd packed away his army uniform and stowed the box in the attic. Charles accompanied him to the clothing store. After so long in khaki, Mel wasn't sure what to wear for the life ahead of him. He needed his father's confident eye for business attire, style of suit, colour and width of lapel. What width of tie did men wear now? Buttons or cufflinks on the shirt sleeves? And what about shoes? One pair? Two? And socks. He'd written a list of everything he thought he would need and showed it to his father. Charles took the pencil from him and added "handkerchiefs."

Before he'd boarded the boat for England in 1939, Mel had owned one suit, dark brown. A boy's garment. On his return, he tried it on and found that whatever body he'd possessed as an eighteen-year-old had been left behind in Europe. The brown suit was the physical evidence of who he had become in the intervening years. He donated the suit to the clothes rack in the church basement.

The grey had been his choice. He thought the medium shade suited him and had the added unspoken attraction of not being mistaken for military dress. Charles insisted he buy the dark blue pin-stripe.

"It's standard," he said to his son. "A businessman's suit." When Mel hesitated, Charles said that he would pay for this one, as well as the two ties and the black shoes that Mel didn't especially want either. He preferred new brown shoes to replace the boy's pair he'd let go to the church along with the brown suit.

"You'll have both," Charles informed him. "You'd be surprised what clients notice. You don't want them thinking you're only doing well enough to afford one pair of shoes. And three suits, that's one too many. They'll see that and be sure it's their money you're wearing. So, two—suits and shoes—is what you want."

Mel bought five shirts, all white (cuffs on the sleeves, not buttons). Theresa wouldn't be cleaning and ironing these shirts along with the regular washing as she had always done with his boy's clothing. These new ones were sent out to a laundry, along with Charles's business shirts. Mel found the starched collars too stiff. They rubbed and chafed against the skin on his neck grown used to the worn army field shirts.

"You were a soldier, for God's sake. It won't take you long to toughen up and get used to how it feels," Charles said when Mel complained. "You can't go round with a floppy collar and expect to be taken seriously."

Because Mel's bedroom has no closet, he hangs his two suits in what was his brother's room. Each weekday night he chooses the suit and tie and shoes for the following day. Before getting into bed he hangs the grey or the blue pin-stripe on the hook fixed to the back of his own bedroom door. He loops the tie around the suit collar, tracing its curve, following the line of the lapels. And each weekday night, he lies on the narrow bed and looks at the dark shape of the suit against the white painted door. In the same way that the khaki army uniform had assured him that the boy had become a soldier, the grey and blue suits offer him a much needed comfort that his new life was taking shape around him.

Mel wonders what his parents see when they look at him these days. After so much time apart, they know each other little more than they ever have. The day Edie disappeared, a lone thread in the cloth that had formed their lives as a family had broken. With their sons' departures for remote army camps and for Europe and their years away, that single flaw of the broken thread unravelled and became an open tear.

They had all locked away parts of themselves after Edie's disappearance, driving their own wild grief deep and deeper, leaving them with little to say beyond the ease of established routines.

After Edie, an unnerving practicality took over their lives. Mel imagined Charles's voice saying: "There's no point thinking about what's done, what you can't change. Accept and move on." And so, in the relentless Clarey way, that is what they do, while the ghost of what they had once been remains to taunt them.

≈

"You used to like oatmeal." Theresa picks up the bowl that, moments before, she had set down in front of Mel.

"I used to like a lot of things."

"You never complained when I made it for you before."

"I didn't complain about a lot of things then."

"So, you're complaining about my oatmeal now?" She places the bowl in the sink with more effort and effect than necessary.

"No, I'm not. Don't be like that. I only said that it reminds me of army food."

"You said 'slop.' That it reminded you of slop."

Oh, Jesus, please, not this early in the morning.

When he was a boy, mornings had not been Mel's best time of day. He'd stumbled about and said little in the time it took him to wake up. He'd sat at the same kitchen table, his head empty of thoughts and words, Edie beside him chirping and giggling, pinching him, messing his hair when his sleepiness rendered him helpless against her assaults. Theresa always intervened, scolded Edie and ran her hands over Mel's hair to smooth down the bits his sister had shaken loose. As all this went on around him, Mel had eaten his oatmeal, one methodical spoonful after another, a sleepy and perfectly contented boy.

"It wasn't oatmeal the way your oatmeal is, Theresa," he says. "We ate anything, mostly because it was all we had. It just… wasn't as good as yours. So I lost my taste for it."

"Oatmeal's good for you."

"I need a bit of a change, is all. I'm fine with toast. No oatmeal."

"Toast won't see a young man like you through the morning. You need more'n that."

"Really, Theresa. That's all I need. A bit of a change is all. Then I'll go back to oatmeal. Promise."

The knife, with the lump of soft butter, rakes the surface of the toast. The bread Theresa now serves him is so different from the loaves he knew as a boy. This is delicate, more like cake. The first day back in his parents' house, his first morning, and the taste of the butter and bread, not in the least like the food that had fuelled him all those years overseas, brought him close to tears.

"And you never got the habit of drinking coffee neither," she says to him. "I thought you might've picked up the habit over there. I was afraid you might be asking for that now." Theresa isn't comfortable with the notion of coffee.

Since he's been home, he's struggled with how to talk to his parents and Theresa. He wants them to understand what he's seen and done, but no space has been made in the household routine to accommodate his last six years. Chin up, he expects his father to say to him. Move forward, nothing to be gained by going over old ground.

He balances the warm tea cup between his hands. No more thick chipped ceramic mugs or metal containers. After such a long time away, he is holding the familiar piece of china with its intricate design of dark blue, orange and gold.

"I only ever drank tea over there. If we didn't have that, I didn't drink anything." He lifts the cup to his lips. His father was right when he observed that tea is the only good thing that comes out of Theresa's kitchen.

The cup warms his hands in the chill of the kitchen. For a moment he holds another china cup, that one also delicate and warm.

"You know, at the end of things, in Holland, it was pretty grim what with people starving and all. The Germans knew they were done, so they handed over some food. Maybe they thought they'd be thanked. Funny, isn't it? After all they did." Mel takes care replacing the cup in the saucer. "Somebody got hold of a few coffee beans. Some kind of miracle, you'd think. You should've seen their eyes bug."

He is in another kitchen, small and cramped, in another country. It's nighttime and the person next to him is just visible in the light of a kerosene lamp.

"We were in a little town, the mayor's house. About a dozen of us. Locals and me and my driver and the guy from the Underground who was taking us around."

Inside the Dutch kitchen again, he smells the coffee and feels the excitement in the room. The anticipation of its taste stirs memories for everyone in the Dutch house that night. With it comes the realization that they're witnessing the improbable. A bit of civilization growing out of the years of misery, like the green shoot splitting the rock. Everyone in the mayor's house understands that the long night is ending at last.

"Here's something they'd longed for, dreamed of, for years, and what'd they do? They give the first cup to the one person who doesn't drink the stuff, can't stand the stuff. Me. What could I do? I had to be polite. So I drank it. Worst thing I've ever tasted in my life. You should've seen their faces, Theresa. I kept smiling and drank every drop. Should've got a medal for that one."

"That part of your life is over and done with, Mel," he imagines his father saying. "Now get on with the rest of it."

"Thing about coffee for me is," he says, "I like the idea of it. Only, it never tastes like what I want it to. It always disappoints me." He puts the last piece of toast into his mouth.

"Do you understand what happened?" Mel wants to ask Theresa. "Does any of what happened to us make the least bit of sense to you? Here I was, quite content, happy. I had a mother, a father, a brother, a sister, and all of a sudden I had no sister. I shipped out and away from a home I had no inclination to leave and survived all those years of training and war and soldiering. And before I knew it, the whole process reverses.

"Imagine," he longs to say to her. "Me drinking coffee with people who just about starved to death. Wearing clothes that hadn't changed in detail or colour for six years. And here I am, back where I grew up, with a cup of tea, a plate of toast, as though none of it ever happened. Normal as hell. I'm meant to forget all of that. Except I can't forget. And I still don't have a sister. And I swear I understand nothing of what's happened." That's what he wants to say to Theresa. It doesn't occur to him that if he did, he would be addressing the only person in the Clarey household who could understand his sense of dislocation and loss.

"What news from your wife?"

Kitty. And the baby. Anne. The framed photograph on top of the chest of drawers in his room. The one he studies every morning.

"Soon," he says. "She's sailing later this month, latest next."

"And then you'll be away again."

"It's not the other side of the world this time, Theresa. Just another part of the city. We won't be strangers."

Theresa listens to him, resting her back against the counter, driving her fists into the pockets of her apron. Her children and family, her husband, Edie, Gus and soon Mel, all gone. For Theresa, life has been a series of disappearances, none easily understood. Once, she blamed herself for the loss of her family. She told herself that she had not done enough, although what practical steps might have saved them she was never able to define. But she had come to know this: love alone cannot hold people to you.

"I don't know why the three of you don't live here. There's plenty of room."

Mel is growing weary of that argument. His father continues to worry out loud about the roughness of the north end of the city where Mel has rented a small house for himself and Kitty and the baby. Charles said: "You'd be better off with a better house in a better neighbourhood." But Mel is restless and in a hurry to have the satisfying order of the next stage of his life. What he never says to anyone is that he's now keen to be away from the big house he grew up in, the house of so many memories. He wants to establish his own home where there is a father, a mother, children, and where no whiff of tragedy singes the air.

A year ago he was in Holland, mopping up, seeing the end of the part of his life that had begun to feel like a permanent state. He sees his life since 1937 as a broken window pane lying on the ground in an unconnected mess. No matter how he tries to fit the pieces of glass together, after all that has happened, after such a long time away and at such a distance, each shard remains unmatched, fitting no coherent pattern or picture.

"I've got to get going."

"Dress warm. Just because the sun's out doesn't mean it's summer."

≈

Outside, Mel loosens the scarf that Theresa tucked around his neck.

Across the street, the front door of the Shines' house opens. Lawrie steps onto the veranda and waves at Mel. Behind Lawrie trails a small figure, his body filling no more space than that of an underdeveloped teenager.

"Mel." Lawrie beckons to him, but Mel is already on his way across the street. "I was just asking Theo if he smelled spring in the air."

Theo is the living remnant of the Shines' European family. He had arrived in Halifax a few months ago, in late December. Charles, Mary and Mel had gathered in their neighbour's living room to meet the new arrival and to raise a glass to his new beginning. Theo sat in a place of honour, Mr. Shine's large wingback, his feet not quite reaching the floor. He wore a suit and tie from Lawrie's pre-war closet. Mel thought the tie hung around Theo's neck like a noose awaiting the hangman's attention.

Nothing about Theo's appearance gave evidence of his age; a child old before his time perhaps or a grown man suspended in a timeless void. Did this man have a family once? What had become of them? Why weren't they here with him? Tufts of hair sprouted in an idiosyncratic pattern on his balding scalp. The effect gave his grave cadaverous face a mildly comical appearance. There was nothing comical about the eyes, though. Brown pools of precisely nothing. Even when Theo smiled at his attentive relatives and their visitors, revealing a mostly toothless mouth, the eyes offered up no expression. His hands and their long slender fingers were the only part of his body that had maintained their adult shape and strength. They became an object of fascination to Mel when he realized that they were entirely without fingernails. All of this was the physical evidence of Theo's time in one of the camps they had read about.

Mel listened as Mr. Shine spoke to his relative in halting Yiddish, translating Charles's remarks, since it was Charles who did most of the talking for the Clareys.

Mary, silent during this rare public outing for her, leaned forward, her eyes never leaving the stranger's face. If anyone had looked at her, they would have seen that the visit to the Shines' front room had brought a temporary light back to her face. And if anyone had asked her what she saw she would have told them: before her was living proof that someone, once given up for dead, was alive after all.

"We're off to Dr. Melanson's for Theo's check-up." Lawrie pats his cousin's back.

Mel and Lawrie, in their civilian clothes, still appear incongruous to each other. Without their army khaki they might be on their way to a masquerade party. They look that uncomfortable in their new suits and hats and coats. Even so, they have appreciated these last months, living again as close friends and neighbours.

"Not so cold this morning, Theo," Mel says. His words are louder and spoken more slowly than necessary.

"Yes, yes," Theo says. "Not so cold. A little warm." Without teeth, the flesh of his cheeks has collapsed and he pronounces his words with a slight lisp. He holds out a hand in greeting and Mel accepts the gesture, although he's uncomfortable touching Theo. He worries that the smallest gesture, the shaking of a hand, will snap the cousin's brittle bones.

"What word on Kitty?" Lawrie asks.

"Soon now."

Lawrie says something to his relative, who shakes his head and shrugs.

"My German's not improving as fast Theo's English," he says, and speaks some more words to the little man.

"I told him your wife is English. That you met when we were stationed there. And that your baby's a month old."

Theo's hand touches Mel's arm.

"What did he say?" he asks Lawrie.

"What else? That he wishes you all a long and happy life. We better get going. I'm already skipping one class to do this."

"How's it going? How're you finding school?" Mel regrets he hadn't put up some resistance when Charles announced that an office had been made ready for him at Clarey Glass and Paint. Why hadn't he told his father that he wanted to follow Lawrie to law school? Nowhere was it written that all Clareys must be businessmen. He had seen and learned things in the past six years that he could put to use in some other profession. What universe would be upset by one Clarey not joining the family trade?

"How're your classes?"

Lawrie considers Mel's question, adjusts his hat, tugging at the brim to spare his eyes from the bright morning sun.

"The world, Mel, is a vast catalogue of questions and it seems they all require answers," Lawrie says. The curious and intelligent boy has become, to no one's surprise, a man of depth and promise. "The law suits me fine, in other words. Might've done you, as well."

"I guess we'll never know, will we? I'm best off where I am, Lawrie."

And with that, and good wishes for the day, the three men part.

Mel watches Theo tug the woollen toque down tighter on his balding head and place a hand around Lawrie's elbow. His body appears lost inside the too big overcoat, taking step after awkward step as if he is only now learning to walk. He had lived a humble life, Theo, of no particular interest to anyone in the wider world until politics and ideology declared him unwelcome on this earth. He should have died on the cobbled lanes of his town or in the unimaginable squalor of the camp. And yet, in defiance of all intent and expectation, some accident of chance conspired to ensure that he lived to walk down a residential street in a foreign city on a sunny spring morning, the unlikely offspring of a relenting bureaucracy and the undefinable luck of the survivor. Who, Mel wants to know, was the arbiter of that equation? And was it too much to ask that along with this man, his sister be spared as well?

17

This morning Mel chooses to walk along Inglis Street to Barrington, a left turn, past the the big hotel and onto Lower Water Street.

His childhood playgrounds are now the avenues of the businessman in the dark overcoat and grey fedora. The boy is now husband to a wife he last kissed several months ago as he prepared to board a troop ship in England and father to a child he's never held.

The sun on his face reminds him of another morning, the day the big airship flew over the city. Is it possible that happened ten years ago? Wasn't it last week or just yesterday? The three of them: Mel, Lawrie and Edie. Lawrie telling them they were headed in the wrong direction, Edie staring in wonder and himself, alive with the boy's thrill of giant mechanical things.

"One day I'll fly away with it," Edie had said to Mel. He knew that was impossible and yet, in a way, it was true. She had gone somewhere.

"I'll always come back to you," she'd promised. Conspirators, the two of them. Everyone said that. He'd buried her secret along with the anguish and guilt he carried about it. He hadn't told his parents or brother what he saw out of his bedroom window that night. He hadn't shared it with Lawrie either, and he told Lawrie pretty much everything.

"Edie's flown away on the *Hindenburg*," he could have said and they all would have stared at him, a boy confused by grief or simply a liar or a fantasist. But looking out of his window that night he had seen her going somewhere. He'd waited for her to come back as she'd promised to do. She didn't come back, though, and later, too much time had gone by to tell anyone about what he had seen her doing. And when more time went by, there was no point in saying anything at all. Why stir up more hurt and confusion? What was done was done.

"Let it go. Move forward." He hears the older pragmatic Clarey voices. "Edie is gone," they say to him. Except his sister will never be gone.

Someone holds the answer to the question of his sister's disappearance. One day I'll know where you are, he says to her. No reason to get out bed otherwise. The answer exists at some point of time in the future, he tells himself, and each morning brings him one day closer to knowing.

≈

The air is cooler closer to the water. His scarf has come loose. Mel tucks it deeper into his coat and picks up his pace. What will Kitty make of this place, her new home? She isn't a city girl. That they'd met at all was one of those stories from wartime that leaves people shaking their heads and smiling, marvelling at a tale of happenstance, or even luck, they call it.

Mel was the passenger in an army transport truck after an unhurried stop at a pub, driving on a narrow country road, the way ahead almost impossible to see in the moonless black of the night. The pin-holed headlights picked up the outline of a figure in the road waving at them.

Mel stumbled as he hopped down from the truck and squinted into the inky blackness.

"Can't beat the view around here," he said and he heard the driver's hoot from inside the cab.

The voice of the figure on the road, when it came, surprised him.

"Do you know anything about motorbikes, then?" He hadn't expected this uniform to contain a woman.

This was Kitty, a Wren dispatch rider filling in for someone that night. One moment her machine was running fine and then it sputtered to a stop, she explained. They left the motorcycle where it was and he helped Kitty climb into the truck where she settled in between him and the driver. So close to her, Mel sensed the tension running through her body. He understood. These were strange days. No one ever knew if, in the dark of a lonely country road, a soldier offering to help a single woman had other intentions.

The home where she was billeted was down the lane, she said.

"Drop me here." Not a question, a command. This is my territory, my people, my rules, she was saying. She made it clear to the soldiers that she'd grown up around farm machinery and wasn't intimidated by a broken-down bike, but the dark made inspection impossible. So she'd leaned the machine against a tree and prepared to wait for first light or for a white knight like this tall, good-looking Canadian soldier. That was how they met. That was in 1942.

Her nervousness eased after they'd driven a distance and her chatter bubbled with amusing detail about the kind of work she was doing. The war allowed her to do things that a few years ago would have been out of reach for a girl like her.

As Mel helped her down from the cab, he put his hands on her waist and felt her slenderness under the heavy fabric of the uniform. She weighed next to nothing and with that simple thought he was struck by how much he missed the company of women. And this one with her quick high laugh and chatty manner had captivated him.

"Can I see you again?" he asked before she could turn away.

"Again? You haven't seen me once, have you?" she said. "It's pitch black out here. Only you might take one look at me in the light and head for the hills."

"I doubt that," he said.

When they did meet up, later that week at a dance in the nearby town, right away he picked her out of the crowded room.

She was standing with some other girls, talking, their high voices fluttering with expectation. Seeing her, he felt carefree for the first time in a long while. Until Mel left for Italy in 1943, they saw each other as often as time and opportunity permitted. All that had been such a long time ago.

He carries a black-and-white photo in his wallet, a small version of the one that sits on top of his bedroom dresser. The beautiful woman, her dark hair waved around her face, falling to her shoulders. He struggles to remember her eyes. They're an odd blue-green colour, so vivid against the almost black hair and the white and pink English complexion. Her smile is tight, lips drawn back in a nervous reaction to an impatient photographer's command. She wears a long-sleeved dress, probably the deep red colour she favours. Propped into the corner of her arm is a solemn-faced infant, her eyes locked on the exact centre of the camera lens.

"A picture for your daddy," he imagines Kitty telling the baby Anne. "Smile for your daddy." This baby, she wrote in a letter, was "good as gold" throughout the photo session, although she could not be cajoled into smiling for anyone that day.

"It's like she needs explaining as to why she should do something," Kitty wrote. "And I don't mean just with this photo. She's like that with everything. The girl has a mind of her own. I don't know who she gets that from!"

When he read that, Mel considered the Clarey stubbornness and how no one had been as stubborn as Edie. This baby had arrived a little early, not full term. "She doesn't want to waste any time," Kitty observed.

Some mornings, as Mel looks across his bedroom, he's startled to see the framed photograph of Kitty and Anne. They might as well be a made-up story; their meeting, the courtship, the marriage. There is so little sense to any of it. Mel had grown up in a very ordinary house in an insignificant place, gone off to a war and done his growing up there instead of here, in Halifax, where it should have happened. And what of the chance encounter with

Kitty? And now this woman and this baby are arriving any day. Thank God he has Lawrie across the street to remind him that this is real, he hasn't dreamt the wife and daughter. Everything bad the two men had seen will be wiped out by their arrival. Mel, Kitty, Anne. A new beginning for all of them.

Mel crosses the street in front of the big railway hotel. A cold breeze is blowing off the harbour. He tugs his hat closer to his head and picks up his pace.

He'd proposed to Kitty in a letter he wrote from Holland, the morning after a night of celebration and rough Dutch gin. The next day, the formal surrender of the Germans to the Canadian general would be signed in the hotel in the middle of town. The war was all but finished and a delirious lurch had propelled them, the Dutch and the Canadians, into an oasis of new possibilities. What that meant in practical terms was nothing that age or experience had prepared them for. In a mad rush to establish normalcy, letters were written and promises enshrined.

The morning after the night of Dutch gin, posing with the rest of his company for the Army photographer in front of the newly historic hotel, a weary and happily hungover Mel began to consider the letter he would write to Kitty.

"This will only have been worthwhile if you say yes to marrying me," he wrote to her later that day. Overnight the world had become brand new, limitless and filled with the potential for happiness. Gaping holes would close. And he was sure that pain and guilt would ease and, with time, be driven out of his life altogether.

≈

The first of the day's sparse grey clouds approach the harbour. Mel pauses in front of the Clarey building on Lower Water Street and tilts his face toward the sky. Early May in Halifax. Feel the warmth of the sun while you can.

A new sign had gone up on the front of the building not long after he came home. "Clarey Glass and Paint" it reads in glossy black letters. Charles defended the enormous signage, covering almost the entire width of the building, as a good investment. To be prosperous, he said, a man must make customers believe in a company's prosperity.

"You want to get the girl, put on your best suit," he said when pressed by Mel about the cost. Or another time: "It's the prettiest girl always gets asked to dance."

Mel, the child of the penny-pinching '30s, isn't sure he would have made the same decision. He does admit it is a handsome addition to the front of an otherwise nondescript building and adds a fresh touch to the street lined with grey industrial structures. The appearance of the sign speaks of hope and stubbornness in the face of change that no one understands yet. A decade ago, such self-promotion would have been viewed with suspicion, whispered about as too grandiose a gesture for such a modest town. The war has changed so much. There was a building boom going on, readying quick constructions for returning soldiers and their new families. This is a new time with new ways of doing business. Even slumbering Halifax recognizes that.

Most mornings, Mel stops and looks at the Clarey building or hesitates before opening the door. He's waiting for the day he doesn't feel that he's there under a false pretense or as a visitor. He longs for the morning to arrive when he's sure that this is where he is meant to be. Instead, he finds himself wishing he was somewhere else, more at ease, still in uniform with the army's certainty of purpose and direction. The ingrained habits of saluting and calling anyone older than himself "sir" were difficult to shake off until he realized that was because he didn't want to let them go.

By joining the family business, showing up as he does every day, groomed and polite, Mel is doing what is expected of him and what he tells himself he must do. He is living his life in a forward gear when so much of him wants to find reverse.

≈

The door closes behind him as he steps into the wood-panelled reception area. He glances over his shoulder at the large round wall clock that his father hung there a decade ago. "And still running fine, thank you very much," Charles likes to add. When he tells the story of installing the clock, he omits one detail: that he'd put it there to remind his daughter of standard office hours.

Eight-thirty-eight, Mel sees. A few minutes later than usual. He'll pick up his pace tomorrow.

"Mrs. Brown."

The woman sitting at the desk gives a small squeak and jerks in her chair.

"You startled me. You need to make a little more noise when you come in." She speaks to him as she always has, with kindness, but today with the steely tone of a mother reminding her child of his lapsed manners.

After Edie, one of the uncomfortable practicalities that Charles had to confront was hiring a woman to take his daughter's place in the office. Hilda Brown was not the sole applicant for the job. She was, however, the first to show up, and hoping that this was a position filled only until Edie returned and so it didn't matter who sat there, Charles offered her the job right away. He thought he saw in her broad frame and her unfussy hat someone who was reliable, who didn't need a clock to remind her of the hour. She'd been there ever since.

As a teenager, Mel had called her Mrs. Brown. She had called him Mel and neither of them sees any reason to change that now. She runs the office with pleasing efficiency. There isn't anything she doesn't know or can't find out. There isn't any employee in the office or the warehouse she can't acknowledge by name.

"How was your weekend, Mrs. Brown?"

"Restful, thank you, Mel. Yours?"

He suspects that Mrs. Brown's weekend wasn't restful at all. The lines across her forehead are deep. Her husband had died early on in the war, in the Dieppe raid, and she was left to provide for and raise their son and daughter. Mel knows that the daughter is married. The son had aged in time to catch the last year of fighting overseas and never adjusted to being home. He worked for a short time in the Clarey warehouse, but couldn't keep regular hours and when the crew sought out their bootlegged Friday treat at the nearby barbershop, they often returned without him. Generosity and forgiveness, even of the Clarey variety, stretched and at last broke, and the boy was let go. Now he sits at home, spending his days smoking, drinking bootlegged liquor, and waiting for life to change or end. Mel knew of other cases like this, ex-soldiers locked in some despair that made no sense to anyone who hadn't been there.

"Cup of tea, Mel?"

"I'm going to talk to my father first, Mrs. Brown. Maybe after that."

"He's not here. Gone to talk to someone about something. It all sounded a bit mysterious, if you ask me. Said he'd be gone all morning."

Mel struggles with his coat. He still isn't used to wearing the expensive garment and silk scarf that Charles insisted a businessman needed to wear. He's used to tossing the khaki army jacket on the ground, over the back of a chair or whatever surface was closest. He realizes how awkward he must look at that moment, like a juggler rehearsing an unfamiliar trick.

"Can't be long now."

"What?" He's moving towards his office, folding the coat over his arm as he does so. Too late, he notices the scarf trailing on the floor and his foot on top of it.

"Your wife and baby. You must be counting the days."

A sudden flush of anger takes hold of him as he fusses with the scarf. He wants the talk about Kitty and the baby to stop. He's sick of taking the photo out of his wallet, hearing the same banal remarks and making the same simpering sounds himself. Leave me alone, is what he wants to tell them. What do you want me to say? That these people are as good as strangers to me and I won't know what to do with them when they do get here? I'm afraid

Kitty will hate Halifax and want to go home. Is that what you want to hear? I didn't think so.

"Here. Let me help you." And Mrs. Brown takes the coat and scarf away from him and already is in his office, arranging them on the hanger. Her simple gesture consoles him.

"Thank you," he says.

She pats his arm as she leaves the room.

"I'll get you that cup of tea."

The surface of Mel's desk is a tidy arrangement of papers, work that needs tending. He sifts through the assortment of details, schedules, orders for paint and glass products, most with numbers arranged in tidy columns by Arthur McDougall, the company's bookkeeper. As he rearranges the papers one more time he wonders if McDougall is in his office yet.

Father and son had not discussed what Mel's actual job would be once he began work in the office, or how he should go about doing it. There was an assumption on Charles's part that inheritance, the Clarey blood and levelheadedness, was all Mel needed to absorb his duties and get started. Everything else would sort itself out soon enough. But he was lost in his early days here. He was a soldier by training and often found himself longing for the soldier's reassurance of orders and detail. This is what it must be like, being a performer with a new act at a circus. You've been a lion tamer for so long and one day, out of the blue, you're told you're an acrobat. And always, the audience expects you to excel, when you fear that disaster is only one misstep away.

In the reception area, Arthur McDougall's exuberant Monday voice hails Mrs. Brown. Mel gathers his papers and prepares to greet the affable bookkeeper as his first act on the first day of a new week.

18

The soldier casts a sidelong stare at the Clarey building and warehouse as he passes by on the far side of the street. He seems uncertain, hesitating, not sure if he might turn around and go back the way he came or walk across the street and march right up to the front door.

From his office window, Mel has watched and counted the number of times the soldier has passed, back and forth. Three, four times, and with no indication of intent or reason.

When Mel began work at the family business, the bookkeeper Arthur McDougall offered his own office to him, a larger space and with a window facing the harbour. Mel, as the newest and least experienced employee, assured him that he'd be happy in the smaller room with no view to speak of, only the traffic along Lower Water Street and, this morning, the soldier.

He recognizes the uniform, the cap, the rucksack slung over the khaki shoulder as belonging to a British soldier. What's a Brit doing here, in Halifax, walking this way and that along the sidewalk? Looking for work maybe and hoping the uniform might lend some cachet to a sympathetic prospective employer.

The collar of Mel's shirt feels especially confining this morning. He runs a finger around the inside of the stiff fabric and tugs at the knot of his tie. He is overwhelmed by his need to talk to the soldier. He wants to ask where he's been and where he's served. Who knows? Their paths may have crossed in some crazy wartime coincidence. They're bound to have some moment, some place, in common that would cause the two strangers to clasp hands, slap each other's backs and reminisce like old friends meeting by chance.

The boom of the Citadel's cannon signals noon. He lifts his coat and scarf off the hanger and pulls them on, pushing his hat onto the back of his head as he hurries to the door.

"Can I help you?" Halfway across the street, he sees the startled look on the soldier's face. Stop running, Mel tells himself. You'll scare this guy off. "Are you looking for someone?"

The voice, when it reaches Mel's ears, isn't British at all, but very Canadian sounding.

"Maybe. I haven't decided yet. Who're you?"

Mel holds out his hand. The soldier takes it. His grip is tight, confident.

"Mel Clarey. Signal Corps. Canadian Army."

The soldier pulls his hand away as though he's touched something too hot.

"You're the brother."

"The…"

"I used to work here. A long time ago. Your father hired me."

Mel searches the soldier's face for a feature he might recognize or remember. Under the cap, he sees dark curly hair that needs cutting. The man is thin, a wiry compact body gone too long without enough to eat, yet looking prepared to take on anyone. Mel had seen men like this throughout the war, all semblance of fat burned away by nerve and fear and bad food.

"When did you work here? How long?"

The soldier doesn't answer right away, measuring the trustworthiness of the inquisitive stranger.

"Started in the fall of '36. Stayed about six months or so. Left round this time of year in '37. So not long."

Mel studies the face again, hoping for a familiar feature or mark that he could recall having seen as a boy. Most of that time, the spring of 1937, was lost to him. He had been adrift in the fog of shock and confusion that followed Edie's disappearance. There was so much he could not, or did not want, to remember. Is it possible that he had met this man once, all those years ago? But nothing about his features was familiar. He would have remembered the eyes, so dark they're almost black. You don't forget eyes like that.

"You're back home now? You after some work?" The words tumble out of Mel, fast and anxious.

"No, I…"

Mel's hand rests on the soldier's arm. "Please. Don't go away. Have you eaten? I was on my way to a restaurant around the corner." A lie. Theresa expects him at home. "I'm buying."

The soldier hesitates. His curiosity about this particular Clarey overcomes his natural reluctance to trust anyone. Mel hadn't begged, but there was a desperation in his voice that might have turned the most suspicious heart.

"Well, okay," he says at last. "But not the kind of place you'd go. Another place. Where we can get a beer. Or do they still lock you up for trying to get a drink in this town?"

"It's not that bad anymore. Things are changing here. Things are…" Things are what? "You're right, there're laws, but it's pretty open what goes on. And I know of a place."

"I'll go with you if we can get a drink."

They walk along Lower Water Street, an odd pair, the rough-looking soldier and the tall businessman in the expensive coat.

"I didn't ask your name," Mel says.

"That's right. You didn't."

"Would I know your name from before, when you worked here?"

"I doubt that." The soldier answers with a gash of a smile, not meant to be friendly, and giving nothing away, although if the man was offering free food and beer, he could return the favour and give him the least of what he's asking for. "It's Micah Gessen."

"Micah Gessen." Mel doesn't recognize the name. Gessen. Jewish maybe. Like Lawrie. That's something.

"I'm sorry. You're right. I don't know your name. I didn't have much to do with my father's business back then. I was just a kid." He's sure that the first chance, the potential for holding some illuminating coincidence, has slipped away.

$$\approx$$

The faded sign on the weathered house off of Lower Water Street lets anyone know that this is Ma Oickle's Café. In the years before the war, it was a family home, one of many in the area that sold bootlegged rum and whisky from the kitchen door. When it became clear that upholders of the province's tortured liquor laws were also upholders of glasses of booze, many of the homes became "cafés," serving food and, in a separate room, something to wash it down with. The back room at Ma Oickle's Café on the day Mel and Micah enter is almost full. The smaller front room, the "dry" room, the room any inquiring passerby could peer into, is empty.

Fifteen tables, each only large enough to hold two bowls and two glasses, dot the stained and cracked linoleum floor. The chairs are plain, wooden, crafted with no one's comfort in mind. Mel and Micah sit at the only available table. Nearby, two uniformed policemen are chatting, taking their time over their noontime food and drink.

"They won't be leaving a tip," Mel says in a low voice with a discreet nod of his head in their direction.

"Regulars?" Micah says.

"Likely won't be paying, either. More like someone's going to pay them. No one really cares these days."

"You a regular too?"

"First time for me here."

Without having asked for them, two small glasses of beer are placed on their table. The man who brought them has a sturdy build, wide and muscled through his heavy shoulders and chest. No concern registers on his face about gracious customer service. It is understood that dealing with a certain clientele will be no problem for him.

"We'll have something to eat, too," Mel says to him.

"We got chowder," the man says.

"Good to know. You have a menu?"

"As I said. We got chowder. That'd be the menu."

"Chowder then."

"Two," Micah says.

Throughout the war, Mel drank beer because that's what soldiers did and it was a cheap way to get drunk when that was needed. The thin bootlegged liquid here is very different from what he drank in England. The soldier, Gessen, shows no great reluctance for what he's drinking. Already his glass is almost empty.

"Why'd you come back to Halifax after all this time?" Mel asks. He's careful to keep his voice conversational, not too curious or prying. He doesn't want this soldier bolting.

"That implies I had a choice. I didn't. I was in hospital for a while after it ended. Then someone put me on a ship and this is where it docked. I could've ended up in Montreal. But I didn't. How's that for chance?"

"You staying long?"

"Well, here's the thing, you see. I'm catching a train at three."

Mel swallows some of the thin beer. That can't be right, he wants to say. We have too much to talk about and a couple of hours in Ma Oickle's Café won't be enough for everything that needs saying. As soldiers are when they meet away from the battlefield, he's certain there must be a juncture at which their lives intersect. He's sure of that and a little more than two hours can't possibly be enough time to discover what that is.

"You sure you don't want to stay longer? I can help. I can find you a place in the warehouse again if that's what you need." His first careful sips of the beer, befitting a responsible businessman, have become mouthfuls.

Micah shakes his head and smiles. These Clareys.

"Thank you, no. It's not work I'm after."

Mel raises his glass to the server and nods. Already the beer, on his empty stomach, is making him feel like a balloon released to float and drift. His mind is fighting to stay on track.

"Where're you going then?"

"Toronto."

"That's where you're from?"

"It's the only other place I really know." The soldier's voice is flat, matter-of-fact. "There're people there, from before the war, you see. I'll contact them again. If they're still alive." With his right hand he scours his head of dark curls as though doing that will stir a long-forgotten memory and bring it to mind. "And I believe my father is still there."

"You believe? You don't know?"

"It's been a while since we had contact, but yes, I suspect he's still among us. Some people hang on long after they've given up on everything except getting up in the morning and going to bed at night. You know what I mean. I've no idea what keeps people like that going. We've all met them, and I'm betting he's one."

"Well, I'm sure any father can't wait for his son to get home." Even though Charles had seen Mel off and welcomed him home with only a handshake, there was no mistaking what he was feeling as he gripped his son's hand.

Micah laughs at that. Clareys. Always so keen to put a nice polish and shine on everything. Isn't that what the girl tried to do, too?

"The only thing my father's waiting for is death. That's when he'll be truly happy."

Micah knows in his bones that Chaim is there, in the tailor's shop on Baldwin Street. Ten years Micah's been away, a decade with no word written to his father and so no reason to expect any word from or about him. He harbours no doubt that the tailor is alive. If the sorrows that Chaim Gessen endured throughout his life had not killed him, then these years without word of his son would be a drop in his ocean of time as he anticipates the inevitable.

"I took some money from him, you see. My father. I needed help to get me to Halifax back then. Eighteen dollars." He winks at Mel, meaning to share the humour of the idea: a fellow could rely on so little money then to keep himself alive for a month or more. He thinks of the night in 1936 when he robbed the tailor's cash box. "The least I can do is pay it back," he says.

"You stole?" Mel says. "From your father?"

"I needed the money and it was the only way I could get it. I knew he wouldn't give it to me if I asked. Desperate times." His hand holding the glass of beer pauses at his mouth. He must make one thing clear to this Clarey man. "I always intended to pay it back."

"That's very…" Mel isn't sure what that says about this soldier. Travelling all this distance after ten years to pay back eighteen stolen dollars? "That's very, ah, honest of you," he says.

"Maybe," Micah says. He's never doubted his own honesty. For ten years the eighteen dollars has been an enduring echo, an unfinished sentence demanding a full stop. And something else: there is his need to search the tailor's face for anything that might resemble a longing for a lost child come home.

"Is Joe Dan MacLean still with you?" The warehouse manager when Micah worked there was a kind and intelligent man with an easy manner, solid. When Joe Dan spoke, the men listened. His was one of the faces Micah sought as he walked back and forth along Lower Water Street.

"He left a while back," Mel says. "When his boy was killed in France, as I understand it. Normandy. Made it all the way through the landing and then got it. Joe Dan and his wife went home to Cape Breton after that. I met him a couple of times when I was a kid. My father told me he kind of faded after the boy died. Didn't want to work anymore."

"And Ralphie Campbell?" What of the warehouse worker, the lumbering soul who had been responsible for Micah being christened "the Spanish boy"?

"Sicily, I heard. Least, he was on his way to Sicily. The boat was hit. Sunk before he even got there. Funny, isn't it? You spend three years training and you never survive the first chance you get to show off what you can do. That was Ralphie's luck, I guess."

Micah's hand tightens around his glass. He's reminded of someone and unsure if he wants to say the name out loud.

"And what about the bookkeeper?"

"Who? Arthur?" The genial MacDougall is the only bookkeeper Mel has known.

"No. Another one. Gillis, I think. Yeah. Raymond Gillis."

"Oh, him. I heard he didn't stick around long once the war started. Signed up and went off like the rest of us. No idea if he made it back."

"But he's not here."

"Nope. Not here."

"Sanctimonious little prick he was."

"Can't say. Never knew him."

"I did. Quite a bit more than I wanted to. Always thought he knew what's best for everyone. Holier-than-thou little shit." He thumps the table with his left hand.

Until that moment, Mel hadn't noticed that three of the fingers on Micah's left hand are curled into his palm, leaving only the index finger and thumb to move about. There must be a story there. He knows men who were wounded, disfigured, some badly, others less so. Many were angry at how they were left, scarred or limbs missing, as though the bullet or bomb that did this to them had been intended for them alone. Was the Gessen soldier angry in that way?

"You have to understand, Micah, these are just names to me. Strangers, really. People talk to me as if I knew them. So I hear the stories. But they're just stories to me."

"Right. Just stories."

"I'd say only a few of the ones you knew're still around. The rest, they either died in the war or moved on to other things. I'm pretty sure."

Micah stares at an uncertain point in the distance and considers the memory of Raymond Gillis, the bookkeeper who embraced all rules for the sake of being allowed to enforce them. He was the man who handed out the weekly pay packets like a grandee dispensing favours, and was the presence at the head of the boarding house table, dampening the mood at every meal with his one-sided observations. He'd paid particular attention to Micah, goading him, always trying to best him. For all he wants to say about the Gillis fellow, he's done talking about him, thinking about him, for today. There are enough in this world like him to take his place.

"I only worked there, your business, to get up enough money for a boat to Spain." Micah says. "That was the easy part. You hear words like 'seasickness.' Fairly harmless sounding until you're in the middle of the ocean and wondering if you're going to die before you get off the boat. I didn't though. Die. I got there."

"You were in Spain for how long?"

"About eighteen months."

Eighteen months of being terrorized, shot at, starved, bombed, freezing in the winter cold, feigning death in the heat of a shallow trench and unable to overcome his frustration at the bickering and in-fighting between the various factions until he wasn't sure whose side he was on. Micah proved himself a capable soldier there, steady under fire, among the first to advance and the last to obey the order to retreat. He saw some of the Canadians and Americans he met on the ship bound for France die there. Others he never saw again once they arrived in Spain.

"After Barcelona fell, early '39, most of us got out. I was done. The whole fucking thing was done. We lost."

He left along with the other foreigners who'd gone there to fight, ideals unshaken, yet feeling more isolated than ever in the wider world.

Mel doesn't remember enough about Spain, who was fighting whom and for what. Spain was a strange place for this Canadian kid to wind up. What makes a person want to fight a war your country has no stake in?

"You came back here after that?"

"There was nothing for me here. I went to England. London. I grubbed around, managed to stay alive and, guess what? Before we knew it, time for another war."

"Why the British army?"

"One country's uniform's as good as any other, long as it's the good side. My side. Where's the guy with the beer got to?"

Micah talks more about Spain and what came after. He holds back other memories; the young fair-haired woman he met one evening in a London pub. He was alone and she started talking to him, nattering, he thought, unable to keep still. When he tried to ignore her, she didn't give up, and at last she accomplished something of a miracle, as Micah began to talk and to laugh along with her.

What was a Yank doing here, she wanted to know, done up like a British soldier? He set her straight.

"Name's Frances," she said. "Frances. Don't even think of trying Fran or Franny or any of those other F names." She asked for his and he told her.

"That's a new one on me," she said.

"Russian," he said and, in case she knew or cared, "Jewish."

"They're all the same to me, religions," she said. "One person's poison…"

"Prisons," Micah added, nodding and relieved to have found such a like-minded spirit.

"Well, then." She touched her glass to his. "Micah Gessen. If that doesn't mean anything to you, what does?" He talked about Spain and Germany and fighting evil. And much later, long after that night, he wished he'd known her well enough to say: "You. You mean that much to me."

They married, despite her father being very clear that he didn't much care for the scruffy Canadian, never mind whose uniform he wore. He left for the countryside where he was training to be a proper soldier. Frances stayed in London and continued to work in her father's grocery store. She died during a night bombing raid in 1941. The fires from the German incendiary bombs destroyed most of the neighbourhood where they'd met and where she lived.

Micah was left with one photograph of her, taken soon after their wedding. He carried it with him through northern France and into Germany. The photo of the young woman who loved to talk was with him during the liberation of Bergen-Belsen and it was with him a few weeks later when a German civilian fired a pistol into a crowd of British soldiers and one of the bullets hit Micah's forearm, damaging a nerve and leaving him with the three useless fingers on his left hand. The photograph of Frances is with him as he sits with Mel in the café. It's inside his rucksack, along with the only other possession that means anything to him, the ragged birth certificate he took from Chaim Gessen's cash box the night he left Toronto so many years ago. That piece of paper, and the photograph of his wife, are folded in a sheet of clean paper and placed between the pages of a book.

Mel opens his wallet and takes out the small black and white photo of Kitty and the baby, Anne.

"My wife and daughter," he tells Micah. He recounts the story of their meeting on the dark country road and subsequent courtship in pubs and at local dances. He doesn't talk about the moments in the midst of the music and dance that robbed him of words and left him leaning against a wall, ignoring Kitty's puzzled questions at the sudden change in her cheerful Canadian. Those nights, Lawrie, a lively and popular partner among the local girls, left the floor to stand beside him. These were the times, in the exuberant figures and voices all around him, that Edie came to him. Solace from grief and forgetting wasn't found among such cheerful nights, but somewhere else during the rough and dangerous days of fighting. All that goes unsaid, too.

Mel finishes his chowder and notices that Micah has only eaten half of his.

"You don't like it?" he asks, gesturing at the bowl with his spoon. "Better be careful. You don't want to offend the guy who brought the beer. He might be the cook, too."

"Habit. I started doing that a long time ago, trying to get used to being hungry. When I was getting ready for Spain," Micah says and he remembers the times he sat with the girl, Edith, by the water. He'd asked Mel about everyone else and hadn't asked about the sister. She was a high-spirited girl, but despite her enthusiasms about Spain, he was certain she'd always revert to type and class. She'd probably married and settled into one of those big roomy houses he'd always sniffed at. Still, he wants to know, wants to hear his own beliefs about her confirmed by one of her own family. He opens his mouth to ask about her when Mel interrupts and starts talking.

Micah isn't listening to a story Mel is recounting. Italy wasn't part of his war. He glances at the clock hanging on the wall.

He interrupts Mel mid-sentence. "Two-thirty. I gotta go." He stands up and reaches out with his crooked hand to brace himself against the wall. Steadied, he picks up the rucksack and slings it over his shoulder.

Mel slaps his hat onto his head, off to the side and back a bit, the way they always manhandled their army caps. He fumbles in his pocket, draws a five-dollar bill from a money clip, another of his father's gifts to him, and puts the bill on the table.

"Quite a tip," Micah says.

"Quite a day."

They make their way through the empty front room to the door, the two of them swaying like saplings in a summer breeze.

The men blink as they emerge from the café. The morning's blue sky has become the afternoon's inevitable spring grey. They walk along Lower Water Street in the direction of Clarey Glass and Paint, both spent, tired in the way that midday drinking renders a body. They shuffle along, having emptied their cache of memories suitable for public airing.

On the sidewalk across from the Clarey building with its immense signage, the gleaming black letters remind them that everything they talked about in the café is gone. You live in a new world, the sign says to them, and you cling to the past at your peril. Forget what has been, embrace what will be.

One last thought creeps back into Micah's head.

"By the way. That sister of yours."

"My…" Mel's jaw works up, down, creating no words.

"Edith."

"Yes. Edie." Mel's words are faint, carried off by the breeze from the harbour and Micah isn't certain if any more will follow.

"I knew her," he says to Mel. "A little. We used to say hello."

He considers telling Mel about the bicycle and about the night she gave it to him. When he told her that she wasn't getting on the boat with him, he expected her to dissolve into the tantrum of a spoiled teenager. Instead, as she said she would, she gave him her treasured possession. In one war and then another Micah had seen unexpected gestures of grace, and even though Edie's would never be counted among memorable battlefield sacrifices, her surrendering of the bicycle had touched him in a similar way.

He'd boarded the ship bound for New York that night and lain on the narrow lower bunk in his cabin. He'd managed to shoehorn the bicycle inside the cramped space. That had taken some convincing of his cabin mates, telling them that in a day or two he and the bicycle would be gone, on to another ship, sailing to France.

Micah had stretched out on the bunk and listened to the thrum and rattle of the ship's engine. He'd wondered how long Edie stayed on the pier. It didn't matter to him, really. She'll move on to some other fancy, he'd told himself. She was like that. He'd done the right thing, leaving her behind. She wouldn't cry for long.

He rode into Paris on Edie's bicycle and down the length of France to the Pyrenees where he bartered it for the food that helped keep him and another Canadian and their guide fed until they reached the Spanish frontier. The bicycle had served its purpose and he'd wished there was some way to let her know that. He was certain that would have pleased her. But he thought of her less and less after he arrived in Spain. That was a long time ago and she'd probably gone on to have the kind of life all Clareys were destined to lead.

All of this is too complicated to explain to Mel as they stand on the sidewalk. He's already said too much. And Micah has run out of time. He has a train to catch.

For Mel, the shock of hearing this soldier say his sister's name has frozen him. When they'd met, Micah had said "You're the brother." Not "You're the son." Mel hadn't picked up on that then.

The soldier says he knew Edie and now he wants news of her. What can Mel tell him? That she's gone and no one knows what happened to her. He would have to tell Micah that he might have saved her, stopped her from going wherever it was she went and never returned from. If he'd only knocked on the window or called to her, everything would be different. He'd still have a sister, his parents a daughter. Instead, he'd watched her ride away, swallowed up by the night.

There is no time to say all of that and, crushed by fresh shame and grief, he doesn't know how to begin.

Micah holds out his hand to Mel who takes it and they stay like that, young men who've already lived a lifetime. Whatever comes after this is redundant. They have lived their lives backwards according to any conventional narrative, the drama having arrived at the beginning.

"Travel safe," are the only words Mel can manage.

The soldier makes a quick saluting gesture, the last token of what they both believe binds them, and turns to begin his walk to the train station. He'll arrive at Union Station and make his way to Baldwin Street and into Chaim Gessen's shop. He'll return to Goldstein's, re-acquaint himself with whoever remains from the smoky back room, and find some other fight to fill his days.

Mel remains on the sidewalk for several minutes, watching the solitary figure recede into the distance, up and over the little rise at the end of Lower Water Street, until he's gone from sight. Mel crosses the street and opens the door to the Clarey building.

Mrs. Brown looks up as he walks in. She hasn't been at that desk for as long as she has and remained oblivious to the lunchtime swagger.

"Is my father back yet, Mrs. Brown?"

"He called and said he's gone for the afternoon as well."

"Thank you, Mrs. Brown."

In his office Mel closes the door and removes his hat, coat, scarf. At his desk, his forearms rest on the surface of the pristine green blotter. As his head drops to his arms he tells himself this will only be for a few minutes. When his mind is clear again he'll open the door and, in his father's absence, resume the responsibilities of the man in charge. His tears, when they come, are no surprise to him.

19

In a pattern established years before and rarely broken, Charles arrives home a few minutes after the noon gun sounds from the Citadel, his place at the long oak table in the kitchen already set with plate, cutlery and white damask napkin.

"Mary?" he asks Theresa.

"Her usual place."

From the doorway to the front room he looks at the woman seated in a chair by the window. She sits there for hours after Theresa helps her with her morning bath and dressing and after she's been convinced to take a little nourishment for breakfast. Charles still holds a faint flicker of hope that after so many years he'll arrive home one day to find his wife moving about, ready to chat, ask how his morning has been; that one day the woman he once knew would greet him with her shy smile and a caring word.

Theresa's sewing basket is on the small table in front of Mary. Today, she is emptying it of its contents, placing each object on the table's surface before she returns every spool of thread, each needle, every button, to the box. She'll stop, from time to time, whatever she's in the midst of doing, tidying a thread that has spun away from its spool or sifting through a jar of buttons, to stare out of the window.

As he does every day, Charles says: "Mary, will you join us today, dear?"

And her answer, which never varies: "Not today, thank you."

That formality sealed, Charles returns to the kitchen.

"How is she?" he asks Theresa.

She stares at Charles before putting down the bowl in front of him.

"What do you think? Chicken with rice and potato today," she says.

He moves his spoon through the contents of the soup and wonders how this distinguishes itself from the chicken stew she served him yesterday. He reaches for the bread and butter.

"Where's Mel?" he asks.

"Haven't heard from him."

"Must have got held up at work."

Charles watches Theresa move around the familiar space, stepping from counter to stove to sink and back again. How often in the course of a day, at moments like this, does she think of her own children or her mother and sister and husband? Next year will mark thirty years since the Explosion and in that time he can't recall Theresa referring to any of them more than a handful of times. To ask her about them outright would be impolite, and worse, might only serve to upset her. If she ever told him the names of her children, he can't recall them.

He eats as much of the soup as he can and tells Theresa that he needs to lie down.

"I didn't sleep well last night," he says. "Need a bit of a nap is all."

Charles looks in again on his wife as he makes his way to the stairs. Mary is using an index finger to stir a pile of loose buttons with the focus of someone scouring the grass for a four-leaf clover. If she knows Charles is standing a few feet away from her, she gives no sign. She is lost in the dense thicket of her hopeless search. The pretty young woman he'd fallen in love with so many years ago is gone. The sensitive girl whose china-doll looks and low-voiced manner had enchanted any number of eligible men, chose to marry him for reasons that he never understood, and never questioned. Theirs had been a happy union and they had been a happy family for much of their life together. Does she regret her choice now? After all that has happened to them, does she ever consider how her life could have escaped its sorrow if she'd said "no" to Charles Clarey all those years ago and married someone else?

She might be dressed to receive visitors or go outside to an appointment. Even now, Mary is particular about how she looks. That part of her remains unchanged and evident for anyone to see. His wife's strict standards of dress and personal grooming are being maintained even as her mind gently unravels.

≈

Upstairs, not bothering to remove his shoes, Charles lies on top of their bed.

"This mattress," he says out loud and gives it a thump with his fist. "Too old, too soft, too giving. Like me." It has had its best days and needs replacing and he'll do that soon, as he often promises to do, but not today. Today, he sinks into its soft surface. There was a day, at a beach, many summers ago when the children were very young. He lay back into a sun-warmed sand dune and felt its fine grains yield under his weight. The voices of his three children carried to him along with Mary's warning to them to be careful of the tide. They were such a happy family and that had been such a happy day.

Charles had spent this morning at the big hotel, next to the train station, with two American businessmen. They were nice enough people who didn't hesitate to let him know that they were ready to let the smooth surface of their confidence show its rough underside if things didn't go their way. They represented a company based in Pennsylvania that manufactured paint and glass products. The war had been good for their business. They had money and they wanted to spend it, and how they wanted to spend it was the reason they'd invited Charles to meet with them. Their plan was simple: expand their business into the northeastern states and into Nova Scotia by acquiring small privately owned companies like Clarey Glass and Paint.

"We buy up all the businesses round here till you're surrounded by one big company offering the same products as yours and at a lower price than you can afford to charge." This was all said with the friendliest of smiles, as though the bear-sized American was explaining how to pour water into a glass or how to switch on a light.

"Whether or not you like what we're offering," one of them said to Charles, "do the arithmetic. This is two plus two equals four. For everybody."

The impact of what they proposed was clear to Charles. They were giving him notice that he could sell his company to them for a tidy sum that would see him and Mary into old age. Or he could remain doggedly independent and fight a gallant but losing battle in the marketplace. Either way, the business that had been run by his family for almost a century, the company that bore his name, was doomed to extinction.

He listens to the sounds of Theresa moving about downstairs in the kitchen, tidying up after his lunch. Soon she'll carry a tray of food into the front room and he'll hear her voice coo and whisper, encouraging Mary to take the spoon, just one mouthful, and if Theresa persists and she always does, just one more. It is all part of the accepted routine these days. Funny about Mel, though. He's usually so conscientious. If he knows he's going to miss the noon dinner, he tells one of them.

Charles had worked hard to keep his grandfather's legacy intact. Throughout the Depression when other storefronts locked and shuttered their doors, he ensured that Leo Clarey's legacy did not wither and die. The deal proposed by the Americans would make him the last of his grandfather's line to own the business, selling it to carpetbaggers hungry as sharks in bloodied water.

A fight would cost him everything: all of his savings, Mel's future, attached as it is now to a wife and baby, and who knows how many jobs in the warehouse and office. If he fights, what will happen to this house, how could he care for the vacant woman sitting downstairs by the parlour window?

Nothing had been right since the year Edie disappeared. Gus, home from the seminary, so sick and desperate to tell his father that he wanted out, that he was not capable of maintaining the expectation that as the oldest son of a Catholic family, his life belonged to the Church. There were those stuttering conversations Gus tried to complete. Then Edie was gone and there was no question of anyone causing further upheaval in their home.

Charles had leaned in to Gus one day and said: "It'll break your mother's heart if you don't finish this, don't go back to the seminary. You know she can't take one more thing." What he didn't say was that one more tragedy would finish him, too. His daughter had vanished. He could not lose the woman he had loved for so many years. Saying this to Gus, he knew, placed a terrible burden on his oldest child.

No, nothing has been right since Edie disappeared, the same year he'd insisted she come work for him at the family business; a good and sensible solution to the problem of how to keep her occupied when school no longer served that purpose. He should not have given in to her demand for the bicycle, the object of such dissent between him and his wife, between mother and daughter. It had been her price for working in the office for pocket change. He should have refused her demand and dropped his idea for taming the excitable girl, hired a professional woman. If he had only done that one small thing. Edie would be married by now, settled down and still the funny, loving person she'd always been, but with responsibilities and, more than that, she'd be here.

One more time he runs through the last day, the last moment he remembers seeing his daughter. They'd finished dinner and he was on his way to the front room with his newspaper and cup of tea. She brushed past him. He heard her say one of those funny things she'd picked up from the movies: "Squeeze me, Pops." And she skipped up the stairs on her way to her bedroom, two steps at a time. He paused to watch her. He'd reprimanded her a thousand times to mind how she took the stairs, stop acting as though she'd never been taught any manners. That night, though, he said nothing, issued no warning to her. Such an innocuous image, so commonplace. Why had he stopped that night of all nights to watch her even for the few seconds it took her to reach the upstairs hall, as if he'd known something, and needed to mark the image?

In the days after she'd gone, a woman knocked at their door. She was respectable looking, didn't smell of alcohol, and spoke in a quiet, articulate way.

"Your daughter has spoken to me," she said and smiled.

Charles grabbed her arm and pulled her inside the house. He didn't want any of the newspaper people hanging around outside to hear this.

"What'd she say? Where is she?" Charles wished Gus was home. He'd gone to the pharmacy to get something for Mary to help her sleep.

"She said she's happy and that she wants you to be happy. She's where she wants to be."

"I don't understand. Where is she? Take me to her."

"Well, you see, I don't know where she is precisely. Her voice came to me…"

Charles didn't slam the door behind the woman. He didn't want to risk alerting Mary or Theresa. Let her tell her story to the press boys outside. Let them deal with her. He had offered a substantial reward of $2000, money he didn't have, for anyone with information that led them to Edie. That produced a long line of the desperate and the needy, all saying they wanted to help when what they really wanted was the money. That woman, though, was the only one who said she'd heard Edie's voice, assuring them that she was all right. It was a perverse disappointment for Charles when the woman didn't return after that day.

She was a crackpot, Charles was certain of that, but sometimes even crackpots have insights. If she had returned, he would have asked her why on that last night, of all nights, had he stopped and watched his daughter run up the stairs? Did she believe he might have sensed something at that moment? Ever since that night, whenever he conjured the image of Edie running, there was the same peculiar feeling inside his chest. He must have stopped to watch her for a reason. Why hadn't he called out to her? She was his darling girl. He would have done anything for Edie and yet that night he had failed to do the one thing that might have saved her.

He closes his eyes and sees her chestnut hair bounce and sway. She's wearing her dark green dress that brings out that colour in her hazel eyes. The shade so suits her and the colour of her hair. Her long legs reach the top stair and disappear and then the final flickering image of his daughter, her hand on the wooden railing and loosening, and that too is gone. What had he missed that night? The following days blurred, Gus taking charge and dealing with the hapless police detectives, the newspapermen camped on the front porch, his wife's collapse and young Mel, unable or unwilling to speak. All around them, a pitch black void of silence developed and grew every day Edie wasn't there.

"She's run away," the police told him. "Happens all the time. She'll turn up out of the blue one day. You watch."

Edie hadn't turned up, though, and they had no explanation for why that was except the most obvious and unthinkable. He announced at one point that he thought the family should hold a memorial service. Gus talked him out of that. Charles understood it wasn't his daughter he wanted to bury. He wanted to bury the useless corrosive hope that one day Edie would come home, arriving in their midst with a clear explanation of where she'd been and why.

She'd stand in front of them, hands on hips, grin spilling across her face.

"An absurd misunderstanding, that's what this is," she'd say. "You've all been very silly to worry so much about me."

And she'd fold each one of them in her arms and laugh at what fools they'd been to think she wasn't capable of looking after herself. The Clareys would be a family again, intact and loving, as they were before all this happened. After all the public fuss that had been made, Edie showing up would be an embarrassment that the family could weather. Just as long as she came home.

He'd spoiled her. Every one of them had, each in his or her own way. Who could resist Edie's openness, her enthusiasms and exuberance? Not her parents or her brothers, because all of them knew that inside that skin of wanting and convenience was a real kindness, a thoughtfulness, a true Clarey by looks and by nature. Of all his children and despite her weaknesses, Edie was the one Charles himself wished he was more like. They all wanted to be a bit more like her and less like who they were, anchored by the conformity of their routines. Family, faith, duty. That's who the Clareys were. And Edie had been so much more than that.

Her presence had bound them together. Her absence rendered them solitary creatures, unable any longer to find comfort in each other's company, and yet afraid to remain apart and lose the last vestige of her.

They'd taken for granted their happiness as a family. Edie's going had cast them out of their Eden.

20

Mel returns home with a headache, a sour stomach from the beer and chowder, and no appetite for the evening beyond a cup of hot tea and a comfortable chair.

"I'm sorry," he says and leans down to kiss Theresa on her soft creased cheek. "Won't happen again."

"Words are easy…"

"…the doing's hard. Yes, I know." She's said that for as long as he can remember. "Something came up all of a sudden. You know. Someone I ran into and had to talk to. Hard to explain."

Theresa hadn't looked at Mel since he walked through the door, bringing with him the breath of cold spring air.

"Is there anything I can do for you, Theresa? Set the table maybe?"

She's being unreasonable with her irritation at such a small thing as him missing the noon meal. Having him back home after such a long time away can't be as easy as anyone inside this house expected or wanted it to be. A boy had left and someone else returned to take his place. Their own war years were a mystery to him, beyond hearing Theresa and his parents refer to the endless days of waiting for word of him. Only then did he sense the unspoken fear they all harboured: that the family could not survive the loss of one more child.

"Go ahead," Theresa says and points her chin in the direction of the doorway leading to the dining room and the table waiting to be set. "Do your worst."

The world had changed in many remarkable ways in the past six years and, as a soldier, Mel had seen some of the effects. On his return from overseas, he saw one more change. A single mutated atom of the world's transformation, yet no less significant to this household. They still eat their evening meals at the dining room table overhung by the crystal chandelier, the wedding present to Charles and Mary from her parents, the Sullivans. The food is still eaten off of the Royal Crown Derby service, the wedding present from the Clareys. Charles still retains his position at one end of the table as Mary does her own place opposite him. The one change to all this familiarity occurred during Mel's absence when Theresa was absorbed into its configuration. She sits at the table now, close enough to lean towards Mary like a parent observing a child whose eating habits are of general concern. This transformation happened without anyone asking or proposing it as a topic for debate. Theresa simply sat at the table one evening and Charles, the survivor of so many remarkable moments in the years preceding this, barely registered the change.

Mel sets the four places at the table. Fork to the left of the plate, knife to the right and soup spoon to the right of that.

"That'll do. Now go get your mother and seat her, please." Theresa unties her apron and pulls its bib over her head. Her tone has softened since he arrived home this evening. Mel believes that placating the irritated woman might be his one real accomplishment of the day.

≈

At the dining room table, Mary gives the appearance of someone engaged in eating. She cuts her meat, she spears her vegetables, her spoon scoops sauces and soups. Little of it ever makes its way to her mouth. She is adept at giving the appearance of eating while taking in not much of anything at all.

Theresa reaches out her hand and touches Mary's wrist, the signal that she wants her to try one more mouthful of food.

From time to time, Mary breaks through her silence and contributes to a conversation, proof to them of a mind still capable of being engaged. They seek in vain, however, the pattern of whatever it is that creates these reactions. From one meal to the next, they're never certain what prompt might fire the light inside her head.

Over the soup course, they discuss the house that Mel has rented, the first home for him and Kitty and Anne.

"It's not too late," Charles says. "I can get you out of that lease. Look for something…"

"A little closer to home?"

"A little closer to what you're used to." A little closer to respectability, he means.

Charles was clear that he didn't approve of the small white house in the north end. It was not even on the best street of a bad area, he reminded his son. He advised finding something a little farther south on the peninsula, a place that would be safer for his wife and children.

"I like it. It'll suit us fine," Mel said. He had taken to the little house right away, with its peaked roof over the front door, different in look from the rest of the houses on the street, and he had assured himself that the neighbourhood wasn't so bad. If his father had bothered to look closer, he would have seen that there were a lot of young people living there, people like him and Kitty, soldiers back from the war and starting families, living where their wages dictated they could.

"I was lucky to find it. There's not much out there, but there're lots of guys like me looking for a place. Besides, there's lots of kids around," he tells his father. "Kids for Anne to play with and the mothers, Kitty'll make friends with them right away. She's like that."

"It's a mistake, you know. All these decisions you're making on your own. Women like to have a say in these things," Charles says.

Mel wonders if his father is right, if he should have waited for Kitty to arrive from England before deciding where to live.

In his impatience he thought that Kitty, with an infant, would appreciate settling into her own place straight away. It was the gesture of a thoughtful man and also a practical Clarey who believes it is his role to take on the big decisions as his father had always done.

"It's a rental, Pa. If Kitty doesn't like it, we can always move on."

"Don't wait too long." Mary's words are spoken so quietly that the other three diners have to look at each other for confirmation that they'd heard her at all.

"What's that, dear?"

Mary places her spoon on the edge of the plate holding the soup dish. Her china blue eyes look at each of them in turn.

"I'm only saying that if you stay too long in one place, well then, you tend to stay there for a good long time. That can come as a surprise. You get used to a place. Becomes part of you. Without you noticing."

The three of them wait for more, a further amplification of the thought, an indication of what had jogged those words loose. Mary picks up her spoon and, eyes lowered, resumes the slow stirring of her soup.

One by one, they return their attention to their food.

I'm doing all this for Kitty, Mel reminds himself, renting the house, already furnished, even down to everyday plates, glasses, and cutlery.

He's done his best. He'd always tried to live his life following the example Charles had set. In the Clarey house guided by Charles, one stage progressed along a well-trod path to another. Mel was raised to believe that there is a satisfying order to things and that had been so until 1937. What he wants more than anything in this new world is to establish a soothing rhythm of his own, separate from the past. He wants to say all of that to his father.

"She won't have to do a thing, Pa. You'll see. She'll be so thankful. She can get on with her life," Mel says and with that, the subject of the rental house and its incoming occupants is closed for discussion.

≈

The evening stretches out in its familiar pattern. Mary drifts upstairs to sit at her vanity and begin her routine of buffing and tending to her nails and hands. Charles settles into his armchair with the newspaper and a cup of hot tea at his side. In the kitchen, Theresa fusses with final details of clean-up and tidying as she has done for thirty years. Mel turns on the radio and takes a seat on the sofa, near his father.

Charles riffles the paper, hoping the sound might focus his attention on the newsprint. His mind is locked on the events of his day, the meeting with the Americans and their proposition. He'd struggled with whether or not to talk about it over the meal and decided to leave it for the moment. There is nothing to be gained if what he says upsets his wife. A takeover of the business means he will be expected to step aside. He must have an agreement that Mel's job remains and that his son continues to be the face of this new company, the shotgun marriage of the Americans and the owners of the Halifax business landmark. Maritimers are a suspicious lot, he'll explain to them. We don't much like change and when it does come, we don't absorb it as easily as others might. "We've been let down and lied to too many times," he'll say. Only by keeping some of the faces and names of the old company will they stand a chance of convincing their regular customers not to turn their backs on the new people from away.

The sale of the Clarey business will taint Charles as someone who has sold out, a man who went for the easy money rather than holding his ground for a fight. He'll be talked about as having folded at the first sign of aggression and, worse than that, an opportunist. Generations of Clarey hard work, good deeds and concern for the community are about to dissolve with any news of a sale. He does not yet possess the right words he needs to explain this to Mel and the rest of the family and to allay their fears. He'll sleep on it and perhaps by tomorrow, in the office, he'll be ready to make sense of what he sees as inevitable.

"I'm sorry, what's that?"

"I ran into someone today. Interesting sort of fellow. Canadian, but in a Tommy uniform."

"That must have given you plenty to talk about."

"He was hanging around outside the office. That's where I noticed him. Said he used to work for us, before the war, '36, '37."

"Name?"

"Micah Gessen."

Charles shakes his head. "Doesn't ring any bells. Lots of men came through the warehouse then, from all over the place and usually on their way to somewhere else. Joe Dan took care of them mostly."

"He asked about Mr. MacLean. He was one of the people he remembered."

"Joe Dan. Shame about him. Good man."

"He mentioned Ralphie Campbell, too. And he got quite worked up about a bookkeeper. Raymond something or other."

Charles puts down his paper. "Gillis. Raymond Gillis."

"The one McDougall replaced? What happened to him? I never heard."

"He left. Late '37 if I recall. Went back to Cape Breton. His parents were old and sick, needed his help, he said. Just as well. MacDougall's been a real boon for us. Way more experience than young Gillis had, although he was diligent, I'll say that for him. He did his work well and always tried to do more. For some reason he was very concerned people listen to him. He tried too hard. Every time I thought I was on the verge of liking him, he'd get under my skin. It's hard to explain. As much as he wanted, he had no natural affinity for being a regular fellow. Kinda sad that way. Every time I thought I should cut him some slack, I couldn't summon the energy."

Charles recalls the broad-shouldered fellow with the curly brown hair and pink skin. A good-looking young man with blue eyes so sharp you'd think they'd cut glass. And he remembers that the only time he'd ever had to reprimand his daughter for outright rudeness was when he heard her talk to Raymond Gillis.

"I don't like him, Pa," Edie had said to him later, her chin down, her words soft and sad.

"Your mother and I won't have you being rude to anyone, my girl. Manners first, when you're talking to people. No exceptions. Understood?"

And she'd looked at him, one side of her mouth pulled up, her acknowledgement that the fight was over and that she was allowing her father not an outright win, more like a draw.

Edie was so clear that she didn't like Raymond and everyone knew that if Edie Clarey wasn't disposed to say something good about you, you had a problem. Charles wants to say that to Mel, but like all of them, he's fallen into the habit of not mentioning her. And after the day he's had, he does not possess the stamina to deflect the inevitable wave of grief that the saying aloud of her name always brings.

"What'd he say about Raymond, this soldier?" Charles looks at his tea cup. Empty. Would there be any left in the pot in the kitchen? Should he bother Theresa for another?

"Called him a sanctimonious so-and-so," Mel says.

"That's about right. He was always on his best behaviour around me. But 'sanctimonious.' Yes, he had that flavour about him. Which was odd because he went overseas and got some medal for doing something or other. I suppose sanctimony doesn't stop a person from being brave, does it? Still, I was surprised when I heard. Never thought he had it in him."

"Where's he now?"

"When I was in Sydney last year at some meeting, a guy I met said he was related to Raymond. No surprise. They're all related to each other down there. He said Raymond was working for one of the mines. Up top, of course, in the office. Probably suits him, being back with his own people. Was he asking about anyone else, the soldier?"

"No, he didn't mention anyone else. Not that I recall."

"They're mostly all gone, of course."

"I told him that."

"Was he looking for work?"

"In transit. Just got off a ship and killing time 'til his train left for Toronto."

Charles takes his attention back to his newspaper.

"Your brother's in town next week. Did I tell you that? Something he's involved in. Means meeting the Archbishop. I never understand what he's talking about these days. The Church is changing so much. You try to figure it out when we see him and then explain it to me, will you?"

Mel sits for a few more minutes, listening to the sounds of the radio, absorbing none of it.

"I'm going to Lawrie's for a few minutes. See if I can interrupt his studying."

"Best to Jack and Betty." Charles's voice comes from somewhere behind the newspaper. "And Theo, of course."

≈

Mel tells Lawrie about meeting the soldier in the British uniform, this Micah Gessen, and what the two of them talked about over beer and chowder; where Micah had fought and what he'd seen and about the mangled hand. Lawrie leans forward in his chair and listens as Mel tells him what he hadn't said to his father, that Micah had asked about Edie and said she used to say hello to him. But Edie said hello to everyone. The fact that one person, this Gessen fellow, confirmed that she was exactly who they knew she was, well, there is no nugget of gold in that bit of news to be dazzled by or treasured.

Lawrie pays close attention to every detail. Talk is the soldier's balm. And for the two friends, the simple act of speaking Edie's name gives them assurance, if only for a second or two, that her presence is with them and that she is not forgotten.

≈

The Clarey house is dark and quiet when Mel returns. A single light burns in the upstairs hallway.

He hangs tomorrow's suit, the blue pin-stripe, from the hook on the back of his door and drapes the red tie around its collar. He smoothes the sleeves and closes the buttons so that the suit doesn't develop any lazy ripples in its fabric while he sleeps.

He visits the bathroom and creeps back to his bed, careful not to make any noise that might disturb his mother or father.

He slides between the cold sheets of his narrow bed and pulls the blankets up to his chin. Mel had lived so long in spaces with other men, their smells, their noises, and their talk. In the stillness of this room he realizes that as much as he complained about living with the disruptions then, he is lonely without them. What will it be like with Kitty in one large bed, the two of them together, not for the few nights they had together after their quick marriage and before he shipped out from England, but forever and for the rest of their lives?

The image of Micah in the British uniform comes to Mel's mind. If he hadn't had so much beer to drink he might have been quicker to respond when Micah said he'd known Edie and that she used to say hello to him. He might go to the library, ask if they have a Toronto phone book and write to every Gessen listed there and ask if they know the soldier. Can there be that many people with such a last name in one Canadian city? But what could this Micah tell him about his sister that he doesn't already know? That she was thoughtful and kind to everyone and that's why she said hello to him. No, he's sure there isn't anything more than that to know.

Mel closes his eyes and as always, his last thought, as it has been for ten years, is of his sister.

1957

21

"The church." Mel points to the ornate building farther down the street. "Over there. It's Catholic?"

"You're in Montreal, Mel. What else would it be?"

They'd left the imposing hotel and walked to stand at the busy intersection. His colleague, Harry, is as tall as Mel but bigger around in an uncomfortable-looking way. The buttons of his coat strain against his middle, the sign of the prosperity gained by his move last year from the salesman's beat to an office job. Montreal is Harry's city and he's showing some of the out-of-towners a good time. There will be no churches on his tour today. There are more interesting places to go, more interesting things to see.

Mel is watching the revolving doors of the hotel for the other two, Burt from Ontario and Emile from New Brunswick, all of them in town for the annual meeting of the glass and paint corporation they work for. The official business is over. This is Saturday, the day their itinerary set aside as "travel" for those heading home or "sightseeing" for the ones looking for a bit of fun.

A burst of cold November wind grabs at their overcoats. Mel reaches up to steady his hat. He doesn't want to lose this one so soon and certainly not to the unpredictability of a gust of wind. The charcoal grey fedora was an extravagance, but when he saw it in the shop window during a lunchtime stroll, he wanted it right away. The excitement of the big city and its fashionable people made him feel embarrassed by the hat he was wearing, the one he'd owned since his second daughter, Susan, was a baby, and she'll turn ten soon.

"You're due," he told himself. "Way past due." So he entered the store and bought the grey beauty and put it on his head. He left behind the old one, the veteran piece of headware, on the counter.

"Keep it," Mel said to the man who'd served him. "It's all yours."

"Look at my sign," the salesman said. "Does it say I sell antiques?"

The story of buying the hat is a good one. He'll tell it to Kitty when he gets home. At best, the story will entertain her. At the very least, it will distract her or in some way justify his purchase. "You see, don't you?" he'll say to her. "He called the old one an antique." He'll have to remember to laugh. Then again, maybe he won't say anything about the purchase. He doesn't want her thinking he enjoyed himself too much on this trip, his first to Montreal. His wife has a sharp eye for detail like a new hat. He doesn't want Kitty going on about how he spent money on himself when she, never mind the kids, could use, what? A new winter coat, he's guessing she'll say. He'd been taught that hats have an indispensable place in a man's wardrobe. Charles Clarey never left the house without one, except some days during the summer when "it's very hot, so everyone understands."

But going without a hat on cooler days? "Might as well forget to put on your trousers," Charles had instructed a younger Mel.

If Kitty makes a fuss about the new hat, he'll give her the money for a new coat. She'll want something else for the kids and if that happens, he'll find the money for that, too. Anything to keep the peace.

He'd arrived in Montreal unprepared for its early winter. Halifax weather is still mild in November, so he's here without a scarf or gloves. He won't be spending any more money. A hat is one thing. A new scarf and gloves, in Kitty's eyes, would constitute a whole new wardrobe. His neck and hands will have to endure the biting winds for the sake of some feeble expectation of family harmony.

He sees his two colleagues emerge from the hotel's revolving door, pause and stamp their feet as if trying to wake them up, preparing them for the cold walk ahead. Mel waves to get their attention. He adjusts his coat collar one more time and wishes the men would pick up their pace.

"Christ, but that's cold. Gets right into your bones, doesn't it? Snow's on the way." Burt is the short spherical-shaped dispenser of weather wisdom from the Ottawa Valley. He's followed by the slender Emile from Moncton, the Acadian who refuses to speak French in Montreal.

"What's the use, eh? They pretend they don't understand me," he'd told Mel. "So everybody's happy if I just mangle the English."

Here they are, the three who have chosen to stay in Montreal one more day to see the great city, along with their congenial guide. The rest all had their own reasons for going and hurried off to their homes and families. They weren't interested in exploring this big place, or they were just plain homesick.

"Ready, boys?" Harry asks.

Mel, Burt and Emile nod at him like nervous schoolboys on their first unchaperoned outing.

"Where to first?" Mel asks.

"Well, we're going to say a prayer, Mel. Only not down the street. We're going to Montreal's other great cathedral. I'm gonna show you boys the Forum. Home of Saint Maurice. The Rocket."

With a whoop and a tug at their collars against the wind, the four of them set off.

≈

Harry's time at a company desk hasn't robbed him of his salesman's powers. His smooth patter gets them a free pass into the Forum and from the stands they watch the Habs, true hockey royalty, finish up a practice. Moore, Béliveau, Plante, Geoffrion, Harvey.

All are there except the one they've come to see. The mercurial Rocket, the unknowable, the dazzling one, is missing. Maybe he's already left the ice. Maybe he's hurt again and is home nursing some unacknowledged pain.

"He's a real tough guy," Harry says. "All fire. Does things his own way."

"Not like that Béliveau," Emile offers. "A prince, that one."

They all agree this is so.

"But the Rocket," Emile says. They all hear the awe in his voice created simply by pronouncing the words. "And not just tough the way that Doug Harvey guy is tough."

"What makes him great," Mel adds for emphasis. The four heads nod in solemn agreement.

The practice finished, they follow Harry onto the empty ice, the centre of the hockey universe, giggling and punching shoulders. Even Burt from Ontario, and so by default a Maple Leafs fan, can't contain his excitement. After several minutes of this, a maintenance man, deaf to Harry's charms, hustles them away. They've seen enough, spent enough time in this temple that they can keep their family and friends entertained for years with the story of the day their feet touched the ice that Maurice "The Rocket" Richard skated on.

Who will Mel tell his story to? Certainly not Kitty or his children. Lawrie will be amused by the richness of detail that Mel will add for him, but not much more than that. Lawrie isn't a hockey man. Not like Gus. Yes, his brother will share the thrill he felt today.

They find a tavern, a place where Harry is a familiar presence. The talk is of business and soon gets round to the two Canadian religions: hockey and politics. At a certain point, as Harry is about to order the third round, Mel stands. He has reached some comfortable limit of both the alcohol and the company of these relative strangers.

"I'm off," he says to his colleagues and, with care and more than a little satisfaction, settles the new hat on his head.

They make the expected sounds of protest. Whether there are three of them or four of them, after the next round, won't matter. This is Harry's town. Let Harry lead his tiny tribe of glass and paint executives. Mel will go to the hotel, order room service, pack his suitcase and get a good night's sleep, ready himself for the plane ride home tomorrow.

Outside, in the frigid Montreal late afternoon, he tucks the coat's lapels around his neck and waits to feel the air begin to clear his head. Next time he won't go anywhere at this time of year without throwing a scarf and gloves into the suitcase. One more time, he fingers the rich band of trim kissing the brim of his new hat. Worth every penny he'd paid. It'll last until men stop wearing hats, although he can't imagine when that will ever be. Men without hats; an unnatural thought, like a cake without icing or a Christmas tree missing the angel.

In less time than he expects he reaches the hotel. From the far side of the street, he takes it in. A luxury hotel with the best of everything. He can see through the glass doors into the bright lobby with its marble walls and floors, modern and shiny. The doorman is dressed in a burgundy overcoat with gold braid and buttons arranged to have him resemble a military sentry. To Mel, it all appears a little silly. He still feels the buzz of the strong beer. In this state, he has no urge to rush across the street just to see the doorman touch the bill of his peaked cap as though he's being saluted.

Farther down the street, he can see the doors of the imposing Catholic church, its ornate stone walls blackened by decades of the city's weather, car exhaust and sin. He'll have no time for mass tomorrow morning before leaving for the airport. Family, faith, duty. The Clarey mantra calls. Even if there isn't an evening service, he'll stop for a while and say some prayers and light a candle.

≈

The heavy wooden door gives up a weak groan followed by a solid thump when it closes behind him. He's in luck, a mass has just started. From the vestibule, he hears the rumble of the priest's voice inside the enormous space.

He might have stridden in and chosen any place on a pew, but a sudden need not to feel like a stranger overcomes him. So far from his home, he wants to belong to this congregation, if only for an hour or so. He unbuttons his overcoat and hangs it on an empty hook beside the other coats left there. He removes his hat and, for a moment, considers taking it inside with him. Won't that look silly, though, and he sets it on the ledge with a dozen or so others. He hesitates again, looking at this object he admires so much. Anyone could take it. No, no one will do that, not from here, not this place. Have some faith, Mel. Just in case, he looks for the second nicest hat on the shelf and puts his own beside it, hoping that by putting it there it won't stand out quite so much. He's ashamed to think he worried that someone in this church might break the covenant and steal a hat. Faith, Mel, have some faith, he tells himself again. He hurries into the church, dipping his fingers into the font of holy water, making the sign of the Cross, genuflecting before the altar and taking a seat in an empty pew about halfway up the aisle.

Mel listens to the familiar Latin verse, the low roll of voices from the congregants like faraway thunder, the sharp clatter of the bells as the altar boy flicks his wrist. Decades of high masses in the place have left the air thick with the dense spiced smell of incense, a long-ago scent of his childhood and a reminder of home wherever he travels.

He taps his chest with his fist along with the other worshippers scattered among the pews and mutters the familiar pleas.

Kyrie eleison. Lord have mercy.

Christe eleison. Christ have mercy.

He kneels to receive the Holy Communion wafer and later bows his head as the priest dispenses the closing benediction.

Ite, missa est. Go in peace.

And his own answer: *Deo gratias.* Thanks be to God.

As the small crowd rises and files out, Mel lingers in his pew. He wants to be alone after the busy day, to sit in a solitary place and hear nothing, especially nothing of hockey or weather or glass and paint.

The few stragglers sit or kneel, head in hands, head tilted back, eyes open, eyes closed, hands clasped, lips trembling in prayer.

The warmth of the church's interior, the effects of the beer, the intoxicating scent of the incense and the long day itself, all have their effect on him and Mel closes his eyes. "Just for a moment," he tells himself. He exists only inside this church. If he disappeared tonight no one would ever know where he'd got to after he left his friends at the tavern. Sitting by himself in this hushed place, for the first time in a long while, he feels comforted and calmed.

To the sound of the shuffling feet passing by him, he dozes, dreamless.

≈

The church is empty except for Mel and two others kneeling in a pew several rows ahead of him. The hiss of their voices carries to him as they recite their prayers. However long he napped, he feels refreshed and wants to go to the hotel, get something to eat and prepare for the re-entry into his life.

He genuflects, dipping his head in respect as he'd been taught to do as a child. The final drops of the cold holy water dot his forehead when he makes the sign of the Cross and steps into the vestibule.

As he shrugs on his coat he glances at the shelf, not believing at first what he is seeing, or not seeing. There is a lone hat there. It is not his hat. The charcoal grey beauty is gone. There is no anger. He had owned it for such a short period of time that it might as well have been an object on loan to him, as if he was only holding on to it for someone else.

"My own fault," he murmurs. "I could have…I should have…" He knows it's done, the hat is gone. Someone else saw it, admired it, and walked away with it. Whoever it was, must have hung back while everyone else retrieved their belongings. He would have looked around to ensure he was alone and, at that moment, snatched Mel's hat. He would have heaved his body against the heavy wooden door and stepped into the cold night and scurried off before someone could call out for him to stop.

"I hope you really need it," Mel says.

22

The bright lights of the hotel lobby dazzle after the dark of the church and the night. Mel enters through the revolving doors and reaches a hand up, a gesture as automatic as his genuflecting and signing had been in the church. He registers an instant of surprise when his hand touches his bare head.

He glimpses his reflection in one of the mirrored walls of the lobby. The brown Clarey hair is still thick, blown about by the wind as he ran up the street. At this distance, he can't see the grey strands that have begun to show up. He still carries himself with his soldier's back and shoulders, straight and broad. The expensive dark blue cashmere overcoat has held its shape and shade after several winters. His arms hang loose and aimless by his sides and his hands, with no hat to hold, lack purpose. He stares at his face as he might stare at a portrait of an ancestor, marking certain familiar features, and hoping it will tell him who he is or who he is becoming.

"Can I help you, sir?"

A young man, dressed in a neat blue suit and burgundy tie, hotel logo embroidered on his left breast pocket, smiles and bobs at the waist. There's a small red line where he must have run a ragged razor over his chin this morning. When he speaks, Mel hears his accent and is reminded of a soldier in his company who made it as far as the Liri Valley before disappearing there one bad day.

"Thanks," Mel says. "But I'm…" He's not sure where he's headed. Certainly not his room to begin his packing. Perhaps he should go back to the church to look one more time for the missing hat.

"If it's the bar you need…" and the young hotel employee is pointing to one side of the large lobby.

"Yeah, sure. The bar. Why not?"

He steps into the dim wood-panelled room with its maroon velvet banquettes and slender green plants. The cocktail hour is past; the usual late Saturday crowd and the guests demanding a final nightcap have not yet arrived. In the near-empty room, notes of piano music echo, tinny and grating to his ears. Mel's relieved that he recognizes no one and moves to the bar where he sits on one of the white leather-cushioned stools.

"*M'sieur*," the barman says.

Mel has no idea what he wants to drink or if he should drink at all. The beer at the tavern had been enough for him. What he longs for is a cup of strong hot tea to get rid of the sour taste left in his mouth by the afternoon beer. But he knows this isn't the place to order cups of tea.

"Scotch," he says, the first thing that comes to mind. "*Beaucoup de…*ice."

The second and third glasses, at Mel's request, carry less and less ice. A woman takes a place two stools away from where he sits and lifts her chin to the bartender, so subtle a signal that only someone expecting it would know how to respond. A glass filled with red wine is placed in front of her. Mel has seen her before. He noticed her the first night he was in the hotel. She was sitting at one of the banquettes, close to a man he assumed wasn't her husband, although there was an ease between them that spoke of familiarity, as if they weren't strangers to each other. He'd noticed her because she was so pretty, with her round girlish face and her large brown eyes and small nose with its slight upward tilt. And there was some other intangible thing about her that he found attractive, something special that French girls have, like they know a thing or two about the ways of the world that English girls don't or never will.

She takes a red package of DuMaurier cigarettes from a silver sequined clutch purse. Her hands are covered with expensive white kid gloves that reach half-way up her forearms.

"*Du feu?* You gotta light?" She shifts on her stool toward Mel.

"I don't smoke." He follows her gaze to the ashtray holding a paper book of hotel matches. He fumbles with it until he ignites one of them and touches the tip of her cigarette.

"*Merci.* Thanks."

"Okay," he says. He can't remember how to say "it's nothing" in French or "you're welcome." He must seem very rude to her. They sit, she sipping and drawing on her cigarette, Mel sipping and trying to piece together her jigsaw image reflected in the bar's glass backdrop behind the array of coloured bottles.

She's perched on the stool with a straight-backed confidence. A teacher or nun might have placed a yardstick there once and impressed on her the importance of good posture. Mid-twenties maybe, dark hair pulled into a neat knot on top of her head. A fringe of hair covers her forehead. Her lips are full and painted deep pink and even though she's a little thin for Mel's taste, her breasts look good, with enough size to fill out the satiny ice-blue dress she wears. Her bare arms are firm, those of someone used to physical work. A farm girl maybe, who'd left behind the relentless labour of her family's holding to seek out an easier life. All she needed to do was learn some English and acquire the knack of talking to strangers.

"I'll get you another," Mel says. She turns to look at him and her mouth moves into a crooked smile.

"*Non.* Thanks anyway. This one is good for me."

He likes the sound of her accent and he wants to tell her so, but that might sound condescending. What does it matter what anyone sounds like when they speak? Kitty, now Kitty, with that English sensitivity about your accent pegging your class, would not have hesitated if she heard this woman. "Your accent," his wife would say. "So charming. Where are you from?" as though the woman sipping the red wine hailed not from this province, not even from one of those places with funny-sounding names like

Chibougamou or Rouen-Noranda, but from another planet much farther away from the sun than this one.

"But maybe I won't stop you if you insist to order me one more," she says. Her lips part and he sees a row of small white teeth, even, except for one incisor that seems unsure of its place.

"Well, okay," he says and rattles the ice in his glass at the bartender and nods in the woman's direction.

"It's not that cold here yet, you know," she says.

"What?"

"Your coat. Your coat is on. We're inside. You won't freeze here. Not yet anyway. It's only November."

Her way of talking is direct, no coyness, as though she's used to giving orders to reluctant cows or younger siblings.

Mel struggles with the coat, his arms useless and flopping. "I don't know why…" and all of a sudden he wants to tell her about the hat, such a beautiful thing, and his for such a short time. Now someone else in Montreal is walking around with it, accepting compliments on such a fine piece of headwear.

"'*ttendez*," she says. "Just wait a minute, eh?" and slips off the stool to pull the coat off of Mel's fumbling arms. She knows an item of quality when she sees it, folds it with care, and places it on the seat between them.

"Thanks," he says and remembers. "*Merci*."

"You're not used to so much Scotch, eh?"

"You're right about that. I'm not."

"So why do you drink so much of it then?"

And, again, he wants to tell her about the hat. He can't summon the energy to unravel the story and to tell her in a way that makes sense about one hat being as old as his second child and no longer stylish and about the new one, what Kitty would say about it, and what happened at the church.

"Last night here," he says instead. "Want to make it a memorable one, I guess."

She takes a fresh cigarette out of the pack, hands Mel the book of matches, and leans in for the light.

"You said you wanted another?" He gestures at her glass with the spent match.

She exhales the cigarette smoke and shrugs. "Okay. Sure. Why not? You seem a nice man." And again, there's the almost imperceptible lift of the chin, the well-rehearsed signal to their server.

Mel wonders how much the man behind the bar gets as a cut for allowing her to work the room. If he asked her, she'd probably climb down from the stool and leave him and that's not what he wants right now. He wants the company.

"We went to the Forum today, me and some pals. Got right inside, too. Saw The Rocket practising and everything." Why is he lying to her? Richard hadn't been there. Because he wants to. Because he wants to believe that if he can make Maurice Richard appear at the Forum then he can believe what happened with the hat, hadn't. He can believe that he wasn't so stupid as to leave it on a shelf, for anyone to see, a brand new expensive hat, a glaring temptation alone and unguarded, available to anyone with the nerve to steal it. Of all the lies he wants to tell this woman, the one about seeing The Rocket is the easiest and the least harmful to him.

"Don't you guys know to do anything else when you're here, in Montreal? You talk only hockey and *le saint* Maurice." And she laughs. When the men she meets don't know what else to say, they tell her about sightseeing and always about the Forum. Only later, they tell her what they really mean to say; how unhappy they are.

"You…" she says and laughs again. *"Les anglais,"* and she gives her head a tiny shake.

"Hey. I'm Catholic," Mel says. For Mel, a true *"anglais"* must be Protestant as well as English-speaking, a small but crucial prejudice. In this stewpot of a country, doesn't such a subtle distinction allow us to maintain a measure of identity? He knows his Catholicism sets him apart a little, even in his own culture. Doesn't a shared religion bond him and this woman as the faithful Catholic David pitted against the godless Protestant Goliath?

"Okay," she says. "So maybe we have a better chance to understand each other then." She touches her glass against his.

And like that, he begins to tell her about the hat, how much it meant to him and going to mass and the moment he saw that the hat was gone and what that felt like.

He finishes the story and they sit, Mel wishing he hadn't gone on at such length and the woman, by the look on her face, wishing he hadn't either.

"Christ," he says. "It's the randomness of it, you see?"

"*Comment?*" she says. "The what?"

He tries the word again, slower this time, his thick tongue struggling with every syllable.

"*Ran. Dom. Ness.* You see?"

"Not really."

"I mean…why me?" he says. "Why us?"

"It's only a hat, *m'sieur.*"

"What did we ever do to deserve this?"

"Okay," she says and pats his arm with a gloved hand. "Sure. Okay. Whatever you say."

If he'd done what he was meant to do, if he'd got on the plane the minute the last meeting ended, gone home to his wife and children, none of this would have happened. He'd only yesterday decided to stay, to have some fun with Harry and the others. Didn't he deserve to have a little fun?

"The random…" The word will not leave his mouth sounding the way it should. "The *ran. Dom. Ness.* Of everything, you see? And I don't just mean the goddamned hat."

He could tell her about Edie. There's an example of randomness, as if he needed one more.

The woman rests her head in her hand, elbow propped on the shiny surface of the bar, feigning interest. She's used to hearing men discover the meaning of life in a hotel bar.

"Look," she says and rests gloved fingertips on his hand. "I'm very sorry about this hat of yours. But I need to know first, are we going to your room, or no?" The voice again, not demanding, quiet and matter-of-fact. He can even believe he hears in it the gentle nature of someone who wants him to understand that with enough encouragement she might be persuaded to share the pain of his loss.

Mel had started out his day in a tiny buoyant skiff, tethered securely to a dock. Before he could understand what was happening, the line holding him there loosened, came away, and set him adrift into open water.

"Yes. We'll go to my room." His voice sounds to his own ears as if he stuttered. Someone had stolen from him today, so he will steal something too. Why not one more totally random act this day? "Yes. We will do that."

The barman places the bill in front of him as though he's been anticipating this moment and watches Mel scrawl his name across the bottom of the paper.

She picks up his coat, brushes her hand along its smooth surface and hooks it over her arm. "Let's go then," she says and slides off the stool. Standing beside him, she's smaller than he thought she'd be, the top of her brunette head hardly reaching his shoulders.

The bright lights of the lobby hurt his eyes and make him blink.

"Whoa. The key," he says and walks to the desk, where he leans across the marble counter, grateful to have that to hang onto. He pronounces, with care, his room number and is handed the key along with a piece of paper, folded once. He opens it and reads: "Call home immediately. Urgent."

He holds out the paper to the woman. She reads, folds it and slips it into a pocket of Mel's coat, which she takes from her arm and presses against him.

"Another time then," she says and turns to make her way back to the bar.

"I need to make a long-distance phone call," Mel tells the young man at the desk, the same one he'd spoken to earlier, who points to the far side of the lobby and a row of telephone cabins.

23

Mel's daughter, Anne, answers on the fourth ring. "Clarey residence."

Kitty had taught her to answer the phone that way. They'd argued about it, such a small thing. He said it sounded ridiculous, especially having children say it.

"It's charming," she'd said. "And they're learning some real manners," as though no one in his family, or in his city, knew how to answer a phone properly.

You're a farmer's daughter, he'd wanted to yell at her. What do you know about things like that? What angered him was that he knew this had nothing to do with manners and everything to do with a spitefulness growing out of Kitty's corrosive unhappiness.

"Anne, it's Daddy."

"Oh, Daddy. Where are you?"

"Still in Montreal. I just got the message to call. What's happened?"

"Well…" He'll have to wait while Anne dribbles out the details to him. His oldest child enjoys being in control. Which one of them did she get that from?

"Anne, for Christ's sake, what's going on?"

"Language, Daddy, please. I was about to tell you. But you need to settle down first."

This girl, almost twelve and going on forty, will do this her way.

"Anne. Is anyone…"

"No one's dead, if that's what you're going to ask. Mummy's hurt herself is all."

"What kind of 'hurt herself'?"

"Well. She was boiling some water, you see, and it sort of tipped off the stove somehow. She burned her foot."

"Jesus God. How bad is it?"

"Language, please, I said." Her words are crisp, distinct, even down the scratchy long-distance telephone line. "I tell you, when it happened you'd think it was the end of the world. The way she went on about it. It's not so bad. Once she settled down, I mean. I cleaned up the mess, of course. Susie and Charlie got hysterical right along with her, wouldn't you know it. So someone had to take charge."

"When did this happen?"

"Oh," the syllable is long, drawn out, as Anne considers a precise answer. "Two...really more like two-and-a-half hours ago, I'd say. I'm the one who called the hotel, by the way, in case you're wondering."

"And where is she now?"

"In bed. What's wrong with you? You sound funny. I can hardly understand what you're saying."

"It's the phone line. Makes people sound not like themselves."

"If you say so. I can try to get her to come to the phone, but she's taken some...you know...medicine." Her voice is arch, sarcastic. The tone comes so naturally to her.

"What medicine?"

"You know what I'm saying." Anne's voice dips, a whisper shared between collaborators. "You know. The alcohol."

Mel had adored Anne from the moment he first held her. Even as he began to understand what a demanding baby she was, his love was not shaken. "A real handful," he and Kitty said about her, which was as generous as they could be during her waking hours. Mel told himself that the infant Anne's fretful behaviour was a signal that she had inherited Edie's high spirits. With time, though, he saw that while his daughter shared his sister's determination, she lacked Edie's big-hearted generosity. For Anne, the need to express disapproval trumps all else.

"Could you please try to get your mother to come downstairs for me? Just for a minute? I need to know if she's doing okay."

A sigh of resignation. "I'll try."

"Hurry, okay? This is long distance. Put someone else on the phone. Where's Susie? Let me talk to her."

He listens to Anne's voice pester her younger sister. A ribbon of sweat unfurls down the centre of his back. He reaches into his pocket for his handkerchief and dabs at his forehead and the back of his neck.

"She can't talk to you right now. She says she's too upset."

Susie is the excitable entertainer of the family. She is also the ten-year-old whose immediate response to any situation is an emotional unwinding.

"She wants to know, though…"

"…wants to know what?"

"What you're bringing home for her."

He'd bought an expensive hat for himself and hadn't thought once of his own children or his wife.

"It's a surprise," Mel says. Are there shops at the airport? A souvenir. Something. Sunday morning. Would the airport shops even be open?

Anne conveys the message to her younger sister.

"Susie says she wants a scarf." A high-pitched burst from the background makes its way down the line to the telephone cabin in the Montreal hotel.

"A *smart* scarf, she says. Don't forget that. The scarf must be *smart*. And Daddy?"

"What, Anne?"

"I don't want a scarf. So don't think you can buy two of something in different colours and expect we'll both be happy. Anything but a scarf for me. Understand? Anything. I'm going to get Mummy now. Here's Charlie."

Oh, God, no. Not Charlie.

"Hello? Charlie? Are you there?"

A soft, rhythmic pulse of breath. Not the static of the phone line, but the faint signal of another human presence.

"Charlie?"

The words, when they come, at last, are only a little louder than his breathing.

"Yes. Here."

"How are you, son?"

Again, the soft undulating wash of the boy's breathing.

"Charlie, I asked how you are."

"Okay."

He was a heartbreak, this boy; eight years old next month and with his small size, he was often mistaken for a younger child. He has Kitty's dark curly hair and blue-green eyes. Other than those recognizable features, he doesn't seem to belong to either one of them. His blank face is too round and there's an unappealing flatness to it. No playmates swarm the house or yard. Teachers tell Mel and Kitty that Charlie is often the subject of cruel pranks at school. One day the principal called Kitty to come collect him. Bring some clothes with you, he said. A group of older boys had stripped Charlie naked and stuffed what he was wearing into a toilet. Mel longs for the day he'll hear his son say: "Okay, I know what you want. I'll be a regular boy now." But that's not what Charlie is. Unreachable. Unknowable. And never a regular boy.

Some nights Mel lies in bed, staring at the ceiling, the thought churning inside of him: What will happen to Charlie when Kitty and I are gone? Who will care for him then? Kitty dismisses such talk and assures Mel that their son will "snap out of it" and some days he's sure they're about to see that happen.

And the worst thought: what if Charlie dies first and he and Kitty are left to grieve? For what? For the boy who never was and for their own failing at having produced so sad a creature. Why do we love our weakest the most?

"Daddy?" Anne is back on the phone.

"Where's your mother?"

"She can't speak to you right now."

"Can't or won't?"

"You see," and here Anne's voice dips again so that Susie and Charlie can't hear. "She took the bottle to bed with her. She's mostly asleep at this moment."

"Anne, look. This is what I want you to do. You must call Dr. Melanson. Right away. Tell him what's happened, tell him everything, just what you told me, and he'll come over and take a look at Mummy's foot. He'll understand. Can you do that?"

"Yes."

"I'll be home tomorrow afternoon. You'll be okay till then?"

"I know what to do."

Mel doesn't doubt for a moment that she is the most capable person in the house.

"If there's an emergency, if Dr. Melanson wants Mummy to go to the hospital…" Then what, Mel? Then what does this girl do? "I want you to call Grandpa and ask for Theresa to come stay with you. You got that?"

"I can look after…"

"Anne." His voice is louder, sharper, than he uses with his children. "Listen to me. It's important. You do what I'm telling you to do. Understood?"

The phone line hisses at him for several seconds.

"Anne?"

"Yes, I understand."

"You know, on second thought, I want you to call Grandpa anyway and tell him what's happened. He'll figure out what to do. All right?"

He hears his daughter's faint, grudging reply: "Yes."

"Good. I'm going to hang up now. This is costing a fortune. I wrote down the number of the hotel for your mother."

"It's here."

"If anyone needs to call me, you tell them it's okay. You got that?"

"Yes."

"Good girl."

"Is there anything you want me to tell Mummy?"

"I'll be back tomorrow afternoon. She knows that. I wrote down all the flight details, too. She has that somewhere. I'm hanging up now."

"That's all?"

"Hanging up."

He isn't sure if the sound he hears on the line is his daughter's dismissive "bye" or the phone disconnecting.

Mel presses the handkerchief against his face and looks into the lobby. The woman from the bar is at the front desk, holding out an unlighted cigarette to the young clerk. He offers her the flame of his lighter and she rises up on tiptoes to lean across the marbled top. She says something to him and a brief, knowing laugh passes between them.

The whoosh of the big revolving doors brings Mel's colleagues, Harry, Burt and Emile into the hotel. They think there is something very funny about the way the door has pushed them into the building. It seems to be the funniest thing of a very funny day. They must have stayed at the tavern long after Mel left. They're all talking at once. Harry is still leading them. This is Harry's city, Harry's show, and he's going to make sure that the day has a memorable finish for the visitors. He steers them in the direction of the bar.

The woman in the satiny ice-blue dress watches all of this from where she leans against the counter of the front desk. With a last amused look at the clerk, she crushes her cigarette, brushes the skirt of her dress and runs a hand up the back of her hair, from the nape of her neck to the thick knot on top of her head. Ready, she follows the three men into the bar.

≈

Outside the hotel, Mel shrugs on his coat. He wants to walk, needs to feel the cold air on his face. He sets off down the street, stops at the corner and looks at the ornate facade of the church. It's too cold to walk. No amount of Scotch can protect him from that reality.

The church is empty and dark except for the dim overhead lights near the altar and the flickering glow of the votive candles in their trays. Inside the church again, he's aware that the world outside is gone, has ceased to exist. The sound of the street, the hotel, his daughter, disappears now that he's within the safety of the thick stone walls.

His footsteps echo along the centre aisle. He'll light a candle for someone. Mel does this whenever he visits an unfamiliar church. Sometimes he says a prayer, a general request for health and happiness for everyone he knows. Other times, there is a specific mention of an ailing parent.There are not enough candles in this church for every heartbreak and worry he's able to mention.

He drops a coin into the donation box and picks up one of the slender wands, touching its tip to a flame while he decides which of the candles will be his. There's one on the top row, the single unlighted candle there. That one. The flame of the wand touches the cold black wick. He hesitates, not sure of what to say or how to say it.

"Where'd you go?" he says out loud. "You said you'd come back and you didn't. You promised me.You promised me, Edie. Everything would be so different now if you'd just come back like you said. I need to know where you are. Please."

He stares at the candle's flame, the brightest of them all.

If he'd only said something that night when he saw his sister in the street with her bicycle. Opened his window, leaned out and called to her to come home. Wouldn't everything still be the same if he'd done that one small thing?

A voice carries from the side of the altar, startling him. A man steps out of the darkness, holding a broom. He's talking to Mel in rapid French, not angry, more surprised to see him there than anything else. Mel recognizes the word *fermé*. The church is closed, the door should have been locked, he shouldn't be in here.

He gestures to the man. I understand. I'm going. Don't worry, I'm going.

Down the aisle, through the vestibule, he leans his shoulder against the heavy door.

Snow is falling, whipped by the wind, eddying across the concrete steps and around his feet. He lifts his face to the sky and feels the icy pinpoints of the flakes as they melt on his face. Winter had arrived as he was inside the church.

The cold wind holds him there, batters his bare head.

"I'm sorry," he says. "I'm so sorry."

24

Mel sits on the edge of his bed and scans, again, the sheet of paper. He folds it once, twice, struggling to line up the edges the way he likes to see them; squared, precise, with no overlap. The mattress wobbles and makes his task more difficult. He's complained about this bed. It's too soft, he told them, his back aches every morning because of it, but ,nothing has been done. How many pained bodies have lain here before him? How many tried to do something and were left resigned to administrative apathy, the bed's spongy surface one more of life's final lost battles?

He shifts his weight and eases the folded schedule into the back pocket of his grey trousers. One of these appears every morning on the carpeted floor of his room. Although the information changes very little from day to day, it's a useful thing to carry with him in case he gets lost or isn't sure what to do next or where to go. The schedule reassures him, gives his days purpose and routine. The dependability soothes him, most often during those times when his body feels ragged and jumpy and his memory isn't any better than incomplete. He never thinks to ask who delivers it or when, but as with the day's sun, he's always relieved to see it there.

The red dot in the corner of the clock radio screen blinks at him. Seven fifty-eight; two minutes until he begins his walk down the hall to the residents' dining room for breakfast.

Outside the window of his ground-floor room is a small garden. The tulips are long gone. The gardener was by, when was it, last week? Last month? Mel was sitting on the bench when the man arrived with his tools and flats of annuals. They'd talked as the gardener turned the soil and planted the pink and white flowers in the dirt. His name is Ignacio. Ignatius. A patron saint of soldiers. That's why Mel remembers the gardener's name. Ignacio is from away, Mexico, a country Mel once thought he might visit except that he doesn't like the food with its gummy beans and cheese that always give him digestive complaints. Their conversations are friendly, even when one of them isn't sure what the other is saying.

The red dot on the clock radio pulses. Eight o'clock. Mel pushes himself off the bed and stands until he feels steady enough to walk to the door. He pauses for a last look in the mirror to ensure his thick white hair is holding its place and that his morning's shave has left no shadows on his face. Some days he's surprised to see his father staring back at him; the long face, the straight line of his jaw rendered indistinct by age, the hazel eyes now hooded by drooping lids. So much a Clarey in looks everyone always said and here, before him, is the undeniable evidence.

He's relieved to find the hallway empty. There are days when he has to walk the length of the long corridor with someone he isn't sure he's met or even seen before. The ensuing conversations are usually about sleeping patterns or pains or, worst of all, bowel movements; theirs, never his own. He shares his mother's sensibility about mentioning those private matters to anyone but a doctor and only then when absolutely necessary. He doesn't want to know about the health problems of these strangers whose bodies ceased, long ago, to register pleasure before pain. If he has to talk to anyone he wants to talk about something besides all that. He hopes Ignacio's duties take him to the garden today.

A handrail runs along the wall at waist height. Mel's pleased that he's never had to reach out and hang on to it as he's seen others do, gasping for a breath or waiting for some spasm of pain to subside, or for balance. His posture is still good. The army training, his straight back with shoulders engaged, has never left him. He's sure his physical sturdiness is helping his body fight the inevitable soft sag of old age.

Mel leaves his room at eight o'clock every morning. He doesn't like getting to the dining area early to wait with the other residents for the doors to open. At that hour of the morning, their names are lost to him. If that same concern bothers any of the others, they don't show it or they make jokes about it, and their good-natured chatter at that time of the day annoys him.

At the final corner of the hallway Mel stops, leans against the wall and listens for the voices of other residents fade as they enter the dining room. "Shorefront hide-and-seek" he calls this game. He checks his wristwatch. Eight-oh-three. Time to find breakfast.

Arriving later than this means that one of the other residents assigned to his table might take his favourite chair, the one with the view out the window onto the sidewalk. From there, he might see a dog or a young visitor, a small child hand-in-hand with a parent or wheeled in a stroller. He enjoys watching the cars come and go, the new models, how shiny some of them are in the early sun. All this provides him with a distraction from his tablemates and the room's other diners.

A man waves at him from across the room.

"Mel. Come on."

What is his name? Bill? No, Bill died a couple of weeks ago. Everyone knew that Bill had died although no one's death is ever announced by the people who run the Shorefront Residences. Such news is left to meander through the labyrinth of the daily tittle-tattle and if you miss it you're left to wonder, with alarming frequency these days, "whatever happened to…" Mel knew about Bill's death because Bill was one of his assigned tablemates. He was one of the lucky few who never had a sick day, and for that reason alone Mel considered him reasonable company. He'd vanished in the middle of the night; one day there for meals and the next day, a vacant chair.

"You don't suppose it was the corned beef, do you?" a woman at the table next to Mel had asked. "My stomach always has such a time with it. So tough."

Carl. The man waving at him from his table is called Carl. A name like that. When he's eaten his breakfast, the brain will get going and the name will come to him.

"Big news, old chap," Carl, or whatever his name is, says as Mel eases himself into his chair. Is the man's name Alan? Yes, he remembers now. The man's name is Alan. A veteran, one of those irritating anglophile Canadians who has never shed the mannerisms and phrases he picked up while training in England, as though it happened last week and not sixty years ago. If it wasn't mealtime and if this man whose name he's sure is Alan wasn't assigned to this table, Mel would avoid him altogether.

"I say, d'you hear 'bout Cec? Cecil. Last night. Gone. Like that." And this man, who might be named Carl or Alan, snaps his fingers. "Bill's chair barely cool and now Cec. Bad run of it here, this table, wha'? Just the two of us now. The whole table to ourselves. Wha'dya say to that? Wha'?"

"I don't say much of anything to that, Alan. Except I'm sorry to see him go." Cecil, or Cec, as everyone called him, was a sour man whose every word resonated with complaint.

"Sid."

"Pardon?"

"You said 'Alan.' My name's Sid, Mel."

"Sorry. I was thinking of someone else."

"No one here by name of Alan," Sid says. "Hmmm, eh? Better watch out, old man. You keep on like that, they'll be making room for you on the second floor." And he gives Mel's arm a chummy punch and booms a laugh that feels like broken glass inside Mel's ears.

He might risk offending Sid and ask to be reassigned to another table. He needs a new line of conversation or, better than that, no conversation at all, and someone whose name is worth remembering.

The young woman serving breakfast puts their plates down in front of them.

"Eggs again," Mel says.

"What do you mean 'again'? Always have eggs on Thursday. Mondays, Thursdays and Saturdays. My favourite." And with that, Sid picks up his fork and circles his mauve tongue around his pale lips. "Tally ho, old chap."

Mel picks up the menu card propped against the salt and pepper shakers. "Omelet with chives," it reads, but it tastes like nothing. As he has done all of his life, he eats everything on his plate.

≈

After breakfast, Mel returns to his room and brushes his teeth. Unlike a lot of the people at Shorefront Residences, what is in his mouth has always belonged to him; no dentures, no implants, no bridges. Since he was a boy, he's taken good care of his teeth. Even when he was overseas he carried a toothbrush with him.

"Extraordinary," said the young dentist who'd taken over the practice Mel had visited for decades. "Your age and still got all your chompers. Extraordinary." Mel's chest puffed a little with the words. His parents and Theresa would have been especially proud of him.

Teeth brushed, he stands at his window, hoping to see Ignacio. The garden is empty of anyone and anything except the birds. This time of the morning seems reserved for the tiny brown sparrows who hurry to make quick work of their search until the moment when the bully blue jays shoo them away. He takes the folded paper out of his back pocket and studies it.

Just before ten o'clock, he walks to the lounge for the "singalong." Mel isn't much for singing, by himself or with anyone else, but this will help eat up his morning.

After the singalong, he drinks a cup of tea and pretends to be interested in a conversation Sid insists on drawing him into about reforming immigration quotas. Back to the dining room for lunch, again with the insufferable Sid, and after that to his room to tend to his teeth and take a nap. When he wakes, he looks again at the schedule of daily activities, checks the time on his clock radio and starts down the hall to the lounge.

Story Time is led by a young woman whose enduring smile makes the best of a plain face framed by curtains of lank brown hair. Not much to look at, although she has a good voice for reading. He's wedged into a corner of one of the uncomfortable sofas. Something isn't right in his mouth. He'd missed a piece of food when he brushed his teeth. His tongue worries the grain-sized bit between two molars.

"This is a story by one of this country's greatest writers," the young reader says. "One of the *world's* greatest writers. Alice Munro." An appreciative sigh goes up from the female members of the small audience. She begins to read and Mel listens for a while, but doesn't understand the story and, besides, it's set somewhere in rural Ontario and so means nothing to him. He's never been much of a reader.

He touches his index finger to the piece of plastic in his ear and turns down the volume on his hearing aid. He must remember to buy more batteries for the device. They never last longer than two or three weeks. Over the reader's shoulder, he can see the trees and grounds. When the young woman finishes the story, Mel offers polite applause along with the rest of the gathered residents.

He eats a cookie and drinks more tea. Then dinnertime, and more food, with the annoying Sid. When that ordeal is complete, he walks to his room and lies on his too-soft mattress, head propped up by the too-hard pillows. Why hadn't he thought to pack his own feather pillow when he moved out of his house? Too late to ask anyone now of its whereabouts. It will be long gone, taking up some lonely space in a rural landfill. He'll ask his daughter, Anne, to help him buy a replacement for it as well as getting new batteries for his hearing aid.

The television remote rests on top of his flat stomach, rising and falling with each of Mel's breaths. The red dot on the clock radio blinks at him from the bedside table. At some point he drifts off, the noise and the light from the television set no impediment.

≈

The piece of toast, coated in shimmering strawberry jam, lands in the centre of Sid Dodge's chest. That exact placement was not Mel's intended target, but both time and timing had betrayed his eighty-four-year-old arm. He had aimed for his tablemate's face. Now he must settle for the triangle-shaped brooch decorating Sid's tie.

"What the hell? What the hell?" Sid's voice grows louder with every repetition.

At tables around the room, fingers dig into ears, turning up or turning down the volume on hearing aids. Others sit with pained expressions on their faces.

"What's he saying?" echoes around the room.

"Tie was a gift from my granddaughter," Sid says.

The fuss has brought Sheila, the manager of the Residences, to their table.

"Do we have a problem here?" she says.

The crease running between her eyes is deeper than usual this morning. At a social event for residents not long ago, Sheila had confided to Mel that her preferred tipple was rum and Coke with a slice of lime ("For the Vitamin C, you know.") He thinks she may have overindulged her vitamin intake last night.

"He threw it at him. That one. We all saw it." Millie Butts is the dining room's unofficial news announcer. "Just picked it up off his plate and let Sid have it." Her voice fills the crowded space. Everyone can see which bullseye the red-tipped arrow of her finger is pointing at.

"Mel Clarey did it," she says. "We all saw him. Ask anyone."

Mel crosses his arms in front of his chest, his face hard and unsmiling.

"Now, Mr. Clarey," Sheila says. "This isn't like you." Some other members of the staff talk to the residents as though they are in a day care, every word loud and slow. Not Sheila. She doesn't condescend to them and so they listen when she speaks.

"I didn't catch that, Mr. Clarey. You'll have to speak up."

"I said I want a divorce." Mel summons his best voice. He wants to make sure Millie Butts doesn't miss a word.

"You want a…"

"From this guy," and he gestures at Sid Dodge. "This is your official notice, Sheila. I'm calling it quits with Sid and me. It's over. I want to move on. I've had it."

"Well, they're not putting you here." It's Millie Butts again. "Mel has no right to shut Sid up just because he doesn't like what he's hearing. My first husband died so people can say what they want. And he was just a boy."

As if on cue, her words move a chorus of diners to signal their own thoughts on the matter.

"Not here either."

"Not with us."

"Millie's right."

Sheila picks up Mel's plate of scrambled eggs and hooks her other hand under Mel's arm.

"Come with me," she says.

≈

They stand at the counter of Mel's tiny kitchenette. With his fork he prods the lump of congealed eggs grown cold during the three-minute walk down the hallway to his room.

"Mind if I sit?" Sheila settles into the only chair available without waiting for Mel's reply, an armless piece of institutional furniture meant neither to offend nor comfort. It will do for now. She only wants to take some the weight off her left foot and its troublesome bunion.

"Now tell me what happened, please." Without taking her eyes away from Mel, she eases off her left shoe and flexes her toes. Out of its prison, the painful foot is bearable. "What were you thinking?"

"I can't stand that guy. I told you already. I want to sit at another table."

"Well, Mr. Clarey, you're aware of our policies regarding seating in the dining room. Minor disagreements are inevitable, but we can't go moving people around because somebody takes a notion that's what they'd like, can we? You know what we'd have then, don't you?" Her voice is steady, calming. "Don't you? That's right." She nods her head with its limp greying hair, up and down, in small but definitive movements. "Chaos. Hmmm? We'd have absolute chaos. A mess. You're a smart man, Mr. Clarey. You ran a business. You understand give and take. Don't you?"

Mel doesn't want the scrambled eggs. For one of the few times in his life, he's refusing to eat what's on a plate in front of him. This is what people must mean when they say they've lost their appetite.

"We had a disagreement. All right? He's going on about George Bush being some kind of hero for invading Iraq. George

Bush is an idiot." He can't leave the scrambled eggs alone and pushes the yellow mess around the plate. "Sid Dodge is an idiot. Anybody asked, I would've said so. I just want a little peace and quiet when I eat. Is that too much to ask for?"

It isn't just the sound of Sid's voice and his inane comments. The way bits of food stick in his moustache and dribble onto his tie disgust Mel. And he hates the sound of Sid's dentures, clicking and sliding in his mouth as he chews and lectures. Mel wouldn't be surprised to learn that George Bush also spits food crumbs onto his plate as he talks. Bush and Sid deserve each other, and when no one else cared enough to tell Sid to shut up, that's when he threw the toast at him.

"We know it's okay to disagree," Sheila says. She crosses her legs, left over right, and massages the toes of her left foot. "That can be healthy. But we don't do it this way, do we, Mr. Clarey? If we move people to other tables whenever they have a bit of a…"

Mel tosses the fork onto the plate. The sound it makes is satisfying, dangerous even.

"I don't want to move tables," he says. "I want to move out. I don't want to be here anymore."

Sheila slips her foot into its narrow-toed shoe, sighing as she feels the sharp pinch. She'll call the podiatrist's office today. She's been promising her daughter for the last month that she'll do that, although he'll only tell her what she already knows. Lose a few pounds and buy sensible shoes.

"Your family, Mr. Clarey" she says. "They love you. They want you in a place where you're looked after, where you've got friends, people to talk to. Stimulation."

"I had plenty of stimulation where I was."

"You were in a great big house, going up and down stairs you couldn't manage anymore. What if you fell? You couldn't drive your car anymore, couldn't shop for yourself, couldn't mow the lawn, couldn't shovel the sidewalk."

"I did okay."

"You remember those visits you made here, don't you? With your daughter…"

"Anne."

"…That's right, Anne. Took you three times before you understood this is the best place for you to be. Remember?"

Mel remembers. Three visits; the first one more than a year ago. He'd agreed to visit Shorefront Residences to placate his daughter, who'd been so insistent. Anne had driven him to suburban Bedford, outside the city proper and away from everything familiar to him. They sat in Sheila's tidy office with its framed photos and tasteful seascapes on the walls, perched on hard chairs, and listened to her talk about all the facility had to offer. A tour of the premises was unnecessary since Mel had already made up his mind that he wouldn't leave his house.

There was a second visit, again at Anne's insistence, and Mel's second refusal to consider moving into the Residences.

Anne, an experienced litigator, recognized the need to change tactics. She would wait and let the right moment come to her and it arrived, as she knew it would, as inevitable as the final April snow.

Mel had developed a cold that had turned into pneumonia. He was weak in ways he never imagined he could be; feeble and tired of body, tired of mind. He had the energy of a wounded bird and the moment he was shown, for the third time, into the Residences' model suite, all he wanted to do was lie down on the bed and sleep.

"He caved," Anne said that evening to her husband, Norman. "Ha." Another strategic success. "I knew if I waited long enough…"

Mel moved into the Shorefront Residences less than a month later. He sold his house to Anne and Norman, the rambling three-storey on Vernon Street where he and Kitty had raised their children. The sale money topped up his various pensions and allowed him to meet the high monthly costs of living at Shorefront. There were some testy exchanges between Anne and her siblings about their inheritance being drained away until she reminded them that their father would have to live to a very great age to go through all the money. There will be enough left over when the time comes, she assured them. As a small reprimand for their selfishness, she thought to add: "We have to think of Dad first."

Mel pushes away his plate of cold eggs.

"You're right, Sheila. I didn't make a fuss when I moved in. I was sick then. I'm better now. So I'm making a fuss."

"Do we need to have a sit-down with Anne?"

"Call her. Call anyone you want. Just move that turkey, Sid Dodge, or let me eat my meals here, in peace, in my room."

"You know we don't cater, Mr. Clarey. We only do that for the second floor and I'm pretty sure you don't want to be included among them, those poor dears. You're meant to mingle, get along with your fellow residents. That's what the Shorefront experience is all about. What our stakeholders pay for. You know that."

"I'm well aware what I'm paying for, thank you very much. And the privilege of being bombarded by bits of Sid Dodge's brain was never part of the deal."

Sheila pushes her hair back from her forehead. For so long, Mel Clarey has been off her radar. He is one of the least likely of her clients to offend or cause trouble.

"Well, just say, Mr. Clarey, and I'm not promising anything here, but just say we could do what you want. Is there another table…"

"Yeah. That couple." He sees them so clearly. What are their names? They'd had a nice conversation not long ago. What had they talked about? He might have gone to school with one of them. "The…you know the ones I mean."

"I'm afraid I…what do they look like?"

"You know. Not too tall. Kind of average, I guess. My age or so."

"First names? Last name?"

Mel's hand grips the fork as if holding it tighter will squeeze the names out of his memory like toothpaste out of the tube.

"Robert?" Yes, he's sure the man's name is Robert. No, not Robert. "Donald maybe. And hers is…oh, I don't know. I forget. They were nice enough though."

"That doesn't really narrow it down for me, Mr. Clarey. Maybe a few more details when you remember them. That would be helpful."

"It'll come to me. I'm just upset is all."

"Well, in the meantime, I'll see what I can do," Sheila says. The call to the podiatrist's office has already slipped down her list of the day's priorities.

25

Lawrie Shine drives the short distance from Halifax to Bedford to visit Mel three days a week. Monday, Wednesday, Friday. They had been boys together, known loss and war, and now they are old together. Through it all, they have remained best friends; steadfast, supportive and loyal.

They walk, or sit outside, in the good weather. When there is rain or snow or high winds, they spend their time inside, although never in Mel's room.

"It's not comfortable in there," he's told Lawrie. "No real place to sit and relax, you know." What they do not say is that Mel's room is too much a reminder to both of them of how small his life has become.

So on the bad weather days they look for quiet corners of the building where they're not likely to be interrupted. This being Halifax, though, with its centuries-old warren of family and business connections, there is always another resident in search of company and usually curious in the way that the people of that city are. They stop to ask after a member of Mel's or Lawrie's family or to reminisce about a moment that no one except Lawrie seems able to recall with much clarity these days. And from time to time, someone says to Mel: "I've been meaning to ask. That sister of yours. The one with the red hair. You ever find out what happened to her?"

Mel has a standard response to such intrusions. "No," he says and turns his head away, ignoring any follow-up questions.

Lawrie, always the stickler, and never more so than when it concerns the subject of Edie, points out that her hair was a very particular shade.

"Not red," he says. "Chestnut." And he finds some other thing to say to move the conversation or the person along. Lawrie's smile belies his annoyance whenever Edie's name is mentioned in conversation with all the thought of a piece of litter dropped to the ground.

Other times, the two of them wander through the Shorefront complex. Mel points out areas of interest: the modest library, the nearest washroom if you don't feel like walking to your room or if timing is the issue. Mel also knows the places to avoid.

He points to the door with the sign that reads Crafts Room. Inside, three women, white heads bent, study a jigsaw puzzle or perhaps the top of the table.

"I'm sure that's where they put you right before you die," Mel says. "So if anybody suggests a visit to the crafts room..."

They ride the elevator to the third floor and inspect the gym and cards room for activity.

"What about the second floor?" Lawrie asked during one of his first visits.

"Oh, strictly enemy territory as long as you're still upright. You don't want to get caught wandering through there. The bed cases. You know. No telling what might happen there. Are you sure you don't want to move in here?"

"You won't be offended if I say you lack your father's genius for salesmanship?" Lawrie said and they moved on.

They know Lawrie isn't going to join Mel in this place. Mel is here for the duration, as long as that is. His oldest child resists his talk of another move.

"Where to?" Anne had asked him when he'd recently raised the subject of relocating. "Where will you go?"

"Lawrie's building," he told her. "A whaddya-call-it, a condo. Everything on one level. Like here, but more space for me. And better company."

"You can't afford Mr. Shine's building," Anne said. "And, besides, you don't own any furniture anymore. You'd have to buy all new, and what's the point of that?" Her message was clear: you won't live long enough to get any use out of it. Mel could tell from the look on his daughter's face that even she regretted the bluntness of her remark.

≈

The day after the incident with the toast and Sid Dodge, the sun shines and the outside air is warm. Mel and Lawrie follow their regular route on the boardwalk along the shore of the Bedford Basin. In the distance, an enormous container ship, looking like a skyscraper floating on its side, brings in cargo. Ducks and gulls crowd the water's edge, protesting as they're forced to make way for walkers and runners. A short parade of mothers pushing strollers with infants and toddlers wheels by into chatty oblivion. A lone runner brushes past them and on the surrounding grass, dogs chase whatever it is dogs find to chase. After the isolating months of winter and the weeks of glum spring skies, the clear blue and gold of early summer is a gift, repeated every year, to be sure, although never any less a surprise to the people who live here and never any less welcome with its memories of other days.

These two old men, Mel and Lawrie, are the last of those who knew Edie best. They carry the memory of her and the mystery of her death like pieces of their skin. It covers them, insulates them, and is ingrained in their living cells. They are, when it comes to Edie, each other's sole and final comfort.

Mel looks up at the expanse of sky and follows the white line of a jet contrail. Lawrie is saying something to him.

"What?"

"My shoe," Lawrie says. "Lookit. See what they did?"

Lawrie walks with a cane. It keeps him steady and upright after hip replacement surgery. Mel believes his friend uses it because it lends him the distinguished air that a retired judge should have. It was carved specially for him by a carpenter he'd once done some legal work for and has a smooth rounded bird's head that his hand curls over. It suits him and his carefully put-together outfit of tan pants, brown check jacket, white shirt open at the collar, and all topped by the halo of snow-white hair. Between the cuff of his pants and the shoes, there is a glimpse of Lawrie's sartorial signature argyle socks, these ones patterned in red and black.

"Lookit." He shifts his weight onto his cane and lifts his right foot. "The shoe repair guy in my building. Built up the heel. I'm on the level again." Lawrie came out of hip surgery with the repaired leg half an inch longer than the other.

"If they'd done the job right in the first place…"

"Meh." Lawrie paws the air with his hand. "They told me when I get the other one done they'll even it all up. Thing is, I can hardly wait. You know us Shines. Hip replacements aren't so much a privilege as a birthright. I feel a little cheated I've only got the two to replace. Maybe my knees will give way."

"You always did look on the bright side."

They stroll like this for a while, talking about health issues, children, grandchildren. There are lapses when they say nothing at all.

During more than eighty years of friendship each one of their conversations has been a needle's stitch, each one inconsequential as a single loop. Collected over the decades, these stitches of experience, friendship, sorrow, and day-to-day living have formed the tapestry that is their lives.

They sit on a bench and rest until the moment when one of them says, "Well, shall we?" and they turn back toward the Shorefront Residences to look for a cup of tea and, if they get there in time, a cookie to accompany it.

26

The knocking wakes Mel from his afternoon nap. He shuffles across the grey carpet, opens the door and stares at the pleasant-faced woman in front of him.

"Your daughter's here, Mr. Clarey."

"My daughter?" Mel rocks, unsteady, and holds onto the door frame for balance. "Are you my daughter?"

"No, I'm not your daughter. She's waiting for you in the sunroom, dear. Let's put on your shoes and we'll walk there together."

In the last month, the weather has turned from a cool June to a July that's warmer than usual. His feet swell in this kind of hot and humid air, so he takes fewer and fewer long walks with Lawrie.

"Ow." The shoes pinch his swollen feet. Each step is painful. He puts one of his hands on the woman's arm.

"What did you say we're doing?"

"Your daughter, Mr. Clarey. She needs to talk to you about something."

"What's her name?"

"You don't know your own daughter's name?"

"Pardon?"

"Anne. Your daughter's name is Anne."

"Anne." He turns the word over, trying to find the place where it fits. The word has a funny sound. If he says it slowly, drags it out, it sounds like a baby starting to cry.

Annnnnnnhhhhhhh… But this daughter can't be a baby. They wouldn't leave a baby alone.

There is no sun in the sunroom. Outside, clouds cover the sky. Mel's eyes close against the bright overhead fluorescents as he enters the room. He stays like that until he's sure it's safe to open them and when he does, he sees a blonde-haired woman sitting in one of the chairs, staring at something in her lap. She must be praying because she's holding a small black prayer book and reading the passages. Her thumb gently strokes the page.

"You've been to mass?"

Anne looks up, startled.

"I've what?"

"You've got your missal. Did you just come from mass?"

"It's my Blackberry, Dad. Good God. Church. Why'd you say that? I mean, the last time I was in a church was for Mom's funeral."

"Your mother died?"

She pushes her hair off her face and hooks a strand behind an ear. A quiet release of breath escapes her lips. "Oh."

Mel lowers himself into a chair. "What did you say?"

"Nothing, Dad. Forget it. Nobody's died."

She's familiar, and attractive, but tired, maybe even a little unhappy. The blunt edge of her straight hair brushes the tops of her shoulders. The blonde colour doesn't look entirely natural. She tugs at the tight black jacket she's wearing. She could stand to lose a few pounds around the middle.

"They told me my daughter's here."

Mel hears her sighing sound again.

"That's me, Dad. I'm your daughter."

He studies her face, so familiar. Every time he's about to find that place inside his head where she might belong, it slips away. So familiar. What is it? If only she'd stop fiddling with the little book she's holding so that he could get a good look at her. If she'd sit still for a moment, he could remember where he's seen her before.

"Do you really think…" Mel begins to say.

Anne looks up at him. "What?"

"…that I'm old enough have children?"

There's that look he sees on faces; frozen, eyes opened wide, mouth moving and staying like that until it shuts. Then the eyes go back to normal and whoever it is, swallows. Why do people react like that when he talks?

"You have three children, Dad."

"Three?" It's useless for him to search this woman's face for any more clues to her identity. Mel looks around the room. Another woman walks past the doorway. Her black hair is tied back and braided into a complicated bun. She wears a dark skirt that reaches to mid-calf, a white blouse buttoned to her neck and a cherry-coloured cardigan. Her feet are shod in beige crepe-soled shoes that squeal with every step she takes over the smooth tiled floor. She carries a black leather handbag, its handle looped over her forearm, the way the Queen carries hers. She flutters a hand and smiles at Mel.

"*Buonasera, Signora Guerriero,*" Mel calls out and gives her a friendly wave.

The woman laughs, touches her hand to her mouth, and walks on.

"What'd you say to her?" Anne says.

"I said 'good afternoon' to Mrs. Guerriero."

"Where'd you learn that?"

"Well, I was in Italy, you know. Picked up a bit of the lingo. Just a few words. It's only polite to be able to say hello in someone else's language. Makes them feel you're interested in them."

"Jeez, Dad, that was sixty years ago."

What did she mean, "sixty years"? When does sixty years begin? When does it end? He was only being polite, putting Mrs. Guerriero at ease, making her chuckle. What had he done that was so wrong and so upsetting to this blonde woman?

Anne runs her hand over her forehead and along the side of her face.

"You have children, Dad. There are three of us. I'm the oldest and my name is Anne."

"I see. Thank you. And the…" How many did she say? "The others?"

"Susan. She's just younger than me. Then Charlie. The only boy." Her voice is controlled, her pronunciation precise, but Mel hears something else. Maybe he was right about what he sees in her face. Maybe she is unhappy and doesn't know how to say that. The poor girl.

"I have three children, then?"

"Yes, Dad. Three of us."

Mel lets his gaze wander around the room again. The large fern in the corner isn't happy there. The tips of its fronds are turning brown. Not enough water or perhaps too much water. Maybe, like this woman, this plant isn't happy either. His mother tried keeping ferns in the front room of their house and they turned brown, too. When Theresa voiced her displeasure about having to sweep up the dead bits from the floor, Mary gave up on them and went back to the tidy reliability of African violets.

"These children of mine. How old are they?" Mel asks.

"I'm fifty-eight. Susie's fifty-six and Charlie just turned fifty-three."

"I see. They're very old. For children, I mean. Aren't children very young?"

Anne waves a hand around, her mouth works, opens and closes. "They're…we're…" Her hand drops into her lap like a discarded weight. "Doesn't matter, does it? Look, I've got to talk to you about money and about Susie and Charlie. Maybe it isn't such a good day for this. I can't waste much more time here. I've got to get back to the office…"

"You have an office? What do you do there? Do you answer the phones? My sister does that."

"No." It's a short bark of a word. "I'm not a secretary. I'm a lawyer. And a goddamn good one. Why do you have so much trouble accepting that?"

Why is she talking to him this way? He's done or said something to upset her, but he doesn't know what it is. He pats the top of his head, smoothing his white hair, the way a parent soothes a fussing child. Something is beginning to feel not right about any of this. And there it is again. Just like the other day. He wants to cry.

"I'm sorry," he says. He feels the tightness in his throat and the stinging in his eyes. He can't stop what's happening to him.

"Dad. Dad, please." Anne leans towards him and takes one of his hands. Mel can feel her trembling. "I'm sorry I spoke like that. I don't know what to say anymore when you do this. So just listen to me. Okay? Can you do that? I really need you to snap out of this. Please.We have to go over some things. Focus for a minute. I know it's not easy, but try. Okay?"

He nods his head, unable to utter any word. If he opens his mouth, he's afraid a loud wailing sound might come out.

She sits back in her chair, brushes her skirt, runs a hand across her face. "You remember you gave me power of attorney?"

Mel doesn't know what she's talking about, although the way she's acting frightens him, so again he nods his head.

"Good. Well, you know I always tell you anything I do because A, I should and B, so you don't feel left out. Right?"

He moves his head up and down.

"Great. That's wonderful. See? Just focus. So I only need to tell you that I've written a couple of cheques for Susie and Charlie. They're both a little hard up at the moment and I thought this might tide them over until…well, whenever they need more. They know it's coming out of their share of the estate." Her voice drops. "When the time comes."

Anne is back on track, doing what she does best, explaining, winning a case. Her voice has lost its anxious timbre. She is going over a court process with a client.

"You understand what I'm saying, don't you?"

Listening to her speak calms Mel. He wants to make sure this woman leaves believing that he cares about what she's said. That's the polite thing to do, after all. He nods his head.

"Where do they live? My children?"

Her small black book makes a buzzing sound. She squints at it. Her voice drops again, faint and faraway sounding.

"Susie's here in Halifax. Charlie's out in BC."

"What do they do?"

"Susie's an actress."

"An actress? In the movies, you mean? My sister…"

"Theatre. Local stuff. Some TV."

His sister Edie loves going to the movies.

"She's very good, very busy. As an existence, it's pretty marginal, though. So we help. Charlie? Charlie's a carpenter." She utters a short laugh. "Carpenter. He installs kitchen cabinets. When he's not smoking BC Bud. The work's not what you'd call consistent. Unfortunately, the dope is."

"Are they happy?"

A look of surprise crosses Anne's face. He's been asking more and more of these odd questions. The most frequent topic of conversation these days among her friends is their parents' failing memories, who has been diagnosed with Alzheimer's and who is merely struggling with the expected decrepitude of old age. They all fear that they see their own future in a parent's face or hear it in a voice.

"I don't know," she says. "I don't know if they're happy. I never asked. Maybe. I hope so."

"Are you happy?"

She smiles. "Why do you want to know that all of a sudden? I'm okay. Same husband, same kids, same job. It's not too bad."

"So you're happy."

Anne stands and tugs at the too-tight jacket. "I have to get back to the office."

Mel extends his hand to her. "Very nice to have met you," he says. The impeccable Clarey manners, so ingrained, as responsive as a thump with the little rubber hammer to the tender spot below the kneecap.

Anne sighs, stoops and kisses Mel's forehead. "You take care. I'll see you soon. Love you, Dad."

"Yes. Right." She shakes the hand that's been offered to her, holding it longer than Mel thinks necessary to say goodbye to a stranger, and she leaves the room.

Mel continues to sit. What a peculiar thing to have happen in the middle of his afternoon.

He looks out the window and watches the blonde woman walk along the sidewalk to a bright red car. She's holding the little prayer book to her head. Her lips are moving. She must be saying a prayer. What a curious obsession she has with that book. She is so familiar.

Voices drift in to him from another room. As he shifts in his chair he feels something in his back pocket. He pulls out the folded sheet of paper with the day's schedule.

14.30-15:00 "STORY TIME" IN RESIDENTS' LOUNGE—TEA AND COOKIES WILL BE AVAILABLE.

He lifts himself out of his chair and walks towards the voices. Cups, saucers, an urn filled with tea and a plate of cookies are on a table. He looks at them for a while, absorbing, understanding at last what it is he must do. He pours a little milk into a cup, adds the tea, balances one cookie and then another on the saucer and sits down. The plain-faced woman with the melodic voice is reading. Mel looks around the room at the heads tilting toward her, straining to make out what she's saying. One or two residents hold a cupped hand to an ear. The tea is good. A cup of hot tea in the afternoon always revives him.

Mel looks at the clock on the wall. Two thirty-seven. Anne said she was going to visit him today. Where is she? She's usually so dependable. Must have got caught up with something important at her office. She's so busy these days, never slows down. She said she needed to discuss some money business with him. If she's too busy to come here, perhaps she'll phone him later and that's fine with him because he feels as though he's come out of a deep sleep and hasn't fully woken up yet. He can't remember getting up from his nap or walking from his room to the lounge.

His oldest child is attentive, organized and independent. She always has been. He and Kitty never had to tell Anne anything twice. Not like Susie, who only wanted what she wanted. And not at all like Charlie, who never seemed to be entirely present whenever he was spoken to. Anne was never a worry. He and Kitty were so proud of her. Mel shouldn't be fretting over his grown children, about whether or not they can feed themselves, and yet that's what he does. Susie means well and is always sweet to him when they see each other, bubbling over with all kinds of excitements, but she doesn't stand still for a minute, always distracted. Mel used to count himself lucky if he ran into her at the grocery store. And he hasn't seen Charlie for years and only hears from him when his son needs money. Thank God for Anne.

"What's she going on about today?" Mel whispers to the man sitting beside him.

"Something about Paris."

"Paris? Why Paris?"

"Seems the writer lives there," the man says.

"Hunh."

Mel ignores the story and wonders if he has the energy to get up to fetch more tea and cookies. The man sitting next to him, what is his name? They'd had a conversation the other day or week about Italy. He had served in another regiment so they'd missed each other back then. Instead, they met as old men, memories faded or failed, never sure what was left to talk about.

"Don't look now, Mel, but the Vespers woman is giving you the eye. Showing off a little leg, too."

In the big armchair, big enough and just yielding enough for someone to fall back into and feel comfortable, Ella Vespers's head slumps, tilted in their direction. Her eyelids droop while the skirt of her dress rides up to reveal a stockinged knee.

"Been a while since she's seen two such good-looking guys round here, I guess. Can't help herself."

Mel laughs, not loud, but he's making a noise and his shoulders shake. The tea slops over the rim of his cup and onto the saucer.

"Maybe we should come here more often. I didn't know the pickings were so good," his neighbour says.

"Please." The plain-faced woman stops reading to address at them. "I'm afraid I'll have to ask you two to leave if you can't pay attention. You're disrupting the reading for the others."

Ella Vespers stirs in her chair and smiles.

"Over so soon?" she says. "Such a sweet story."

27

"I've given this some thought, Mr. Clarey," Sheila says to Mel. She moves papers from one corner of her desk to another. A brochure for Weight Watchers falls onto the floor. She grunts as she bends to pick it up.

In the days since the toast-throwing incident, meals in the residents' dining room have been tense affairs for everyone except Mel. The silence that descends on the room when he takes his place at the table with Sid is a bit of heaven for him.

"Now, Mr. Clarey." Sheila taps the manila folder on the desk in front of her with the tip of a company souvenir pen. "You are an exemplary resident. You're the thinnest file we've got here. You also know that I run a tight ship. That I'm partial to my rules and I'm happiest when everyone follows them. However…"

The faint hum in Mel's ears might be the whisper of Sheila's electronic gadgets, the room's air conditioner, or perhaps the battery in his hearing aid needs replacing again. He tugs at his right ear lobe, hoping to interrupt the buzz until Sheila starts speaking again.

"Because you are, because you have been, such a good resident and cause us so little trouble…" and she pauses again.

Mel's gaze drops and he can see the toes of her feet just under the front cover of her desk. She's kicked off her shoes. The static swish of one stockinged foot rubbing against the other joins the general room hum. Sheila's good at her job, and wandering off the path of her prescribed rules and attitudes is difficult for her.

The wriggling feet are the only sign to him of the agitation she feels. She must have learned by now that a change of direction, a correction of course, can head off bigger problems.

"I'm going to give you a choice, Mr. Clarey." Under the desk, her feet come to rest, soles flat on the floor. She stops fidgeting with the pen. "You can eat your meals in your room, all right? Not something we're set up to deal with, but in your case…"

"That would be…"

"I'm not done, Mr. Clarey. *Or. Or* you give the dining room another go. Where I'd only ask that you try your best to get along at another table."

The first time Mel met Sheila he thought she must have been very pretty once, a "looker," as they called girls in his day. Marriage and motherhood and their sacrifices had smudged her prettiness, some days almost erased it entirely, but she was still an attractive woman. From time to time, the engaging face of · the younger Sheila emerged to be admired, and remembering this softens Mel's stubbornness. He had made his point about Sid Dodge and established himself as a person who insisted on being heard. He decides, in that moment, that there is nothing to be gained in complicating Sheila's life any more than he already has. He will let Sheila know that he is a reasonable man.

"I'd like to…" he says. "I'd like to return to the dining room, please, Sheila."

"A very good choice, Mr. Clarey." Her smile is genuine. Mel has pleased her. He's sure that in a desk drawer she keeps a list and at the top of the page, in Sheila's tidy hand, is written "Potential Problems." Mel had had one just like that during his years in business. A neat line will be drawn through his name as he leaves her office today.

"Could I ask though…" Mel puts an index finger to his chin and shifts his gaze to a spot over Sheila's shoulder as though he's actually given some thought to what he's about to say and not the truth, which is that he's making this part up as he goes along. He doesn't want to be seen as a pushover. He takes his time, lets his eyes wander over a framed series of photographs of tots, grandchildren probably, hanging on the wall.

"Rather than you running the risk of me bothering a new group of people…" he says and pauses again.

Sheila taps her cheek with the company souvenir pen. Under the desk, her feet are moving again.

"Rather than that…"

"Yes, Mr. Clarey?"

"Well, you see, I really don't want to be the cause of any more trouble for you. What if I don't get along at the new table either? There's always that risk, of course. So I'm wondering if it might be better for everyone concerned if I sit by myself?"

"Not share, you mean."

"My own table. My point precisely, Sheila."

"I don't know how that will look."

"I don't understand."

"What if others suddenly want to do the same thing?"

Mel's shoulders twitch, not so much a shrug, but enough to let Sheila know that he finds her argument to be without much merit.

"Who else has asked you lately? I guess I missed the stampede to your office."

"I mean you'll be giving them ideas."

Mel wants to laugh at her. The last new idea that bunch had was the decision to go from belts to elastic waistbands.

"The only thing they'll notice, Sheila, is the peace and quiet. Otherwise…" And this time his shrug is extravagant, bringing his stiff shoulders close to his ears. A smile creases his face.

There has always been more of his father's talent for bargaining in him than he was ever given credit for.

≈

At lunchtime, Sid Dodge moves to Millie Butts's table, which suits everyone, in particular Millie Butts. Since Gerald Callaghan died and presented her table with an empty chair and an open opportunity, she's been eyeballing Sid as a possible replacement for Gerald's attentions. Ever the romantic, Millie believes that love is always ripe for blossoming, even over a plate of tuna melts in the dining room of the Shorefront Residences.

Sheila arranged for a small round bistro table and chair to be taken out of a storage closet and placed by a window. Mel sits there with his back to the rest of the room. From this spot, he can see the front of the building and watch visitors come and go. Here, he absorbs his first moments of real contentment since moving into the Residences.

The dust-up with Sid Dodge has made Mel a target for the attentions of other diners seeking easy distraction or entertainment. And his isolation at the single table has freed them to talk about him as though he's not there or that overnight he's been rendered stone deaf. Because of this, in the enclosed world of the Shorefront Residences, he and his ancient history are once again headline news.

Millie Butts's voice from a nearby table catches his attention. It's rumoured that her last husband starved himself to death rather than spend any more of his pain-filled final days in her company.

"You know the story about the sister, don't you?" she's saying. "So odd, that. But they always were an odd family, those Clareys. Very odd." In Halifax, the gossiped history of Edie's disappearance has a particular appeal to people of a certain age such as Millie Butts, those old enough to have a residual, although selective, memory of the time and the event.

"I knew them, you see. And the girl. A little. Quite excitable she was. Yes, very odd indeed. I always said something wasn't quite right there. We all thought so."

The little bistro table wobbles under Mel's touch. Millie Butts and her comments are his penance for upsetting the unwritten commandments regarding the dining room's order. He'd been too clever thinking he'd outsmarted Sheila, getting her to agree to his demand to sit alone rather than jumping at her offer to serve his meals in his room; a foolish old man playing by yesterday's rules.

His cleverness put him here, within earshot of every uninformed opinion in this room. The table's jerky movement stokes his agitation and his anger at the widow's ignorance. What does she know about his family? About his sister? She says she knew Edie "a little." She didn't know Edie at all, only knew about her and what people said.

If Edie had returned home all those years ago or if her body had been found, if there had been some determination of how and when and by whose hand she died, if she had died at all, then the public history of the Clareys would be spoken about in quite a different way. Rather than having to listen to the nonsense Millie Butts is spouting, Mel might hear solemn expressions of sympathy or see a furrowing of brows on the old faces. The enduring mystery of Edith Clarey still resonates as grief in the dwindling few who loved her. To strangers, the story with no conclusion invites only tantalizing speculation and theories. It confirms for them that something the Clareys did or didn't do, rather than a random act of bad luck or whatever else they want to call it, drove Edie away.

Mel grips the edges of the wobbly table. He wants to confront Millie Butts and bellow: "We didn't lose Edie the way you lose an umbrella, you know. We didn't lose my sister because we were careless. We didn't leave her on a park bench and forget to bring her home."

And yet, so many years on, people talk about his sister as though her worth to anyone, including her own family, is equal to that of a misplaced object. A person's grief frees up the bystander to peer and pry and parrot all sorts of nonsense. Edie lives on as fodder for the spontaneous observations of people who never knew her or loved her and never felt the weight of her loss.

Mel knows what Edie's disappearance did to the Clareys. It made them wild with grief and smothered them like a wet blanket. It hadn't made them odd. They were the most ordinary of families. Yet some people who didn't know them at all held them responsible for whatever it was that had happened. After he and Lawrie are gone, the direct line to the memory of Edie will be gone as well. Mel has always believed that one day he'll learn where she went that night, but the time left for that is growing shorter and he fears that no one will ever know the truth. All that will remain of Edith Clarey when he and Lawrie are gone will be a head-shaking puzzle, an historical footnote, a terrible personal pain reduced to a casual public curiosity.

When the priest makes his regular visit this week, Mel will confess to him his own unkind thoughts about Millie Butts. He's forgotten the young man's name, apple-cheeked, and exuding too much youthful spirit for Mel's idea of what a priest should be. What does this freshman understand about life in the Shorefront Residences? Only last week, Mel sat on one side of the portable screen the priest carries with him to create a jury-rigged confessional and explained how and why he used Sid Dodge as target practice for a piece of toast. He heard the start of a chuckle from the young man that became a longer than necessary clearing of his throat. What, Mel wanted to demand of him, did he expect from his geriatric parish? Admissions of bank robberies? Serial murders? Few of the Shorefront residents attend the weekly service to receive the wafer from the priest, even the ones Mel knows had been raised as Catholics. Perhaps they've forgotten the usefulness of faith. Mel will remain obedient to his faith when others have lost theirs.

A young woman, one of the breakfast servers, a little overweight and her uniform straining in a worrisome way over her breasts and across her hips, but the one with the nicest smile, puts down a bowl, a plate of toast, and a small dish holding three prunes.

"Morning, Mr. Clarey." Her voice, the chirp of a small bird, doesn't match her size.

"How are you today, dear?" On every shift, she asks the same question, but with a sincerity that Mel finds touching. And she's gone to the trouble of learning everyone's name.

"Okay. Fine. Thanks very much for asking."

"Oatmeal this morning, Mr. Clarey. Enjoy."

Oatmeal. This must be Wednesday. The morning oatmeal at the Shorefront Residences is always overcooked by some well-intentioned kitchen person who's probably been told it's easier for the residents to deal with when it's in a state of mush. Or they're just lazy and don't watch what they're doing.

"Make sure you put syrup on the oatmeal," another diner had advised him when he first arrived. "I hope you like syrup."

He eats his oatmeal and looks out of the window into the front parking area. No one comes or goes. The inside workers have arrived and it's too early for any residents to be outside. Not a good walking day. Will Lawrie be coming by? He can't remember. Oatmeal. Wednesday. Yes, Lawrie. Lawrie, the constant one. This is what his old age has brought him to, measuring his life against a series of losses, great and small, family and friends, until the only one left of the time that defined him is Lawrie.

Who does he remind himself of, sitting like this, alone at the window? His mother, holding vigil until the day Edie skips up the walk to the front door. Mary is gone. All the Clareys from that time are gone, except Mel. He is the lone sentinel, anticipating the familiar loping gait, the chestnut hair and the easy smile.

His father was the first of them to go. One day in early July 1959 and, by coincidence, his daughter's birthday, Charles was talking to Jack and Betty Shine on the sidewalk in front of their house. The air was filled with the scent of the trees lining their street. They talked about the most mundane and neighbourly things, weather and children and grandchildren. Charles said goodnight and turned to walk home. "He seemed so tired," Betty Shine later told Mel. Halfway across the street Charles stopped and fell to the ground. "Slowly, like he was melting," Mrs Shine said. The doctors determined the cause of death to be a stroke and hurried to assure the family that their father hadn't suffered. Mel and his brother Gus laughed out loud when the doctor said that. They couldn't help themselves. Charles had suffered plenty in his life and if his stroke hadn't caused him any further pain, well, that was only fair after all he'd been through. Charles was not quite seventy years old.

Mary never understood that her husband was gone for good. "He's at the office," she'd say, even when no one had asked after his whereabouts. She never questioned why Charles no longer ate at home or paused to ask how her day was going or came to their bed at night. She never let go of the idea that he was still there, maintaining his daily schedule of sleeping and rising and going off to work. Mary outlived her husband by fourteen years. Noble as a queen and silent as a ghost, she faded with each successive year after his death. Her life, begun as rich damask cloth, was reduced in her final days to the sheerest gossamer.

By Mary's side, to the end, was the faithful Theresa. After Mary's death, she and Mel packed up the Clarey house and got it ready for sale. He moved Theresa and her possessions into a nursing home, embarrassed to see that she owned so little. Whatever luck or toughness had ensured Theresa's survival the day of the Explosion kept her alive into her ninetieth year. When her time came, Mel and Gus took turns at the bedside and waited for her final breaths. Gus, who had been little more than a baby when Theresa first held him, performed the last rites over the dying woman. The thin black tattoo of scar running the length of her face had folded into a deep crease. She was buried near Mary in the Clarey family plot in the Catholic cemetery.

That cemetery is where Mel will be buried, beside his wife, the sad alcoholic Kitty, who never found her place in this foreign country. And he'll be near his brother. Gus, who had waited too long to tell his father that he wasn't meant to be a priest, spent his life tending congregations among the rural poor of New Brunswick. He did so with thoughtfulness and adherence to duty and faith, but no joy, and at the end he was a sad man incapable of accepting or understanding the course his life had taken.

There is no headstone or marker for Edith Clarey in the cemetery. No one spoke the words aloud, but every one of her family understood that to plant such a thing among other reminders of the dead meant they had given up the last vestige of hope that one day their daughter and sister would ever return. To do that would be a loss of faith in Edie herself.

Lawrie's parents are gone too, along with their cousin Theo, who had confounded all odds to find a new life in Halifax. He became the owner of a popular restaurant and later married for love. A man who seemed at peace with everything life had given to and taken from him, he always greeted Mel with a wide smile. Theo was well into his nineties when he died. Was there anyone who deserved happiness more, his friends had asked? No one deserved it more. And yet, his final few years were tormented by nightmares of his time in the wartime camps. In the end, memory had defied happiness.

Mel considers all of them as he sits at the wobbly table in the residents' dining room, gazing out the window. He wishes Lawrie were here right now so that he could express some of the anger he wants to direct at the woman who had called his family "odd." A century and a half of good work in this city, a respected business, decent lives, and their public legacy was that? Nothing of what had happened to the Clareys made them odd. They had lived their lives and had died the way people of their place and station had done for generations. The sole exception had been Edie. How to convince that Butts woman that she was so wrong? A task as futile as trying to make the argument to a colour-blind person that your eyes are green and not blue.

A passing vacuum cleaner bumps his chair. The room has emptied as he sat there. The cleaners and the servers want to get on with their day. Time for him to go. He takes the day's schedule out of his back pocket and studies it.

28

The summer sky threatens rain, so the two old friends drive to the Sunnyside Mall, where they walk the wide concourse and study the contents of the shop windows.

Mel stops at the shoe repair outlet. He buys laces, brown, twenty-four-inch, for a pair of shoes that Lawrie can't recall seeing him wear. Mel's purchase completed, Lawrie wanders over to the specialty candy shop.

"After all these years," he says, "all of a sudden all I want to eat is candy." The two of them are shocked at the prices of the brightly coloured jelly beans.

"Jelly beans, for Christ's sake," Mel says. "They're just jelly beans."

They leave the store with a small plastic bag filled with flavours of coconut, strawberry, espresso, roasted marshmallow.

Mel is tired. He never recovered his physical stamina after the bout with pneumonia last year and, today, he's struggling with the upset of the Butts woman talking about the Clareys being odd. He lets Lawrie steer him to a table inside one of the mall's coffee shops. Lawrie orders a large latte with whipped cream and caramel sauce on top and adds powdered chocolate from a shaker on the service table.

"Have a taste," Lawrie says and pushes the paper cup across the table toward Mel.

"I don't drink coffee. You know I don't." And Mel nudges the cup with his fingers.

"This isn't really coffee. It's like a milkshake warmed up. Try it." Lawrie holds the coffee out to Mel, who, with evident reluctance, takes it and sips.

"Yeah, well, okay. This isn't so bad." The whipped cream leaves a comical white moustache across Mel's top lip.

"Have some more. I always order too big," Lawrie says. He hopes a little caffeine might restore some of his friend's flagging energy.

Mel tries to explain to Lawrie about his new seating arrangement in the dining room. But the telling of it is taking time because he mixes up some names and forgets others. He wants to tell Lawrie something else, too, about a woman calling the Clareys odd. He can't remember why she said that, though, and so he lets it go.

Instead, Mel says, "I need to buy batteries. For my flashlight."

"Your flashlight?"

Lawrie's becoming forgetful. He shouldn't have to remind his friend of their regular nighttime routine of signalling to each other from their neighbouring bedroom windows.

"Mel," Lawrie says. "You know we haven't done that for quite a while." Lawrie's voice is soothing, measured, an observant man correcting the official record from his judge's bench.

"What do you mean?" There's no way Lawrie could forget what they were doing that night, the last night anything in their lives was normal. From their bedroom windows, they'd faced each other across the expanse of the street, and tapped out their messages. "Ahh." He taps his fingertips against his forehead. "You know, you're right. I remember."

"You see? Now have a little more of the coffee. Must be doing you some good."

Mel isn't paying attention to the cup of coffee.

"That was the last night, wasn't it? We didn't do the thing with the flashlights after that. Ever again. That's right. Because that was the night I saw Edie in the street with that damn bicycle and everything got so…screwed up after that."

Lawrie, who has been sipping at his coffee and dabbing at his upper lip with the stiff paper napkin, looks at his friend.

"You saw Edie? In the street? That night? What're you talking about?"

"Edie. My sister. You remember her. That's who I'm talking about. And then she went away. Just..." and he lifts a hand and waves it in front of his face. "Just disappeared. Like that." And his hand drops to his lap.

"Yes, I know what happened, Mel. But you say you saw Edie that night and you never said anything?"

"Because she told me not to tell anyone. It's a secret, she said."

"Tell what, Mel? What secret?"

"That she's going away. And that she'll come back. She says she'll always come back to me. She promises she will. Only I'm not allowed to tell anyone."

They sit at the table off to the side of the wide concourse. The morning traffic of mothers pushing strollers, and other pedestrians, passes by them, alone or in pairs, chatting, whispering, stopping to stare in windows or finger clothes on a rack. Anyone bothering to look at Mel and Lawrie might find them amusing in appearance, an ancient Mutt and Jeff in size, and little more. Even the most observant passerby wouldn't grasp the significance of the moment. The two now share a piece of information that once might have held a clue to one of the city's historic mysteries.

"Mel. Do you know what you're saying?"

"What do you mean? Course I know what I'm saying. Can we head back now?"

"Where did she go? Where did Edie go, Mel? You can tell me. Secrets don't matter anymore."

"Secrets always matter, Lawrie. They do for Edie and me, anyway. She never told me where she was going. Just left is all. If I knew where she was, don't you think I'd go get her? I mean, I miss her so much. She says she'll be back one day. So she will.

She always keeps her word. You know that. But I wish she'd come back because I do miss her. Can we go home now? I'm very tired."

Mel's thoughts have lost their way in the thicket between the past and the present. There will be no more details from him about Edie and that night.

They shuffle along the concourse, two commonplace figures lost among others in the mall; two old men, arm in arm for reasons of friendship and frailty. No one would guess that they had just shared a moment of remembrance of the time that had come to define their lives. The memory reminded them of the burden they carry, the mystery of what had happened to Edith Clarey.

Outside, rain spatters their faces. Mel says, "Why don't you stay for supper? Then you'll see where I sit now."

Lawrie fumbles with the keys to his car. "We should check with the powers that be about that."

"Oh, Theresa won't mind. You know there's always plenty of food. Those jelly beans. They aren't a meal, Lawrie. Theresa'll fix something for us."

The ride back to the residence is quiet. Only the rhythmic scrape of the windshield wipers against the glass keeps the two of them company.

≈

"Wait a second. I think I need to get something here."

Mel stops at the entrance to the mail room.

He takes the key ring out of his pocket and tries to match the shape of the numbers and letters etched on the piece of golden metal with the shapes on the squares in front of him.

Lawrie taps his finger on one of the small silver doors.

"What're you waiting for? It's not going to open for you."

Mel struggles to fit the key into the slot. He turns it to the left and pulls, then turns it to the right and pulls. The face of the box swings open.

"Always sticks a little," he says.

Lawrie helps him pull out the paper, envelopes, flyers jammed into the small space.

"Jesus, Mel. When's the last time you looked in here?"

"Well, you know what it's like. Some days you just don't think to do it. I guess I let it go for a while."

The two men walk down the long hallway, Mel clutching the mess of paper in his arms.

He doesn't have to search for the key to his door. He's been leaving it unlocked, in part because at times he forgets, other times he's afraid that if he does lock it he might not remember how to open it.

The soft mattress yields as he sits on the end of his bed. He places his mail beside him and picks up one piece, a colourful flyer for a pizza special and another, an offer for lower cell phone rates. He holds them out to Lawrie.

"Do I have to buy these?"

"No, Mel. You don't have to buy them. You can throw those out. They're just advertisements."

"I see." He doesn't see, though, not really. "I'm a little tired. If you don't mind, I'd like to lie down now."

"That's probably a good idea. Lock the door behind me, will you?"

Mel continues to sit after Lawrie leaves, his hand fanning the papers out over his bed. He hates not knowing what to do with things, simple things, like this mess. He compresses the paper into a pile and moves it to the top of his dresser. He'll ask his sister what to do. Edie'll tell him what to do with all of it when she comes by tomorrow. Being older, she knows more. She's good about that sort of thing.

29

The clock radio blinks at him. 7:55. The day's schedule is already folded neatly, precisely, and placed in the back pocket of his trousers. Five minutes to go before the walk down the hall to the dining room. Someone has left a disorganized heap of papers on top of his dresser.

He begins sorting, placing the flyers in one pile. Envelopes, possibly bills or notices of some kind, in another. He opens one of them. Someone's asking for money to help cure a disease and they've included what looks like a thousand little address stickers with his name and the street information for the Shorefront Residences. He doesn't want to give them money, although he feels he shouldn't keep the free address stickers without giving them a token amount. And throwing them out would be such a waste.

"Ahhh." This is too much to deal with.

Mel drops the envelope and the sheets of address stickers, along with the handful of colourful flyers, into the blue recycling box under the sink in his kitchenette.

One plain white envelope remains to be inspected. He looks at the handwriting and reads his name, his address, written with blue ballpoint in an uncertain cursive. In the upper left-hand corner, another name, and an address in Sydney, Cape Breton. R. Gillis, he reads. He says the name out loud. Who is R. Gillis and why would he be writing to him?

Mel glances at the clock. 8:01, it blinks at him. The letter will have to wait. He opens the door and starts down the hallway.

≈

The day never becomes clearer for Mel. This isn't one of Lawrie's regular visiting days. There are no phone calls from Anne or his other children, from anyone. A heavy fog has settled over the building and even though some of it dissipates during the morning, the sky remains grey and at noon rain begins to fall. He sits in the residents' lounge listening to others sing. He drinks tea and eats too many cookies and that upsets his stomach. He takes his midday meal alone at the small table by the window and in the afternoon he's back in the lounge to hear the plain-faced woman read a story about a family farming on the prairies. Later, a nap restores some of his energy, but he's back in his room as soon as he finishes his supper.

Sitting on the end of his bed, Mel bends over to untie his shoelaces. The effort leaves him weak. He puts his hands on his knees and pushes himself up to sitting and he stays like that until everything rights itself again. As he walked to his room that evening, his hand glided along the hallway's wooden railing for the first time.

He waits until his breathing is less laboured, until his heart ceases the worrisome pounding that happens when he's tired in this way. On top of the dresser he sees something white; an envelope, with handwriting on it and his name.

He pulls back a corner of the envelope and slips his finger inside, ripping it open. There are several sheets of folded paper, all covered in the same shaky handwriting.

"Dear Mel," it begins.

"I hope you don't mind this familiarity with your name. I am Raymond Gillis."

Raymond Gillis. Raymond Gillis. Mel can't place the name. It will have to join those other words that float around inside his head, looking for a place to settle.

"We've never met, although I remember seeing you a few times when you visited your father's business, when it was Clarey Glass and Paint. You were just a boy then. Your father loved nothing more than to take some of his precious time to show you around the office and warehouse. I always thought he was preparing you for the day you took his place there, when the two of us would work together, I hoped."

Mel had been in his father's office just last week for some special reason, although right now he couldn't say what that was. He enjoyed being in the big wood-panelled reception area with the large round wall clock. The place made him shiver with excitement, so close to the mysterious grown-up world of his family's business. Edie let him sit at her oak desk with all its drawers and secrets. She showed him the latest office contraptions and how to scroll paper into the typewriter and hammer his fingers into the keyboard as the two of them composed a letter to their father making the case for more weekly spending money. When Mel grabbed the ringing telephone and yelled into it: "Clarey Glass and Paint. You need something?" Edie doubled up and covered her mouth to smother her laughter. She wrestled the receiver from him and, struggling to control her voice, said: "This is Edith Clarey. How may I help you, please?" This time it was Mel who turned away to bury his mirth behind his hands. Edie is always so much fun.

"I worked as the bookkeeper for your father's business," the letter goes on. "I met your sister Edith there. It's about your sister's disappearance that I'm writing to you."

He says he knows my father. And Edie. But they don't talk to me about him.

"No soul now living has been privy to any of what I am about to tell you. I begin where I must in order for you to understand why events unfolded as they did."

What is this man going on about? Edie hasn't gone anywhere. Edie comes to visit me. Mel's heart is pounding. The paper makes a rustling noise as it shakes in his hand.

He folds the pages and forces them back into the envelope, opens the bottom drawer of his dresser and shoves the white package with its sheets of paper under the winter sweaters. He listens for any sounds that might remind him of where he is. He closes the drawer and glances over his shoulder at the clock radio blinking, comforting, calming. Mel places a hand against his chest and feels his heartbeat slowing, his breathing ease. Bed. Sleep. After that, everything will be better.

2005

30

Anne finds the white envelope in the bottom drawer of her father's dresser on a frigid day in early January, tucked away under the winter sweaters, presents from her, the ones she never saw Mel wear. She places the sweaters inside one of the green plastic garbage bags she brought with her and picks up the envelope.

She runs her thumb over the handwritten address. Someone old must have written this. In the left-hand corner there is a name. R. Gillis. Sydney, Cape Breton. She attended law school with a couple of Gillises, twins, who were from New Brunswick. It was a common enough name in Nova Scotia, one that wouldn't give a person pause to consider, in an idle way, "what's their story?" She doesn't recall any Gillis among her parents' friends, though. Maybe this was an old business acquaintance writing for, well, for what reason? What is this letter doing under these sweaters? In his last confused moments, Mel must have thought he was filing it as he might have done with a piece of correspondence during his working days. Perhaps he was hiding it. She'd never know.

The ball of regret Anne has felt since her father's death turns inside her again. She should have visited him more often last summer. No one could have known that it would be his last. He seemed healthy enough. She and her husband, Norman, had spent August at their summer house on the south shore. She could have asked Mel to come with them, but it was such a confusing time with the schedules of children and grandchildren and, anyway, didn't her father complain about the damp in these houses built so close to the ocean?

"He's one more level of chaos we don't need right now," she'd told Norman when he suggested they bring Mel with them. Norman had got on well with his father-in-law, had always found common ground for conversation with Mel and even remarked to Anne once that he found her father to be good company. Anne had shaken her head and rolled her eyes.

"I'll make it up to him when we get back to the city," she said. "And, besides, Susie says she'll visit him while we're away."

But her sister visited their father at the Residences only twice during Mel's last summer. She told Anne later she'd been preoccupied with rehearsing a new theatre production, and relying on the buses to take her all the way to suburban Bedford ate into her valuable time.

"What's done is done," she said and shrugged. "I can't let myself have negative thoughts these days. I need all my energy to be positive. And I'm done with blaming myself about anything to do with this family. Even if you do."

"If I do what? Blame you or blame me? What do you mean?"

"Oh, shut up," Susie said. "I'm not on trial."

Anne knows that Mr. Shine, Lawrie, kept up his regular visits. Maybe Lawrie's children are more attentive to their father than she and her sister and brother were to Mel. And maybe Susie was right. What's done is done. Move on.

Anne hadn't cried for her father the way she'd cried when her mother died. She had shed an obligatory tear or two for Mel. There was reluctance on her part to show emotion in a way that she was sure would have embarrassed the youngest child of Mary and Charles Clarey. She told herself that her father had had a good life, all things measured up. He'd had a good war, ended his time with the same best friend he'd started out with, and had had a happy last year in the cozy Residences thanks to her insistence. What was there to cry for? She'd sobbed for her mother's wasted life, the physical hardship of her final days, skin stained yellow with the liver disease that had devoured her. Of the two, Anne believed it was her mother who deserved and would want her tears and grief, not her stoic father.

She looks at the envelope again. There's something about handling the personal effects of someone who's died. Letters, diaries, memorabilia become the property of whoever finds them. Restraint dissolves, all notions of privacy disappear. We are archaeologists by inclination. The material becomes artifacts, clues to an existence that answer as many questions about the dead as they raise questions for the living.

She slips the pages of the letter out of the envelope. The words and lines are cramped, written on both sides of the paper by someone used to making economies. The letter concerns, it says, the sister, the aunt Anne never knew. Her father didn't like to talk about this Edith whenever she'd asked him about her. There were no details beyond the shared essentials: Edith was born, was loved, and when she was eighteen, she vanished one night without a trace. A subsequent police investigation turned up no clues. After that the only material things marking her existence were her clothes and effects and some photographs and a few official documents. And that, Anne thought, is a real shame, because what little she had understood about her father's sister, from Theresa and her Uncle Gus, was that this Edith had been a hoot, a real live wire. Anne liked to imagine how an eccentric aunt might have enlivened parties, brought laughter and fun to summers at her south shore house.

Seated on the floor, her back braced against the bed her father complained about so often, she reads the letter.

"Dear Mel," it begins.

I hope you don't mind this familiarity with your name. I am Raymond Gillis. We've never met, although I remember seeing you a few times when you visited your father's business, when it was Clarey Glass and Paint. You were just a boy then. Your father loved nothing more than to take some of his precious time to show you around the office. I always thought he was preparing you for the day you took his place there, when the two of us would work together, I hoped.

I worked as the bookkeeper for your father's business. I met your sister Edith there. It's about your sister's disappearance that I'm writing to you.

No soul now living has been privy to any of what I am about to tell you. I begin where I must in order for you to understand why events unfolded as they did.

I loved your sister. I was in love with Edith. I cherish her memory to this day. It is still a heartache for me that she never knew how I felt. But she had had her head turned by someone else, a boy named Michael Green. I believe all your family's troubles began the day this Green fellow was hired. And I wasn't the only one who saw him as an instrument of darkness. The others had a name for him. They called him 'the Spanish boy' behind his back for some reason to do with a book he carried around with him. I assure you that this christening was not intended as a sign of fondness on their part. We did not like him and we knew there was reason to be wary. Only Edith was blinded by his sly ways.

We boarded at the same house, this boy and I, you see. So I was able to observe him and how he spoke and acted with the others. We were all suspicious of why he needed to leave the house most nights and not return till late. I thought it my duty to know whether this was someone we need fear. So one night I watched him leave the house key on a table by the door as if he didn't intend to come back. I resolved right then to follow him to find out where he was going and what could be so important to him.

He carried a rucksack over his shoulder, filled, I assumed, with what little he possessed. He kept up a brisk pace and was oblivious to anything around him. Down Morris Street he went and then onto Lower Water Street. I followed him at a careful distance. Never once did he pause and look around to get his bearings. He knew exactly where he was going.

He headed for a ship, one of those old rusting ones that carried things into and, I realized for the purposes of his adventure, out of the harbour. I stopped in the shadows of a building and watched him step onto the pier. That's when I saw something that shocked me deeply.

I saw your sister. I saw Edith turn and look at this boy with something I can only describe as a misplaced girlish eagerness. I wanted to step out of my hiding place and demand to know what was going on, what was she doing here meeting Michael Green? And what do you think she was she holding onto for dear life? Only her most precious possession which was that bicycle of hers.

She was headstrong, your sister, but didn't she know how risky it was to ride around the city alone at night, preyed on by who knew what kind of disturbed individual? And now look what she's done, I told myself. She rode right into the presence of someone that dangerous.

The two of them argued. He wanted her bicycle. There was a tug-of-war between them. When she wouldn't surrender it he walked away. She called out to him. I'm sure she was crying. He took the bicycle. She let him wheel it away. He manhandled it up the gangway and onto the ship with no wave, no call of 'thanks'. Nothing. You see what I mean about him, don't you? That's what he was like.

At that moment, I knew what his game was. This Michael Green had extorted your sister, demanded her bicycle as payment in return for her silence on some matter. Why else would she give up her most prized possession? He took and took, always, that boy. He took money from your father's business. It was money he'd worked for certainly, but without gratitude like me and the others. He was arrogant and insolent in the face of authority. What horrible thing could this so-called 'Spanish boy' have done to push Edith to this extreme?

She stood there and stared after him. Was she thinking that he might reconsider his thieving (I can't think of any other word for what he did) and return her bicycle? If that was the case, I was certain she waited in vain.

I watched her for a long time, so angry at what I'd witnessed, yet feeling so helpless and uncertain about what to do.

We stayed like that, Edith in the cold on that pier, me huddled in the darkness and not sure if I should call out to her and offer to help in some way. I wanted to tell her what I'd seen and I understood what she was feeling, that I hated him too. All of that I wanted to say to her and yet I hesitated.

We waited a very long time in that cold night air. At last, she walked away from the ship, near the place where I was standing.

She passed so close we almost touched. I knew this was the moment I must say something to her. I reached out and took her by the wrist.

My touch startled her and she cried out. With my other hand, I covered her mouth. 'It's all right,' I said. 'It's me. Raymond. Don't be frightened.'

She tried to pull away from me. The more she struggled, though, the tighter I held her. I had to do that, you see, in order to explain to her that she needed to calm down. She pulled my hand away from her mouth and demanded to know what I was doing. She told me to let go of her.

We were so close that I saw the silver tracks of the dried tears on her cheeks. She shivered from the cold. I could see she needed comforting.

'It's all right, Edith,' I said. 'I saw everything. I know what's happened and what he's done to you. We'll tell your father tomorrow, together. Don't worry.'

She was too emotional to listen to me and told me that I knew nothing, as if she didn't believe me when I assured her that I had seen everything. She said that if she told her father anything it would be that I was spying on her and hurting her. My grip on her wrist was so tight, she said, she couldn't feel her hand. But I was afraid that if I didn't hold her like that, she would run away before I'd properly calmed her and talked reason to her.

'We won't wait until tomorrow,' I told her. 'We'll talk to your father tonight, right now. He'll call the police. They'll stop the boat leaving and take him off to jail. We'll get your bicycle back and teach that Michael Green a thing or two.'

'I'll scream,' she said. 'If you don't let go, I'll scream.'

She needed to listen to me, Mel. I was talking good common sense. If only she'd listened to me. That boy had upset her so much I believe she was temporarily out of her mind.

She shouted at me. She called me crazy and said that your father wouldn't believe anything I told him. Who was I to be telling tales about her?

'He will listen to me when I tell him about his daughter and that boy and what he's done to you. Your father respects me,' I said. 'Just wait until he hears how you stood on that pier, crying, abandoned by someone who is nothing more than an ordinary thief. What else has he stolen from you?'

Edith stopped struggling when I said that. I regretted my words right away. Who knows what she thought I meant? That he had taken her virtue and spoiled her forever? My face burned. I knew, even in the dim light, she could see that. I don't know why, Mel, but I felt she hated me at that moment.

Her fist hit me just above my left temple. I remember stumbling backwards as much from surprise as the force of the blow. My hand loosened on her wrist and she jerked her arm away.

If only she'd turned and run at that moment. I'm sure that's what she intended to do. But I know this about your sister, Mel. She was a well brought-up young lady with lovely manners. I'm certain that when she saw the pain she'd inflicted on me, that's why she hesitated. Instead of turning and running, she said: 'I'm sorry.' Just like that, so simply and so quietly.

I hadn't planned to hit her, certainly not the way and with the force I did. She stepped back. A foot must have struck a concrete step and she fell with her arms out, trying to reach for something, anything, to hang onto.

I didn't hear her head striking the ground. All I heard was some very loud noise as though I was standing next to a large machine making a churning and whirling sound.

I'm ashamed and sickened for what I am about to tell you, but I must.

I knelt, grabbed her coat and drove her head into the edge of the step. There was a soft crush as it struck the hard surface. She was limp. I did it again. Her head felt as if it had the weight and density of a large ball of sodden yarn.

What had I done? What should I do? I was in shock. I couldn't think rationally. Should I leave her and let someone else find her body? That would be a heartless thing to do. And there would be questions and who knew what clues or evidence had been left behind?

The pier was empty. I pulled her up by the leather belt she wore around her waist. I thought that someone as slender as she was shouldn't weigh as much as this.

One of my hands gripped the belt, the other the collar of her coat and like that, I dragged her across the pier. I expected to hear someone shout out to me and demand to know what I was doing. But there was no other voice. I tipped her body off the edge of the pier and watched it slide down the side of the rusted hull of the ship and hit the water. Her body should have moved away. The incoming tide would have done that. A part of her clothing, probably that leather belt, was caught somewhere and stopped her body from slipping under the water. I was panicked and sick. Whatever happened to her after this depended on the movement of the ship.

One of her arms was flung up over her head as though she was sleeping. And her hair, that beautiful hair, was loose and swirling in the water.

I did the cowardly thing. I ran and hid behind a building and waited. I was shaking. I had just killed the girl I loved and who eventually I know would have loved me. I hated myself. What I'm not ashamed to say to you is that I began to cry, not just for me and what I'd done, you understand, but for Edith and for your family.

I waited for hours, crouched in the cold, clutching the cloth bag that Edith had dropped. Light began to colour the sky and the ship moved away. I watched it sail past George's Island and McNab's and on to the mouth of the harbour. When I lifted her, I felt the strength of that leather belt, but I knew it would have to give way eventually. By the time the ship reached open water Edith's body would float loose, something for passing ships to carve up or food for whatever large things swim out there.

The first drops of rain fell on my face. A storm blew in from across the harbour and soon my clothes were drenched. Still, I couldn't move from the place. The rain came down as heavy as I've ever seen it. I imagined streams of water running down the city's streets, filling roof gutters and downspouts. It swept across the concrete steps where I huddled with the cloth bag, taking away all signs of blood, the last physical evidence of Edith Clarey's presence in the city.

I have left Edith's bag with my lawyer for you to retrieve. You'll find his name at the bottom of this page. I haven't looked inside it for many years. I remember there is a book, some articles of clothing, some personal things. I never understood what it was she planned to do with it all.

I am an old man, very sick. It's entirely possible I'll be gone by the time you read this. I hope it offers you some comfort to know at last what happened to your sister. There is no suitable penance for what I did except, perhaps, the immense burden of my deed and the guilt I carried with me for so many years. I'm sure you loved her, but you must know this, so did I.

I have to wonder, though, that by not telling you about this for so long, didn't I leave you with some hope? Wasn't her disappearance easier to bear if you thought that one day she might come back, that she was still alive? I have to believe I left you some hope. For whatever unintended pain I may have caused you and your family, please forgive me. I believe that God already has.

Respectfully,

Raymond Gillis

≈

Anne stands, her back and legs stiff from sitting as she had been, crouched on the floor, for so long. At the window, she stares for several minutes at the wintery garden where pillows of snow dot the hard ground and yellowed grass. Her father had told her that he enjoyed sitting on the bench there on sunny days, talking to the gardener as he did his planting, or alone, watching the birds that gathered. She was surprised when, during one of her visits, he'd asked her if she'd like to join him there, and untypically flustered at the request, she'd said: "Not today. I'm too busy. Maybe later." But the later time never came and she was relieved that her father had not asked her a second time.

There is no sound of any other living soul. Many of the Shorefront residents have left to spend the Christmas week with family. She is alone in the room where her father died, having read a letter that he had not wanted her or anyone else to see. What had gone through his mind to do that? Wouldn't he want someone else to know that he had at last learned the fate of his long-lost sister?

Even though Mel's mind was often confused near the end, he must have understood the importance of this letter. During her years of litigating all manner of criminal activity, Anne had never seen a document quite like this one.

She'll contact Raymond Gillis's lawyer, a man she'd attended law school with, and get Edith's bag from him. Perhaps he'll give an old colleague some more detail about this Raymond. And Lawrie Shine, he might be able to make something of the letter, throw some light on all of this. Surely the old friend must remember this girl, Edith, and could tell Anne things about her that her own father never would. She'll phone Mr. Shine tomorrow, to ask him.

She runs a hand over the creased envelope. The postmark is clear: the letter is months old, mailed last summer. If Mel had learned the fate of his sister after all those years, he'd said nothing. For some reason, he put the letter where he did, perhaps for safekeeping or to hide or to ignore. Perhaps it was too painful a subject for him to talk about.

"Is it possible grief lasts that long?" Anne says to no one.

All these many years she had dismissed her father as empty, rule-bound and conventional. She'd shaken her head, time after time, at the legendary Clarey stoicism that guided his life. Was it possible that all that time he had endured great pain, so immense that the mention of it, any physical evidence of it like this letter, was unbearable to him? What had she known about her father? He had never hinted to her that he was aware of the complexity of the time or the dramatic events described by Raymond Gillis.

She was wrong not to have cried for him. One day she would, when she understood more about this girl, this Edith, and her father. Surely Mr. Shine will tell her what she needs to know.

Anne had last seen her father only two weeks before, on the evening of Christmas Day. The renovation of the house that Anne and Norman had bought from Mel, the home she had grown up in, had been completed only a week before the holidays. The interior was now unrecognizable to anyone familiar with its history.

"You'd never know it was the same house, would you?" Anne enjoyed saying to any family member who visited. "All that gloom gone. Finally a place someone wants to live in." She hired a decorator to prepare a special Christmas theme.

Anne and Norman's three children were there, along with their own. Her sister, Susie, made an entrance, held Mel's hand for a few minutes, stayed for the meal and left soon after gifts were opened. They called Charlie, in British Columbia, and left a Christmas greeting on his voice mail.

The mood was lively, with lots of presents and food and drink. Anne gave her father a laptop computer and Mel, ever the well-mannered Halifax boy, thanked her very much.

"I'll show you how to use it, Dad. You'll be able to send me messages whenever you want. All day long if you care to. You don't have to bother with the telephone anymore. Just send me emails. I'll read them and get right back to you. Promise."

Anne was happy in her belief that she had chosen well for her father's gift. She congratulated herself on her own thoughtfulness. The smile on Mel's face broadened as Anne's hands punctuated her words, but his expression was as empty as his understanding of what she was saying and what this strange object could be.

When Mel said that he needed to visit the bathroom and returned with his coat and scarf, Norman offered to drive him back to the residence. Mel gripped his bag of presents and accepted the hugs and kisses of his daughter and grandchildren. He looked tired, but content, as he always was when surrounded by family.

He took Anne's hand and leaned in to her. She offered her cheek for a kiss. He put his lips close to her ear and whispered: "Tell Ma and Pa they don't have to go to all this fuss next year."

She smiled at him and he was gone from the house for the last time.

≈

Because of the holidays, Mel's funeral had to wait until after New Year's. And because of the holiday slowdown and various offices being closed and paperwork delayed, the family couldn't vacate his room before the last day of December and that meant another half-month's rent had to be paid. Although Anne didn't say so out loud it was understood by Norman that his wife thought her father's death was badly timed.

Mel's death was a quiet one, so fitting for a man who never liked to make a fuss. He died in his sleep, sometime in the dark of that last Christmas night. Not a bad way to end, Anne assured herself, after being surrounded by family and voices rich with happiness. If she had one regret about her father's final moments of living, though, it was that the last voice he heard was that of her husband, the stolid Norman, who had driven him home, and not her own or someone else who meant something special to him.

But Mel had gone to bed his last night and thought of his sister as he had done every night for sixty-seven years. He thought of the promise he'd made to Edie so long ago on that golden July morning when the three friends watched the giant airship, the *Hindenburg*, float over their heads. He had promised her then that he would keep her secret. And he had.

And on his last night, he allowed a particular story to visit him, a story meant to comfort and console a heart filled with a grief as old as his memory and as fresh as that morning's snowfall.

The boy is at his bedroom window.

"Edie, what are you doing out there?" he calls to her.

She turns to look at him and smiles at the sound of his familiar voice.

"It's time to come home," he says to her.

And she does. It's as simple as that. She wheels her bicycle back to the house and he hears the satisfying thump as she lets it fall against the outside wall.

The boy lies in his bed and listens to her enter the house through the back door, followed by the sound of her running, taking the stairs two at a time. He hears the tread of her feet along the hall carpet and into her own bedroom.

Then the soft sound of a voice, his sister's voice, Edie's voice, calling softly to him: "'Night, brother."

And he sleeps.

ACKNOWLEDGEMENTS

I owe a great debt to the Writers' Federation of Nova Scotia for including me in the Alistair MacLeod Mentorship Program and, in particular, to Binnie Brennan, whose talent and good sense guided me. The Keaton films were an unexpected bonus.

Many thanks to the first taste-testers of *The Spanish Boy*: Barbara Kennedy, Susan Wenning, Ruth-Ellen Soles, Mary Reardon, Bill Stewart, Deborah Stacey, Cilla Kent, Mary Lou Finlay and, as well, to Marie Thompson and Paul Emile d'Entremont for their help.

Lucy van Smit and Kim Echlin went beyond mere friendship and generously contributed support and advice. David Gilmour did not hesitate to jump in when asked. The solidarity forged in the edit suites of CBC's *The Journal* endures.

Dr. Shirley Tillotson of Dalhousie University did her level best to keep my feet on the acknowledged path of historical evidence. Any mistakes are mine alone.

As well as the fascinating newspaper archive at the Halifax Public Library, several books were useful to me for research:

The Gallant Cause: Canadians in the Spanish Civil War, 1936-1939 by Mark Zuehlke

Renegades: Canadians in the Spanish Civil War by Michael Petrou

Crime and Society in a City of Order: Halifax, 1918-1935 by Michael S. Boudreau

Hindenburg: An Illustrated History by Rick Archbold

South End Boy: Growing Up in Halifax in the Tumultuous '30s and '40s by Jim Bennet

And to Karen Haughian of Signature Editions, "thank you" hardly seems adequate, and yet…thank you.